Lost and Found in Lavender Bay

The Lavender Bay Chronicles Book 2

Michele Brouder

This is a work of fiction. Names, characters, places and incidents are either a product of the author's imagination or are used fictitiously, and any resemblance to actual persons, living or dead, events, or locales is entirely coincidental.

Editing by Jessica Peirce

Book Cover Design by Rebecca Ruger

Lost and Found in Lavender Bay

Copyright © 2024 Michele Brouder

All Rights Reserved. No part of this book may be reproduced or transmitted in any form or by any means, electronic or mechanical, including photocopying, recording, or by any information storage and retrieval system, without permission in writing from the author.

PART ONE

Maureen

Chapter One

"I'm so glad you're here," said Mrs. Kovach, barely giving Maureen Cook Peterson time to set her open umbrella on the porch before pulling her in through the front door.

Mrs. Kovach, Maureen's newest client, lived on the corner of Heather Lane and Vine Street. Her daughter, on a whim, had decided to surprise her by redecorating her house while she was away on a two-week trip to Hawaii. Maureen, an interior designer, had been asked to step in and help reverse the damage.

Maureen had brought along her "book," a binder filled with photos of work she'd done in the last five years. It was the fourth book she was on.

Like many of the homes in this part of Lavender Bay, Mrs. Kovach's house was a small Victorian with the requisite gingerbread trim. Though she was a neighbor of Maureen's mother, Louise Cook, it had been many years since Maureen had been inside the house.

She was taken aback from the moment she stepped inside. The hallway walls had been painted black with white trim. The space was too narrow for so dark a color, the contrast too stark against the white tile floor. It didn't help that it was dark and dreary outside, making the interior appear even darker. March had been a total washout. Lots of rain, the only plus side being the disappearance of the final mounds of snow along the beach.

Mrs. Kovach looked as if she was trying to find the words as she scratched her head. "I know Tracy meant well, but I don't think you should go into someone's house and redecorate for them without their permission." She paused, looking around and grimacing. "This is what happens when you give your daughter a key to your house."

With every room they stepped into, Mrs. Kovach winced. And Maureen could see why. She remembered the house being done up in various shades of peach and maroon, but there had been a total overhaul and the color palette had been confined to black and various shades of gray. The faint aroma of cinnamon and cloves in the air didn't match the dark and depressing effect of the décor.

The older woman put her hands up for emphasis. "It's too much. I don't want to leave my bedroom. I feel like I've entered a house of horrors or something. Now, Tracy was trying to help, and I'll admit that maybe it was time for an update, but I can't live in this house the way it is. I thought it would be easier to redo it rather than sell it, because that's where I was at last week."

Maureen reassured her. "Don't worry, we'll figure something out."

"Come on, let's go back to the kitchen," Mrs. Kovach said with another shake of her head. "Wait until you see what she's done in there."

Maureen almost flinched when she entered the kitchen. The cabinets had been painted a gunmetal gray, and the counters were black granite.

"I liked my white cabinets," Mrs. Kovach cried. She gestured toward the small glass-topped table and four bistro chairs. "Have a seat."

Maureen pulled out one of the chairs and sat, setting down her book.

"Would you like tea or coffee?" Mrs. Kovach asked. "I'm having tea myself. I've had to switch to peppermint because my stomach's been so upset."

"That's fine for me too, as long as it isn't too much trouble."

"None at all. I'll have it in a second."

She turned on the gas burner beneath her kettle and pulled two mugs from the stand next to the stove.

Maureen glanced around the kitchen. She sourced the origin of the cinnamon-and-clove aroma: a small electric potpourri burner on the countertop that sat next to a set of white canisters with a cornflower-blue pattern. The counter space was otherwise occupied by the usual array of small appliances—coffeemaker, stand mixer, toaster, can opener—but all in black.

Mrs. Kovach set down two cups of steaming peppermint-scented tea on the table, sliding one mug over to Maureen as she took the seat next to her.

"Thank you," Maureen said. She opened up her book. "Maybe you'd like to look through some of these pictures and we can decide where to go from there."

Mrs. Kovach pulled the book in front of her. "Mercifully, Tracy did nothing upstairs. It's as it was." She widened her eyes for emphasis. Carefully, she began to flip through the pages, pausing to look at the photos and studying them, commenting from time to time. "That's lovely." "That looks so fresh." "I love that color combination; you would have thought if you put those two colors together it wouldn't look so nice."

She paused, holding a page between two fingers. "How are your children, Maureen? How old are they now?"

"Everett is twenty-one and in his third year at Michigan. He's hoping to go on for a law degree. Lance is nineteen and is in his first year up at UB outside of Buffalo, major undeclared. They'll be home next week for spring break. Ashley is in her senior year over at McKinley High School. She's been accepted to a college out west and will start there at the end of August." Maureen couldn't wait to see the boys and hear all about college life. She was happiest when the whole family was all together under one roof.

"That's great that they'll all be getting college degrees. You have so many more opportunities with that piece of paper in your hand." Mrs. Kovach sipped delicately from her cup.

Maureen was proud of her children. There would be no failure to launch with her group. No living at home in the parents' basement. They all had plans and goals and although she would miss them all terribly, she was eager to see how their lives turned out.

"Allan and I have been blessed," she said. "Other than the usual growing pains, they're good kids."

"Consider yourself lucky, Maureen," Mrs. Kovach said. "The kid next door is relentless."

Suppressing a grin, Maureen asked, "How so?"

"It's not his fault. He's only seventeen, but he's home alone. A lot. Both his parents travel for work. In the summertime, he's either outside playing basketball until two in the morning or blaring music from his bedroom. Let me tell you, I love winter if only for the closed windows and the peace and quiet."

Maureen laughed.

Mrs. Kovach returned her attention to the book, studying the photos of Maureen's work.

She tapped one page. "I like this color scheme."

Maureen nodded. "Those are warm colors."

"That's what I need. Whatever we do, no black! Or gray!"

"Got it." Maureen wrote some notes down on her notepad.

Mrs. Kovach thumped a bony finger on a particular photo. "Do the downstairs in various shades of that."

"Very good. I'll look at different types of textures and fabrics and put together a sample board. I'll be on the hunt for decorations as well." Her first stop would be her garage, where she had a supply of all things related to interior design. "I'll bring over some sketches to show you what the rooms might look like with the changes."

Clearly impressed, Mrs. Kovach asked, "You sketch?"

"Not very well. But I use an app that helps."

"The things technology can do these days."

"May I take some photos and measurements of the downstairs rooms?"

"Of course."

With tape measure and phone in hand, Maureen went from room to room, taking down measurements and recording them on her notepad. She took photos of each room from various angles, making note of which direction the windows faced.

When she was finished, Mrs. Kovach saw her out. "At my age," she said, "it's worth it for me to pay someone to clean up this mess."

Maureen smiled; she loved her job. Like everything else in her life, it was just about perfect.

Chapter Two

Everett and Lance were due home for their week of spring break. Since yesterday, Maureen had been cooking up a storm. She'd made a pot of sauce with meatballs and had also made a pan of lasagna. Her youngest, Ashley, had baked a batch of chocolate chip cookies.

With the change of the month from March to April, the rain had disappeared, and although the atmosphere remained damp, the sun was making an effort to peek through the heavy cloud cover.

Because she wanted a light work week while the boys were home, she'd made an effort to get things cleared off her desk. Earlier, she'd dropped off some watercolor renderings and a sample board of fabric swatches and paint chips to Mrs. Kovach, who'd been delighted with Maureen's prompt turnaround.

Maureen was anxious to see Everett in particular. Her oldest wasn't in touch as frequently as he was when he first went away to college. And when he was home for Christmas break, he hadn't seen his old friends from high school, claiming he'd outgrown them. She tried to chalk it up to new experiences, living away from home, meeting new friends and getting a taste of freedom. But deep down, she worried that something was wrong. Allan always told her she worried too much, but wasn't that her job as a mother? Someone had to do the worrying. Make sure everyone was fine and doing everything they were supposed to be doing.

Lance, her golden boy, was the first to arrive, in the middle of the afternoon. He favored her in looks with his light eyes and auburn hair. She cast a scrutinous glance over him. He looked well. He was eating, but whether properly or not, she didn't know. It was amazing how fruit and vegetables fell right off the menu when they left home for college.

"Hey, Mom, how are you?" Over his shoulder, he carried a large duffel bag, which Maureen suspected was filled with dirty laundry.

She embraced him. "Hello, honey."

When they pulled apart, she held out her hand for the bag. "I bet that's for me."

He had the grace to look sheepish. "Yeah, sorry about that."

"Don't worry about it. I'll get started on it." There was something satisfying about sending your child back to college with a lot of clean laundry and food.

Lance looked around the kitchen. "What's that smell? What are you making? Is that sauce?"

"I made lasagna for dinner tonight."

"Sweet! Hey, is my hockey equipment still in the basement? I'm going to meet up with some of the guys for a quick pick-up game at the rink."

"Everything is down in the basement right where you left it. Better go do it though. The rink will be closing soon for the summer."

"That's the plan. Dad at work?"

"He is. He'll be home for dinner."

"What time is dinner?"

"The usual time. Six."

"Where's Ash?"

"She's going straight from school to her violin lesson."

He grimaced. "She still doing that?"

"Yes. She enjoys it. You like sports and she likes art and music."

"Yeah, I know, hard to believe we're related."

"Well, for better or worse, she's your sister."

He laughed in that easy manner of his and went out the door with a wave, promising to be home in time for dinner.

The duffel bag was heavier than it looked, and she had to drag it with both hands to the utility room off the kitchen. She emptied it on the floor, separating the clothes into piles of darks, lights, and whites. There was enough to get a full load started, so there was no need to wait for Everett's laundry.

When Everett didn't arrive by four, she tried not to panic. She dashed off a text but there was no reply. Later, as she was filling a pot with water for a side of spaghetti to accompany the lasagna, she heard the door open. She turned just as Everett stumbled inside.

With a laugh, she teased, "First day with your new feet?"

"Ha-ha," he replied, but there was no humor in his voice.

"Hi, honey." She frowned slightly. He looked awful.

"Hey, Mom."

She set the pot on the stove and turned on the burner. She walked over to Everett and hugged him.

"I was expecting you earlier." She stepped back to take a closer look at him. He looked thinner than he had when he was last home. His cheeks were hollowed out, and his bangs hung in his eyes.

"I was late getting on the road."

She reached over to push his hair out of his eyes, but he ducked away, out of her reach.

"You've lost some weight," she observed.

"I needed to."

"Are you eating all right?"

He rolled his eyes. "Mom, don't start. I just walked in the door."

She smiled and softened her tone. "I only ask because I'm your mother and I love you."

"Love me a little less."

"Impossible." She persisted. "You're looking a little bleary-eyed, kiddo."

"Pulled an all-nighter for an exam this morning."

"How'd it go?"

He shrugged and looked over at the stove. "What time's dinner?"

"Half hour."

He nodded. "I'm going upstairs. Call me when dinner is ready."

"Come down in half an hour." The lasagna was already in the oven, along with a loaf of garlic bread. The table was already set.

Everett disappeared upstairs, but not before dumping his bag of dirty laundry in the utility room.

Ashley walked in, carrying her violin case.

"Hi, honey, how was your lesson?" Maureen asked.

"Good, she says I get better every class."

"It's all that practicing."

Always a popular, outgoing kid, Ashley had never given Maureen or Allan a moment of grief. It would be hard on them both when she finally went off to college in the fall, all the way out on the West Coast.

"I see the boys are home," Ashley said, sitting at her usual place at the table and pulling up one of her knees in front of her. "Everett was kind enough to park in the middle of the driveway."

Maureen looked up to the ceiling in annoyance. "Why does he do that? Your father won't be able to get by him to pull his car into the garage."

"Where are they?"

"Everett is upstairs, and Lance went to play some hockey with friends before dinner."

The pot on the stove began to boil, and Maureen threw in a pound of spaghetti.

Ashley reached for an apple from the fruit bowl in the middle of the table.

Maureen looked at her. "We are eating in less than twenty minutes."

Sheepish, Ashley put the apple back in the bowl.

"Do you have much homework?" Maureen asked.

"I've got that AP history paper due Monday. I better get started on that." Her spring break did not start until the following week.

"What is it with you and Everett waiting until the last minute to study for tests or do papers?"

Smiling, Ashley shrugged. "We work best under pressure."

"Wouldn't it be better to have it off your plate?"

"In theory it probably would be, but I don't see that happening. Do you?"

"I guess not," Maureen said.

Her husband walked through the door, all smiles. "Well, if it isn't my two favorite girls."

Ashley rolled her eyes. "Dad, we're your only girls."

Allan went for Maureen, placing a hand on her arm. "Hey, you."

He kissed her on the lips, and she smiled, kissing him right back, thinking he was still as handsome as the day she met him. Although there were fine lines around his blue eyes and gray had appeared at his temples, his attractiveness had not diminished in her eyes.

"I see Everett is parked right in the middle of the driveway," he said. "Again."

"Points for consistency."

"Dinner ready?"

"Five minutes."

"Good, I'm starving." Allan took his seat at the head of the table. He looked over at Maureen at the stove. "Do you need any help?"

Maureen shook her head. She removed the loaf of garlic bread from the oven, setting it aside to cool before she sliced it. Then she removed the pan of lasagna, which was bubbling around the edges, and set that on a hot pad. She wouldn't cut that yet or it would be soupy.

She drained the spaghetti, shaking the colander a few times to get out all the excess water, and put it into a large pasta bowl and set it on the table.

She sliced up the garlic bread and arranged it on a long, narrow platter.

"Ash, get up and help your mother," Allan said.

Maureen handed her daughter the tray of garlic bread and followed her with the pot of sauce.

Lance appeared. "Do I have time to take a shower?"

"And hello to you too, Lance," Allan said with a grin.

"Oh, hi, Dad."

"Nope, no time for a shower," Maureen said, going back for the pan of lasagna. "Before you sit down, go call Everett."

Lance walked over to the foot of the staircase and yelled up for his brother.

Maureen rolled her eyes and muttered, "I could have done that."

They waited as Maureen began to dish out spaghetti and squares of lasagna. She started with Ashley's plate. Youngest first.

When Everett still hadn't appeared by the time everyone had their plates, she sent Ashley up after him.

Eventually her oldest son stumbled down the staircase.

Maureen eyed him, concern filling her. "Did you fall asleep?"

"Yeah." He slid into his seat and looked at the plate of food in front of him. As if unsure, he picked up his fork and began to eat. He looked over at his father and said, "Hey, Dad."

Allan nodded. "Good to see you. Good to have everyone at home, all together."

Maureen was the last one to sit down. She sat at the foot of the table with Allan directly across from her, Everett and Ashley to her left, and Lance on her right.

Lance inhaled his meal while Everett picked at the food on his plate.

"Aren't you hungry?" Maureen asked.

"No. I grabbed a burger on the way up."

She didn't say anything, deciding she didn't want any friction.

Lance reached across the table, plucking two pieces of garlic bread from the platter.

"How was your hockey game?" Maureen asked.

His mouth was full. He chewed and gave the thumbs-up.

Maureen looked around the table. It was like the old days, when they were younger, and they were all together. When they came home for a visit, she enjoyed every moment of it.

"Does anyone have plans this weekend?" she asked.

Ashley spoke up first, helping herself to another meatball. "Emma's home from college, so I'll be hanging with her." Emma was the daughter of Maureen's sister Nadine. Although a year apart in age, the two cousins had been close since they were young.

"I'll be away for a few days next week, so please give your mother a hand with things," Allan said.

Lance looked at the pan of lasagna on the table but said nothing.

Maureen stood and, using the spatula, she cut a square from the pan and set it on his plate. She thought Lance was unusually quiet that evening. He tended to dominate the dinner table conversations. But she dismissed it, assuming he was tired.

"Thanks, Mom."

"Anyone want more?" she asked, holding the spatula up.

Allan nodded. "You twisted my arm. It's delicious, Maureen."

She cut another square and reached over the table to place it on the plate he'd lifted toward her.

"Dad, where are you going?" Lance asked.

"Sorry. I was distracted by food." Allan laughed. "I'm the keynote speaker at a dental conference this weekend in St. Paul, Minnesota."

"Florida would have been better, Dad," Ashley told him.

"I agree, but I don't plan these things, so St. Paul it is."

Later that night, Allan was first into bed. He turned on his bedside light, put on his reading glasses, and picked up the newest copy of *The Journal of the American Dental Association.*

Maureen stood in the doorway of the ensuite bathroom, applying lotion to her elbows. It bewildered her how her elbows got so dry, especially since she never used them.

"Lance was kind of quiet tonight at dinner," she said.

Allan continued to read his journal. "It was a pleasant change."

"Do you think he's all right?"

"Yes."

"Do you think Everett has lost weight?"

Allan looked up at her over the top of his glasses. "I didn't notice."

"He doesn't seem like himself." She rubbed more lotion onto her left elbow, which felt bumpy.

Allan laughed. "Honey, he just got home. Give him a break."

That had been a constant refrain from her kids. That she nagged and worried too much.

But she couldn't let it go. "I don't know. I think something's going on with him."

Allan set the journal down on his lap. "Why do you say that?"

Turning off the bathroom light, she shrugged. "I don't know, just a feeling I get." She walked to their four-poster bed, kicked off her slippers, and lifted the covers, getting in. This was one of her favorite parts of the day, getting into bed. Her days were busy and hectic, and bedtime was usually well earned.

She turned on her side, adjusted her alarm clock, and turned off her bedside light.

Allan had not picked up his journal. She rolled over on her back and stared at the ceiling.

Her husband looked at her. "Are you going to worry about this? Will it keep you up all night?"

"Yes, and yes." She couldn't help it. It was how she was built. It was the way her mind worked.

With a chuckle, he set the journal on the bedside table, removed his glasses, and turned off his light. "Turn on your side, I'll rub your back."

Willingly, she rolled over, and Allan's hand slipped under her nightshirt and began to rub her back. Closing her eyes, she could feel the tension seep out of her body. This always did the trick. It wasn't long before she was sleeping.

Chapter Three

"And one more thing, Maureen," Mrs. Whittaker said. "Not *too* much orange. I want a splash of color with all that navy, but I don't want it to be overpowering."

Maureen nodded, did a half turn, and headed toward the door. She had a lunch date and was already late.

But Mrs. Whittaker was at her side with more instructions. "And not a neon orange."

The older woman was a recent widow whose husband had never wanted anything changed in the house. The entire place was dated: wood paneling, plastic covering over the furniture, and serene countryside paintings that looked suspiciously like paint-by-number. The kitchen had an old linoleum floor, dark cabinets, and busy wallpaper. The rest of the house was carpeted wall to wall in sculpted, multi-shaded broadloom. The living room was done up in mauve and gray. Relishing her decision-making freedom and access to a substantial amount of money, Mrs. Whittaker had called Maureen for a consult a month after her husband's death.

On that first visit, Maureen had spent more than two hours going over her services and showing her client fabric books and paint charts. But it had all proved too overwhelming for the woman, who kept looking over her shoulder as if she expected the late Mr. Whittaker to appear in the form of a disapproving specter. Today Maureen had brought only one book along, kindly suggesting to Mrs. Whittaker that she remodel one room first, ideally the living room as that was where she spent most of her time. The one thing Mrs. Whittaker was sure of was she wanted to "lighten and brighten the place up." Maureen had a lot of ideas for the space.

She had her hand on the knob of the front door.

Mrs. Whittaker's brow furrowed. "You think these are the right colors?" She placed her hand at the base of her throat.

"I do. I think when it's finished, you're going to be really pleased."

The older woman laughed nervously. "George is probably rolling in his grave."

Maureen laid a hand gently on the woman's arm. "I know these are big changes for you, but I'll be there with you every step of the way and we'll get it to your liking."

Mrs. Whittaker drew in a deep breath. "Thank you, Maureen."

"I'll be in touch."

"I can call you anytime?"

Maureen nodded. "Yes, of course." She said goodbye and slipped out the door, making her way down the porch steps. She sympathized with the woman, understanding how afraid she was of making the wrong decision. What was needed here was a spectacular job and some handholding. And Maureen was more than up for the task.

She might have gone slightly over the speed limit to get to the Annacotty Room to meet her cousin Esther for lunch. Growing up together, the two of them had been thicker than thieves. Maureen had always looked up to her cousin, who although only a year older, seemed to know the ways of the world even at the young age of twelve. She was the older sister Maureen wished for but never had, being the eldest of four girls herself.

The Annacotty Room was a recent addition to Lavender Bay's restaurants, opening in the last five years. Maureen had been hired to design the interior, and she'd chosen plum, lime green, and turquoise as the main colors. It was a job she was proud of. She spotted Esther already seated at a table for four. As Maureen walked by the length of the bar and past the gray vinyl booths with plum upholstered banquettes, she heard the familiar sounds of cutlery and ice clinking in glasses.

Esther had her head lowered, a pair of cheaters perched on her nose as she scrolled through her phone.

Maureen pulled out the chair and laid her purse on the vacant seat next to her. "I'm sorry I'm late. I got held up with a client."

"No problem." Esther set her phone aside, face down. She had dark hair and dark eyes, and was perpetually tan, not from spray but from actual sun as she spent much of her time traveling back and forth to Florida.

As soon as Maureen seated herself, a server appeared with a glass pitcher of water with ice and sliced lemons and set it down on the table. She handed each of them a menu. "I'll give you a few minutes." She walked away, her ponytail bouncing behind her.

"What's new?" Esther asked.

"The boys are home this weekend for spring break, and Allan has a dentists' conference in St. Paul next week."

Esther picked up the water pitcher and filled their glasses. "Are you going with him?"

Maureen shook her head. "I can't. I've got too much work to do. He'll only be gone for two nights." She had accompanied him to other conferences in the past, hanging out at the pool with a good book or doing some shopping and sightseeing while Allan attended talks and workshops. But not this time, even though the Minneapolis-St. Paul airport was one of her favorites for shopping alone, despite the outrageous prices.

Esther scanned the menu, snapped it shut, and set it down.

Maureen laughed. "That was fast."

Her cousin shrugged with a smile. "I always order the same thing: the burger classic with fries. I guess that makes me dull that I never try anything new."

Maureen would not protest, because she knew her cousin didn't care. Esther had always marched to the beat of her own drum. And Maureen wouldn't have her cousin any other way.

"Anything new with you?"

Esther opened her mouth but no words came out as the server reappeared, plucking a pencil from behind her ear. "Are you ready to order?"

"We are." Maureen quickly scanned the menu. She looked up at Esther. "Go ahead."

After taking Esther's order, the server turned to Maureen.

"I'll have the French dip." Back in college, when things were much simpler, she'd lived on French dips and Reubens.

As soon as the server disappeared, Esther said, "Nothing really new. I've booked a cruise after Christmas."

"Going by yourself?" Maureen knew that this never held Esther back either.

"So far. Mom's on the fence and Suzanne's out," Esther said, referring to her younger sister. "We went on a cruise once and she spent the entire time with her head in a puke bag. I save her for the trips that are on terra firma."

"Good idea."

"How's everything going?"

"Good. I can't complain. Since Allan is going to be out of town next week, did you want to grab dinner on Wednesday?"

Esther grinned. "I've got a date that night."

Pleasantly surprised, Maureen broke into a smile. "That's great. Who?"

"His name is Lou. I met him last year at the Hot Air Balloon festival."

"And you're only just going out now?"

Esther was vague. "Yeah, I had to think about it."

"For ten months?" Maureen was incredulous.

Esther laughed.

"Does he live in Lavender Bay?"

"He does. And I don't know how we've never met before." Esther, her mother, and her sister seemed to know *everyone* in Lavender Bay.

"You must be looking forward to it."

"I am. I figured it was something to do on a weeknight," Esther said easily.

When they were young and while Maureen was dating Allan, Esther had been going out with a guy she was head-over-heels in love with, expecting a ring at Christmas, like Maureen. Maureen got her ring and her guy, but her cousin didn't. A week before Christmas, Esther had been dumped. She never spoke about it. But Maureen thought her cousin had kept careful guard over her heart ever since.

"Do you ever regret not getting married?"

Esther didn't hesitate to reply. "Nah. It wasn't meant to be. I like my life. Love my life. I've got the dogs and cats, and let me tell you, pets are highly underrated."

Maureen laughed, thinking of her cat at home.

"Granted," Esther continued, "it would be nice to have someone around to check for wonky moles on my back every once in a while, but I'm happy."

"I know you are."

"And let's face it, marriage is tough. You lucked out with Allan. Yours is one of the happiest marriages I know."

Maureen knew she was lucky. She and Allan had a good strong marriage, which had helped them weather some unpleasant storms. She couldn't imagine life without him. And she knew he felt the same way.

The server appeared with their meals.

Esther looked at her plate and tapped herself on her forehead. "I almost forgot. I'm putting together a team for the bowling league this fall. I was hoping you'd join."

Maureen groaned. "I haven't bowled since school."

"I know. That's when I got hooked." Maureen already knew that her cousin was a serious bowler. When they were in their twenties, she used to go midnight bowling, but Maureen was too busy having kids.

"Come on, it'll be great fun. Think of it like a girls' night out." Esther could be persuasive when she wanted to be.

"Who else will be on the team?"

"I need five, and you and I make two."

"Your math skills are stellar."

Esther's shoulders shook with laughter. "I'm going to ask Nadine."

"My sister Nadine? Is that a good idea?" Maureen joked.

"Hey, she got the most improved bowler award that first year," Esther reminded her.

"That's what I mean. I think her average went from twenty-seven to seventy-one."

Esther shrugged. "Who knows, maybe she's been a closet bowler all these years. I won't bother with Angie because we know she doesn't do anything but work. I'll strong-arm my sister, of course. And maybe I can ask a friend, and if worse comes to worse, I'll ask either your mother or mine."

"Can I think about it?"

"No. I've already added you to my team." Esther dipped a french fry in ketchup. "In my head."

Considering it a fait accompli, Maureen shook her head, chuckling, and changed the subject. "So, tell me about this Lou," she prompted as she picked up half of her sandwich and dipped it into the au jus.

Chapter Four

The third night the boys were home, Maureen, Allan, and Ashley were in the family room, lights out, the big-screen television illuminating the room in a bluish glow.

"What are we watching tonight, Ash?"

"Can we watch a horror movie?"

She didn't even have the words out of her mouth before Maureen started shaking her head.

Allan laughed and leaned forward, reaching for his bowl of snacks. "You know your mother can't watch that kind of thing. She'll never sleep again." He looked over his shoulder at Maureen, who sat next to him, and gave her thigh a gentle squeeze. "Right, hon?"

"Come on, Mom, it's only a movie."

"That's still a no from me," Maureen said. She turned her head toward the sound of one of the boys running down the stairs. A second son tramped down the stairs but ended with a big thud. This was followed by a bark of laughter from Lance.

Maureen stood to investigate and walked to the staircase. Everett was picking himself up off the floor, rubbing his elbow.

Lance was trying to stifle a laugh.

"Did you fall down the stairs?" she asked. "Are you all right?"

"I'm fine. Just slipped," Everett said, brushing past her.

Maureen returned to the family room and rejoined Allan and Ashley, plopping herself back on the sofa.

Everett and Lance stood in the entrance of the family room.

"We're going to watch a movie. Want to join us?" Maureen asked. "I'll make popcorn."

Everett smirked and Lance scoffed, "Come on, we're not ten."

"It was only an invite; I wasn't asking either of you to donate a kidney."

"If you ever need a kidney, Mom, no problem," Lance said brightly.

"Dad, can we have a few friends over and do a bonfire in the backyard?"

This sounded like a good plan to Maureen; she'd know where they were then. Out of the corner of her eye, she could see that Ashley was mesmerized, scrolling through the Netflix list. Maureen frowned. The movie recommendations for her daughter's profile looked like she'd need an exorcist on standby.

"It's fine by me," said Maureen.

"I'm okay with it, but everything better be cleaned up," Allan instructed. "I don't want to wake up to a mess in the morning."

"Don't worry, Dad!"

"Thanks, Dad!"

And before Maureen could say anything else, they were gone. She turned to Ashley. "Did you find anything?"

"Not yet."

"How about one of those Christmas romance movies? They keep them on Netflix all year round."

Ashley stole a side glance at her father and arched one eyebrow. "Dad, what do you think?"

Allan, who looked like he'd rather have a root canal, put his arm around Maureen. "First, it's almost Easter. Second, don't you have enough romance with me?"

Maureen laughed. "I do, but now I'm addicted to it."

He pulled his arm away, smiling. "My work is done here. How about crime or a thriller or action and adventure? I've been looking into people's mouths all day. I need something high-octane to wake me up."

"Pick something for your father, then, Ashley."

Ashley grumbled. "All right. But some night, we're watching horror."

"Why don't you have Emma over for a sleepover and you can watch horror movies all night long?" Maureen suggested.

Ashley rolled her eyes. "Mom, a sleepover, really? Emma's in college!"

Maureen feigned contrition. "Sorry."

"Dad, how about this? There's a race against the clock, blah, blah, blah, and this guy is an ex-cop."

"Sounds good."

"Mom, what about popcorn? You offered to make it for the boys."

Maureen stood. "Popcorn coming right up." It didn't surprise her that her kids kept a scorecard; hadn't she done it herself growing up with her sisters?

They settled in to watch the chosen movie. Maureen was aware of the lights going on in the backyard and as the night went on, the noise level rose. She hoped the neighbors wouldn't complain. Before they went up to bed, Allan stuck his head out the back door and warned them to keep it down.

Maureen was up early and went downstairs to sit by herself and enjoy the quiet as she drank the first cup of coffee of the day. All she had to do was press the start button on the coffeemaker because she always set it up in the evening, before she went to bed. She padded through the kitchen, still in her pajamas, over to the coffeemaker on the counter. She was greeted by two things: a sink full of dirty dishes and half a carafe of cold coffee. Clearly someone had made a pot overnight.

She poured the cold liquid down the drain, rinsed out the pot, and set up the machine for a new brew and turned it on. As quietly as she could, she unloaded the clean dishes from the dishwasher, then took all the dirty dishes from the sink, loaded them in, and closed the door, satisfied that she didn't have to look at the mess anymore.

Once her coffee was ready, she fixed it the way she liked it and carried it over to the kitchen table. She pulled out a chair and sat, pulling one knee up and wrapping her left arm around it while she sipped her coffee.

The sun was coming up in the east, and in a few hours the kitchen would be filled with sunlight. When they purchased the property years ago, the original house had been in ruins, and they'd had it torn down and built their current grand Victorian-style home. She wished she'd had more forethought when they built it. The house faced south, and while the large windows at the front and back let in a lot of light, there were too few windows on the east-facing wall where all the sunlight was in the morning.

Live and learn.

She cast a glance out the back window to see what condition the yard had been left in by the boys and their friends. Blinking several times, she stood up, unable to believe what she was seeing.

The backyard was trashed.

Empty beer cans, quart bottles, and litter were scattered all over the lawn. Some of her expensive lawn chairs had been tipped over. White-knuckling her coffee cup, she took a big gulp, then set it down on the table. She forced herself to go over to the window to get a better look at the damage. The first thing she spotted was a raccoon making his way through the garbage. She groaned. They'd never get rid of him!

She was rinsing her coffee cup out at the sink a few minutes later when Allan entered the kitchen, whistling.

"Good morning, beautiful," he said, sliding a hand around her waist and kissing her on the cheek.

His good mood evaporated quickly when he glanced out the window.

"What the—"

Maureen sighed. "I guess they had a good time last night."

He scowled. "Too good of a time." He narrowed his eyes to get a better look. "Are those cigarette butts all over my lawn?"

"They are. I'm going to get dressed and go out and start cleaning up. The mess has drawn a raccoon."

"Under no circumstances are you to pick up one thing outside," he said firmly, all business. "It's their mess and they can clean it up." He glanced at his watch. "The party is over. Get both boys out of bed by seven and tell them I want that yard cleaned up. And they can cut the grass and trim that hedge I've been asking them to trim all weekend." He paused and added, "I want every single butt picked up."

Although he was easy to live with, the kids knew not to take advantage of Allan's good nature. He was a big believer in actions having consequences.

"I'll grab breakfast on the way to work." He glanced out the window again. "I've lost my appetite."

He leaned in and kissed her again, his demeanor softening. "Have a good day, and I'll see you tonight."

She kissed him back. "Back at ya."

As he walked out of the kitchen, he called over his shoulder, "Tell them I want a photo sent to me by noon of the backyard and the trimmed hedge."

"Will do."

She sorted out dinner by searing a piece of beef and throwing it into the slow cooker with onions, potatoes, and carrots, along with some water and mix packets. Turned it on low and left it.

She went upstairs to get ready for work. But before she left, she roused both boys and passed on Allan's instructions. Everett mumbled something and rolled over in his bed. Lance grumbled, "I'll do it later."

"Dad wants it done by noon. Send photos."

The shower in the upstairs bathroom started, indicating that Ashley was up and getting ready for school.

Maureen went off to work, glad she didn't have to deal with the mess in the backyard.

It was World War Three at the dinner table that night.

Maureen was tired. She'd spent more time than she'd allotted with a couple who couldn't make up their minds about how they wanted to decorate their home.

Both were professional people, but he preferred the rustic look and earth tones, and she liked contemporary with bright colors. They were proving to be a challenge. Anything she'd showed them was met by one of them scrunching up their nose and saying no. Finally, as it was getting late, she said she'd come up with something that would please them both and would get back to them. But it had set her back for the rest of the day.

It was only four of them for dinner. Ashley had gone out with Emma and Nadine.

Lance was in a foul mood, which was unlike him. His expression was stormy all through dinner. Everett, on the other hand, could barely stay awake through the meal. He sat with his elbow on the table, propping his head up with his hand.

Allan carried the slow cooker over to the middle of the table so Maureen could dish out the dinner. They passed their plates to her.

Lance leveled a withering glare at his brother.

"What is going on with you two?" Maureen asked, filling his plate with beef, potatoes, and carrots and handing it back to him.

Allan interrupted. "Backyard looks great, by the way. For future reference, you have a party, you clean up after yourself and your friends. Don't leave it for your mother or me, or there will be no more parties at this house."

With his fork, Lance pointed across the table at Everett. "Tell him!"

Maureen and Allan looked back and forth between the boys.

"Everett never got out of bed today to help," Lance said. "I cleaned the whole backyard by myself. *And* trimmed the hedge."

Allan looked at their oldest son. "Is that true? You left it all for Lance?"

"I didn't leave it for him. I fell back asleep." Everett's tone was sour.

Maureen sighed. "I told you before I left for work to get out of bed and clean up the backyard."

"I just said I fell back asleep."

"Yeah right." Lance's expression was thunderous.

Everett shot him a look.

Allan speared a carrot and put it into his mouth. "Don't do that again. In the meantime, on Saturday, you can help me paint the garage."

Everett sat back in his chair. "I can't. I have plans."

Allan shot back, "Not anymore. You'll be too busy clearing out the garage and painting it."

"It's Mom's stuff, she should clear it out."

"No, she shouldn't. She does enough." Allan cut up a piece of meat. "It's supposed to be a sunny day on Saturday, perfect for painting."

And that was the end of that discussion.

Chapter Five

Despite the backyard being cleaned up, the raccoon continued to show up daily, either late at night or early in the morning. For a smaller animal, he was noisy, getting into things he shouldn't and making a racket as he rooted around for food. They had to move the wheelie bins inside the garage as a temporary fix because somehow he managed to get the lid open and get stuck inside. Maureen had had to go out and tip the bin on its side so the raccoon could make a run for it. She wasn't keen on the bins being kept in the garage with all her fabrics, paints, and rolls of wallpaper, so she went into the hardware store in town and ordered a storage unit for the wheelie bins that could be kept on the side of the garage. Delivery was scheduled for seven to ten days.

Since she was in town, she decided to walk over to Coffee Girl to see her sister Angie. She walked down the length of Oak until she hit Main Street, turning left and walking past her aunt's antique shop, eventually reaching her sister's coffee shop at the corner of Main and Cedar.

Although the sun was out in full force, there was no warmth. The air still had a nip to it. Angie stood outside her shop in her usual work attire: jeans and a T-shirt, and had her hair clipped up in a messy bun. Her arms were folded across her chest as she talked to the guy who owned the café across the street: Java Joe's.

Java Joe himself wasn't bad to look at. Tall and muscular with a neatly trimmed beard and short-cropped dark hair. There was a rumor that his entire back was covered in a tattoo of the American flag and a bald eagle.

As Maureen got closer, she picked up on the clipped tone of her sister's voice. Angie had taken it personally that Java Joe had opened up his café directly across the street from hers. Maureen and Nadine had discussed this a few times, deciding that their younger sister needed to cut him some slack. There was definitely room for two cafés in Lavender Bay, even if they were across the street from one another.

She approached her sister as Java Joe was taking his leave. "Think about it, Evangeline," he said.

Angie snorted. "I have thought about it."

But he ignored her, stepping off the curb to cross the street. "I'll give you a few days," he called over his shoulder.

Maureen came to stand at Angie's side. "What was that about?"

Angie rolled her eyes. "That man is a dreamer. He's been hired to cater a bridal shower and he wants me to do the desserts."

"Like a team effort."

Angie glared at her. "We are NOT a team."

"Okay. Message received."

Angie did not take her eyes off the retreating back of Java Joe. Maureen arched an eyebrow.

"He would pay you, right?"

"Of course. And handsomely, but I said no."

"But why?" Of the four sisters, Angie was the one most prone to getting her nose out of joint, at times even cutting off her nose to spite her face.

"Because he's the competition. I don't want him to think he and I could work together."

Maureen winced. "Sometimes I worry about you, Angie."

"Don't, I'm fine."

Maureen was about to ask if Angie could recommend someone to get rid of that pesky raccoon, but they were interrupted.

"The coffee and pastry won't get made out on the sidewalk, Evangeline," said a croaky voice.

The two sisters turned to the owner of the voice, and both broke into smiles. Well, Maureen smiled, and Angie wore a bemused expression.

"Good morning, Mrs. B," Angie said.

"And to you two as well." Edith Bermingham, or Mrs. B, as she was called, sported a pair of dark slacks, a short-sleeved lavender blouse beneath a khaki-colored London Fog raincoat, and a faint cloud of Chanel No. 5. She slid her oversized sunglasses down her eighty-four-year-old nose and looked directly at Angie. "Did I see you talking to that Java Joe?"

"You did."

"He's got a little goldmine over there," Mrs. B observed.

Angie scowled, but Mrs. B continued talking.

"I always liked a man with money. My third husband had a lot of it, and I think that's why I loved him best out of all of them."

Mrs. B was refreshingly honest, that was for sure, Maureen thought.

"Now, why are we standing out here on the sidewalk in broad daylight?" The older woman's gaze swung from Angie to Maureen and then back again.

"We're just on our way in, Mrs. B." With a smile, Angie said, "Unless you'd rather go to Java Joe's for something to eat."

Mrs. B glanced across the street. "I'm not tempted by a breakfast sandwich or whatever they call it—a slice of lightly buttered toast with some orange marmalade will do nicely, thank you—but I'm tempted to go in if only to ogle that Java Joe." She shook her head and announced, "Mmm-mmm. He's a mighty fine-looking man." She leveled her gaze at Angie. "If you'd stop feuding with him, you could walk over and see what he's got on display."

Now both sisters burst out laughing.

Mrs. B went on. "There's something to be said for a bad boy." She went quiet for a moment, and then said, more to herself than anyone else, "I wonder if he owns a motorcycle."

Maureen had to stifle a laugh. Angie rolled her eyes, smiling. "Come on in, Mrs. B, I've got a fresh batch of those cinnamon rolls with the cream cheese frosting you like so much."

"I do. Let's go, you can't keep someone my age waiting. Every minute is precious."

Maureen followed them inside, inhaling the aromas of vanilla, baked sugar, and freshly ground coffee. This had to be one of the best-smelling places in town. She decided she'd like a coffee and one of those cinnamon rolls. In fact, Mrs. B asked her to join her, and she did, enjoying a pleasant conversation. She should do this more often, she thought: take the time to sit in a coffee shop and talk with people.

As she was walking out of Coffee Girl, she ran into Edna Knickerbocker, Mrs. B's older sister. The two elderly sisters hadn't spoken to each other in decades.

"Good morning, Maureen," Edna said. "Your mother told me you're having problems with a raccoon."

Maureen laughed. "Good news travels fast."

Not reading her sarcasm, Edna agreed. "It sure does. Did you get rid of him?"

"Not yet. Angie gave me the name of someone who will remove him humanely."

"Why waste your money when you can do it yourself?" Edna asked, and then added proudly, "I did."

"But isn't it against the law to relocate raccoons?" Maureen asked.

"Don't pay any attention to that." Edna waved her hand as if lawbreaking wasn't anything to be worried about.

Maureen raised an eyebrow. She'd never been a lawbreaker, and she certainly wasn't going to start now.

"Over the years," Edna explained, "I've had problems with squirrels and raccoons. I set the trap out, put some walnuts or peanuts in it, capture them, put them in the trunk of my car, and take them over to Lavender Hill Park."

It seemed like a lot of work to Maureen. It would be well worth the money to pay someone to do it for her.

Edna was still speaking. "The park is a great place. They all love it over there."

Maureen was half-tempted to ask how Edna knew they loved it. Did the relocated squirrels and raccoons send her a thank-you note? Did she do a post-relocation survey?

Edna opened the café door. "If you want to do it yourself, call me. I can lend you the traps. I may even have some leftover peanuts and walnuts. I bought them in bulk, you see. Now, I must go in for my triple-shot Americano and a glazed donut. I have a lot of work to do at home today, thus the triple shot. If it was an easy day, I'd go for the decaf."

"That's good to know," Maureen replied, unsure of what kind of response Edna wanted from her, if any.

"Anyway, call me if you want a trap."

"Thanks, I will."

Edna waved her hand. "Ta-ta!"

Take-out coffee in hand, Maureen headed toward the beach.

Chapter Six

Allan left for his convention in St. Paul on Wednesday morning. Maureen insisted on driving him to the airport even though he had to be there before six. She didn't bother getting dressed, just threw on her clothes over her nightgown and headed out with him. On her way downstairs, she noticed the door to Everett's room slightly ajar and the light on. She wondered if he was still up.

"Maureen, are you ready? Let's go," Allan said. He was always anxious about getting to the airport with plenty of time to spare.

For April, the morning air had a nip to it, but the sky at the horizon was a thin strip of pale yellow, and she hoped for a sunny day.

"What time are you going to breakfast with Lance?" Allan asked.

"I'm hoping for nine, if he's up by then."

Lance had surprised her the evening before by asking if she'd like to go to breakfast, just the two of them. She'd jumped at the chance. It would be nice to spend some time alone with him. She'd hardly seen him since he came home. And on the rare occasion he was around, he was upstairs in his room. Maybe she could do the same thing with Everett before he went back to college.

"Kind of odd that he asked you to go to breakfast, don't you think?" Allan glanced over at her. Maureen kept her eyes on the road.

"Maybe he'd like to spend some time with his mother." She chose to believe this rather than assigning an ulterior motive to her middle child.

"You're probably right," he eventually said. "You'll make sure the boys see the list of chores I left for them to do while I'm away?"

"I will," she said.

The boys, halfway through their spring break, had been having fun all week with their friends, hardly home except for meals or to change clothes. No one had cracked open a book, and Maureen wondered how their studies were going but didn't want to nag. They were going to be thrilled when they saw their father's list.

As she steered toward the departures area of the airport, Allan said, "Don't go to the trouble of parking the car, Maureen. Drop me off at the curb."

"I don't mind."

"I do. It's still dark out, and I don't want you walking back to the parking lot alone."

"All right." She pulled up to the curb where other fliers were unloading bags from their cars. Curbside drop-off was well illuminated in the early morning darkness.

"Don't even get out of the car." He leaned over and kissed her goodbye. "Love you."

"Love you too."

"I'll text you when I land."

"Thank you."

"I wish I didn't have to go," he said.

Maureen yawned and then laughed. "You always say this. But then when you get there, you're fine. You're always glad you went."

"You know me so well."

"You'll call me tonight?" she asked.

"Yes."

"You better go, you don't want to miss your plane."

"Why do I get the feeling you're trying to get rid of me?"

"I am," she said with a laugh. "It's still early, and I can go back to bed when I get home."

"One more kiss for the road." He reached for her, pulled her toward him, and kissed her again.

"I'll see you in a couple of days."

Once he pulled his suitcase out of the trunk, he rapped on the car, stepped up onto the curb, and waved goodbye.

She waited until he disappeared inside before pulling away and heading home.

The house was still dark and quiet. The drive had woken Maureen up, but it was too early to get up for the day. If she did, she'd be finished by two in the afternoon, and that wouldn't do. There was a lot on her schedule.

The only light on was the one over the sink. Someone had used the dishcloth and rolled it up into a ball and thrown it on the counter. She ran it under the hot water tap and squeezed it out before folding it in half and laying it over the side of the sink.

Yawning, she pulled herself up the staircase, thinking how nice it would be to slip under the blankets for a couple of hours before she went to breakfast. She loved sleeping with her husband but every once in a while, she liked to have the whole bed to herself.

Her mind started to go into overdrive about all the things she had to do that day. Briefly, she wondered if she should get started.

At the top of the stairs, Roger the cat went racing by, paying no attention to her. Funny how a five-pound cat could make so much noise and get into so much mischief. True to his nocturnal nature, the cat was up every night, walking or running around. He shined between three and four in the morning, when he was at full throttle.

As she reached her bedroom, she noticed the door to Everett's room was still ajar and the light still on.

No wonder he's like a zombie all day.

Maureen pushed the door open and looked into Everett's room. He was prone on the bed with one side of his face showing. Headphones covered his ears. One arm hung over the side of the bed. He was still wearing the jeans and long-sleeved T-shirt he'd had on yesterday.

Oh, Everett.

She approached him, pulling his blanket from the end of the bed up over him. But as she leaned closer, she realized something was wrong. Frowning, she removed his headphones, hearing the muted, distant sounds of whatever music he was listening to. She froze. His face was deathly white, and a bluish tinge circled his mouth.

"Everett?" When there was no response, she touched him gently so as not to startle him. She repeated his name and shook his shoulder. But he did not rouse. An alarm bell went off in her head, and she picked up his hand, the one that hung over the side of the bed, and probed his wrist for a pulse. His fingertips were blue. His pulse was weak, but it was there. She tried rousing him again but there was no response. She remembered from a first-aid course she and Allan had taken a few years ago that she should move him into the recovery position, but he was heavy, practically dead weight, and it was an effort to move him onto his side.

She'd left her phone downstairs, so she ran to her bedroom and called 9-1-1 from the landline on her side of the bed.

"What is your emergency?"

"I-I need an ambulance," Maureen stammered. Her heart raced, and it felt as if it was going to burst through her chest.

The dispatcher on the other end of the line asked a lot of questions.

Impatient, Maureen said into the phone, "Can you please hurry? My son won't wake up."

"An ambulance is en route to your address. Please make sure they can access the house."

"I've got to unlock the front door."

"All right, ma'am, I'll stay on the line."

Maureen ran out of her room and checked Everett to make sure he was still breathing. She ran to the other end of the hall, knocked quickly on Lance's bedroom door, and opened it.

Lance sat up, groggy. "Mom, what the hell?"

"Lance, get up quick. Everett's unconscious and I need you to go downstairs and wait for the ambulance."

Without a word, he sprang from his bed, ran into Everett's room, and raced over to his brother. He shook him vigorously. "Everett, come on, man. Wake up."

In the distance, the faint sound of sirens could be heard.

"Go downstairs and open the front door," Maureen said.

Lance flew down the stairs in his pajama bottoms and T-shirt, taking the steps two at a time.

Maureen knelt on the floor next to Everett's bed, watching his breathing, which was shallow, and regularly checking his pulse. She heard the ambulance reverse into the driveway and closed her eyes in relief.

Soon, there was the sound of footsteps thudding up the stairs. Someone was here to help her son.

Two EMTs stepped into the room, wearing all black, their last names stitched in white above their left breast pockets. One carried a portable case, which he set on the floor next to the bed and opened. He was of medium height and had a solid build, looking like someone who spent a lot of time in the gym.

"Ma'am, could you step out of the way, please."

Maureen remembered the dispatcher she'd left hanging on the line and ran to the bedroom to inform her that the ambulance had arrived.

She returned to find one of the EMTs attending Everett. The other began to ask Maureen questions. This guy was older, maybe her age, with salt-and-pepper hair. His eyes were puffy and deeply lined, and she wondered if they'd worked the night shift.

"How long has he been like this?" the EMT asked.

Maureen brushed her hand across her forehead, sweeping her hair away, not quite believing what was unfolding in front of her. "I d-d-don't know. I found him like this a few minutes ago. I had to take my husband to the airport."

"Do you know if he took anything?"

Not fully understanding the question, her mind went blank for a moment, and then she snapped out of it. *Had* he taken something? "No, no, I don't think so." She looked over at Lance, who hovered in the doorway, arms folded over his chest, biting his lip.

Ashley appeared, her eyes heavy with sleep, and asked, "What's going on?" She glanced into the room and screamed, trying to push past Lance. "Everett! What happened?"

Lance immediately put his arm around her and steered her away. "Come on, Ash, let's get out of the way."

One EMT attended Everett, putting leads on his chest and explaining they were tracing his heart, but Everett remained unresponsive. The other asked Maureen questions, recording her answers digitally.

"I'm going to administer a dose of Narcan."

"Narcan?" Maureen repeated, blanching. She knew what Narcan was used for: drug overdoses. She took a step closer to her son. Frantic, she asked, "But what if it's not a drug overdose?" A child of hers using drugs? Impossible. It had to be something else.

The EMT recording the data said as if by rote, "If it's not an overdose, it won't harm him." The tone of his voice was one of weary indifference.

The EMT tending to Everett administered the Narcan nasally, inserting the nozzle into one nostril, pressing the plunger, and then repeating the same thing with the other nostril.

Everett sat up and came out swinging, but the EMT dodged the punch as if he'd expected it. Maureen threw her hands to her face and gasped.

"Whoa, there, Everett, we're only trying to help you," said the EMT.

"What the hell!" Everett demanded, lunging for him.

"Everett!" Maureen snapped.

Confusion clouded her son's aggressive features. "Mom?"

"What did you take, Everett?" the EMT asked loudly.

Everett looked at his mother, lay back down, and said flatly, "Nothing."

"Okay," the EMT said, deciding he had other hills to die on. They brought in the stretcher from the hallway and transferred her son onto it, wheeling it out of the bedroom and down the stairs. Maureen, Lance, and Ashley trailed behind them.

When they loaded him into the back of the ambulance, Maureen asked, "Can I ride along?"

After getting the okay, she turned to Lance. "I'll meet you at the hospital, all right?"

"Yeah, Mom, we'll meet you there," Lance said and then addressed his sister. "Come on, let's get dressed."

The EMT closed the doors on the back of the ambulance and headed to the driver's seat. They pulled out of the driveway, and Maureen peered out the back window of the ambulance to see if any neighbors were around. All Maureen could think was that everyone would know their business. The second EMT stayed with them in the back, tending to Everett.

The ride to the hospital out on the highway was no more than ten minutes, but it felt like it took forever to get there. They pulled into the bay, and Maureen waited while they removed Everett using a mechanized ramp that lowered the stretcher onto the ground. She followed the stretcher into the hospital.

The EMT pointed Maureen to a set of automatic doors. "Ma'am, go through there to the waiting room for the emergency room, and someone will be out as soon as they can."

"Okay." She leaned over and kissed Everett on his forehead. He closed his eyes and didn't say anything. One of the EMTs swiped their badge to open another set of double doors, and they whisked Everett through, the doors closing behind them. A sign posted to the door read "No Unauthorized Personnel."

Following their directions, she made her way to the waiting room. She'd been there a few times before with her father, and once when Lance broke a leg playing football. Quickly, she glanced around, hoping she didn't see anyone she knew. She didn't want anyone to find out what had happened. The idea of being grist for the gossip mill was mortifying to her.

"Allan!" she said to herself. Her husband had no idea what had happened. She went for her phone to check the time; maybe she could catch him before he boarded his plane. But in all the commotion, she'd walked out of the house without anything. Her purse and phone were on the kitchen table back home. She rolled her eyes. There was a clock in the waiting room, and she realized that Allan's plane had just taken off. She sat on a hard blue plastic chair and crossed her legs. The place smelled of something unidentifiable and unpleasant, and she scrunched up her nose. She was wired. She wondered how long it would take for someone to come out and talk to her.

But the main thing occupying her mind was that her son had overdosed on drugs. *Her* son. She had so many questions. Had it been his first time, or was he using on a regular basis? How had she not noticed? What would happen? And what would she need to do to fix this?

Chapter Seven

Maureen sat in the waiting room, arms crossed over her chest because in her run to the airport, she hadn't bothered putting on a bra. She still wore the clothes she'd thrown over her nightgown when she left the house with Allan earlier.

Lance and Ashley arrived in the waiting room, looking pale. Lance, car keys dangling from one hand, wore his baseball cap, a pair of jeans, and a T-shirt. Ashley had put on the same, minus a baseball cap, and wore a hoodie. She carried Maureen's purse.

Lance sat on one side of Maureen, Ashley on the other. Ashley handed her mother her purse.

"Thanks for bringing this," Maureen said. "I left in such a hurry I didn't even think about it."

"How is he?" Ashley asked.

Maureen sighed. "I don't know, I haven't spoken to anyone yet."

Lance leaned forward in his seat, removing his baseball cap and scratching his head.

Maureen eyed him. "Did you know your brother was taking drugs?"

He didn't reply, simply shrugged.

"What does that mean?" Maureen demanded.

Finally, he muttered, "I kinda knew."

"Kinda?" Maureen questioned. She turned to her daughter. "Did you know?"

Ashley shook her head. "No. How would I?"

Maureen's gaze swung back to Lance. "How could you not say anything?"

He shrugged again. "You brought us up not to tattletale."

Maureen stared at him, eyes wide and mouth open. "You guys rarely listen to me. I can't get you to wipe the crumbs off the counter when you make yourself a sandwich, but that was the one thing you decided to live and die on."

He finally looked up at her, sheepish. "Sorry, Mom."

"Don't ever again keep secrets like this. This is too big and too important." She looked at her daughter on the other side of her. "That goes for you, too, Ash."

Maureen felt a lecture brewing up inside her. This was a teachable moment. But just then, she spotted her mother, flanked by Nadine and Angie, rushing through the doors, looking frantic. Like herself, they looked like they'd come straight to the hospital, her sisters not even having brushed their hair. Her mother's short, silvery hair always looked the same.

Maureen frowned. "How did they find out?" she asked. Panic filled her. She hadn't wanted anyone to know about this, not even her mother or her sisters.

"I called Gram before we left the house," Lance replied.

"I didn't want anyone to know," Maureen whispered.

Ashley spoke up, parroting what Maureen had said only moments ago to Lance. "Mom, this is too big and important not to tell Gram and your sisters." Then she muttered under her breath, "Besides, it's not 1950."

Maureen would have preferred to deal with this privately. But she couldn't worry about that right now. Her first thought was for Everett. If he'd been taking drugs regularly, he was going to need help, but she didn't even know where to start. This sort of thing was not in her frame of reference. It had always been someone else's kid. But now, here it was, not only on her doorstep, but right under her roof.

Angie spotted them, and she, Nadine, and their mother, Louise, made their way toward them. Maureen stood, and her mother pulled her into her arms and hugged her.

"Oh, Mom." It was then that Maureen started crying, and her mother rubbed her back.

"It'll be all right, honey."

There were hugs all around.

"What happened?" Nadine asked. Her face was heavy with sleep and devoid of makeup.

"Lance said Everett was unconscious," said Angie. She'd scraped her hair into a quick ponytail, and there was a small loop sticking up on the top of her head.

To say the truth out loud almost strangled Maureen's voice. She coughed, cleared her throat, and swiped at her eyes. "He had a drug overdose."

For a moment, her mother and her sisters said nothing, and then the three of them spoke at once.

"What?"

"What do you mean?"

"How is that possible?"

Maureen drew in a deep breath. "Apparently, it is." Without looking at Lance, she told them, "I think he's been taking drugs for a while."

Louise Cook's hands flew to her mouth. "No! Not Everett. He's such a good, sweet boy."

She would have said the same about any of her grandchildren. This was why Maureen hadn't wanted to tell her what had happened; she didn't want her worrying needlessly.

"Look," Maureen said to her mother and her sisters, "I'd like to keep this as private as possible, and I'd appreciate your discretion. I don't want this to become fodder for the gossips."

Angie arched an eyebrow, and Nadine slid a sideways glance at their mother.

"Maureen," Angie said. "You can't control this narrative."

Maureen thought that was rich coming from Angie, who was a bigger control freak than her, but said nothing. She wasn't going to start arguing with her sisters while her family was in the middle of a crisis.

Louise spoke up. "Don't worry about that now, Maureen. Come on, let's sit down."

They all looked around for seats. Louise and Nadine flanked Maureen, and Angie grabbed three seats across from them and Lance and Ashley sat with her. Louise took hold of Maureen's hand and reassured her, "It'll be all right, you'll see."

Maureen wanted to believe her but was doubtful. She felt her brow furrow. "Will it?"

"Where's Allan?" Nadine asked.

"He's on a plane to St. Paul, heading to a dental convention. I have to get a hold of him. But his plane only took off a few minutes ago."

They were all quiet. Louise dug through her purse for her wallet and pulled out a couple of twenties, handing them to Lance. "There's a coffee shop in the lobby. Can you go get us coffee? And get some breakfast for you and Ashley. You must be starving."

"I'm okay, Grandma."

"Good. But get yourself some breakfast." She turned to Maureen and said, "What do you want to eat?"

Maureen frowned. "I don't think I could eat anything right now."

"Okay." She patted her knee reassuringly.

Lance and Ashley disappeared.

"I'm glad he called me," Louise said, watching the two of them take off.

Maureen didn't comment. She was back to trying to register the fact that her oldest son was taking drugs. "You know, whenever I think of drug addicts, I think of an emaciated junkie in a dark alleyway, leaning against some abandoned building with a syringe next to him. You never think it'll be *your* son."

Angie spoke up. "It's just as much a problem in the suburbs as it is in the big cities."

This did not make Maureen feel better.

"Maybe it was a one-off." This from Nadine.

"Somehow, I don't think so." Maureen had been going over the last six months in her mind. "He's changed. He's moody, quiet, and he has a different set of friends." She leaned forward, putting her head in her hands. "How did I not see this? How stupid and blind am I that I didn't attribute the changes in my son to something more serious or sinister? What kind of mother am I? Am I that disengaged?"

Her mother reached out and placed her hand on her back. "Don't beat yourself up."

It was hard not to. She'd failed her son. She looked at her sisters, who had their own busy lives.

To Angie, she said, "Don't you have to be at Coffee Girl?"

"I called Melissa and asked her to open," Angie replied. This was big. Melissa had worked at the shop for years, and she was very good at what she did, but Angie had trouble letting go and delegating. This was a major step for her.

Maureen looked at Nadine, sitting next to her. "And what about you? You have a full house at the inn. Don't you have to get breakfast ready for your guests?"

"I woke Emma before I left."

Maureen groaned at the thought of another person being inconvenienced.

Nadine continued. "She's been helping me all week since she's been home, so she knows the drill by now. Don't worry about it. It's more important for us to be here."

"Well, I'm glad you're here." Maureen stood up from her chair. "I need to find a restroom. If anyone comes out, tell them I'll be right back."

"Okay," Louise said with a nod.

Angie yanked on something behind Maureen. "Did you know you've got a big bow hanging out from beneath your sweater?"

Maureen looked over her shoulder and sighed. The sash that tied in the back of her nightgown hung over the waist of her jeans. At that point she didn't care, but Angie tucked it in quickly.

"Thanks." She headed off to the restroom.

When she returned, Lance and Ashley had reappeared with coffee in take-out trays and a large box of donut holes. Lance was in the process of wolfing down two egg-and-sausage breakfast sandwiches on croissants. *Breakfast.* She and Lance had had plans to go out for breakfast that morning. She sighed. It would have to be another time. He was due to return to college over the weekend. She hoped she could squeeze in some time with him, but now everything was up in the air.

She took her seat and waited.

It was a while before the doctor came out to talk to them. All six of them stood. He explained that it had been a drug overdose, specifically oxycodone, and that Everett was very lucky. Had he not been found until later, the outcome might have been different. Maureen shuddered. Louise gasped, and Maureen's sisters went pale. Everett would be admitted for observation and at some point, the hospital social worker and discharge planner would talk to them.

"Can I see him?" Maureen asked.

"Yes." The doctor hesitated, looking at the six of them. "Two at a time only."

Maureen and Louise went in first.

Everett lay on a gurney, one hand thrown over his head, and they approached him.

"Hey, Gram," he said quietly.

"You gave us quite a scare, Everett."

He mumbled something, but it was indiscernible. A paper-thin blue curtain separated him from patients on either side of him. This was not the place for a proper conversation.

Maureen wasn't leaving his side and made herself comfortable in the chair there. They'd been informed that they were waiting for a bed, but for now Everett would remain in the ER.

She'd always hated hospitals, as either a patient or a visitor. The strong smell of disinfectant that didn't totally mask the smells of the sick and dying. And the staff running back and forth, and the look of resignation in some patients' eyes when they knew they'd never leave the hospital. And then there was the emergency room and the interminable waiting.

When Louise left, Maureen instructed her to send in Angie for a quick visit and then Nadine, as she wanted them to get back to their jobs. Allan came to mind, and she realized his plane should have landed by now. She dug through her purse until she found her phone, and there was a text from him, saying he'd landed.

Angie arrived and tentatively approached Everett. "What were you thinking, Everett?" were the first words out of Angie's mouth. The kids were used to their aunt's brusque, abrupt manner, and took no offense. Sometimes she said what needed to be said.

Maureen stood from her chair. "Sit here, Angie. I've got to step outside and call Allan. His plane has landed."

Everett groaned. "Do you have to tell Dad?"

Maureen frowned. "Of course I do. I can't keep something like this from him."

To Angie, she said, "I'll send Nadine in, and then the two of you should go. You've got work."

"Don't worry about it." Impulsively and out of character, Angie reached out and pulled her sister into a hug. "Go make your phone call. I'll hold down the fort."

Maureen weaved through the chaos that was the emergency room. Every gurney was occupied, and there was a crowd of nurses and doctors at the nurses' station, all talking, with phones ringing behind them. The need to step out of this morass and breathe some fresh air, if only for five minutes, was strong.

Passing through the waiting room, she indicated to Nadine that she could go on back, holding up her phone and mouthing, "Allan." Nadine nodded and stood from her plastic chair. Maureen headed through the automatic double doors and stepped outside, inhaling a lungful of air. Overhead, the sky was blue and cloudless. The morning air was brisk, and there was no warmth from the weak sun rising in the east.

To put some space between herself and the hospital, she walked about fifty paces. At the end of the sidewalk, she bent over, put her hands on her thighs, and let out a loud gasp. It still hadn't completely sunk in, the drama of the morning. Her son was using drugs. It was outside the realm of possibilities for her but here she was, standing outside of the hospital, dreading the phone call she had to make to her husband. She liked to think of him now, in St. Paul. The airport so easily came to mind. An image of Allan, fast-walking like he always did and dragging his carry-on behind him, filled her head. He was in another state, blissfully unaware of all the drama that was going on with their family. She hated that she would have to make a phone call and deliver devastating news, hated that she would have to crush his soul. She waited five minutes. Gave him five more minutes of peace and believing all was well with the world and their family.

Finally, she pulled out her phone and called him.

Slipping her hand into her back pocket, she lifted her head, watching another ambulance, sirens blaring, pull through the entrance.

He answered on the first ring. "Hey, I was just going to text you. I'm heading out to grab a taxi."

Maureen's voice shook. "You might not want to leave the airport." She looked down and kicked a small stone with the toe of her sneaker. "You need to come home."

Chapter Eight

Allan wasn't able to get back until late that evening, and it took him being flown to Chicago and then to New York City before the final stretch home to Lavender Bay. It was almost midnight by the time his plane landed. This time, Maureen left the car in the parking lot and went into the airport, waiting for his arrival. To think she'd dropped him off to catch his flight out only eighteen hours ago. It felt like years.

He looked like she felt: old, weary, and haggard. She was so tired she felt like her eyes were crossed. There were no words spoken between them as they embraced, holding on to each other for what seemed like a long time. When they finally pulled apart, they both spoke at once.

"How are you holding up?"

"You must be exhausted."

There was nothing to do but go in for another quick hug.

"I'm so glad you're home," she whispered against his neck.

"Me too."

They walked out together to the parking lot, Allan pulling his carry-on behind him. When they got to the car, he threw his bag in the trunk and they both moved toward the driver's side door.

"I'll drive," he offered.

She shook her head. "No, you've spent the last eighteen hours in airports and have been on four planes. *I'll drive.*"

No jokes or teasing, he went around to the passenger side and got in. They buckled up, and Maureen put the car in reverse. Allan looked behind him.

"All clear on this side."

Exiting the airport, she headed toward the entrance ramp of the thruway.

Once she'd merged with traffic, Allan said, "All right. Tell me again what happened. I'm still trying to make sense of this."

"You and me both." Maureen sighed, then relayed the whole story about how she'd found Everett unconscious that morning. It had been an emotionally exhausting day. She'd remained at the hospital, sending Lance and Ashley home around dinnertime with money to order pizza and wings for themselves. The last she'd heard was that her mother had gone over to stay with the kids. They were old enough to be by themselves, of course, but she figured it would be a comfort to have their grandmother around. Another adult during this awful time.

"How long will he be in the hospital?" Allan asked.

"This afternoon, the doctor said he'd be in for a couple of days to be monitored medically."

Allan nodded.

The sky was a velvety black and the moon a golden orb. Ahead of them, the darkness was punctuated by her headlights and the red bars of the taillights ahead of them. She went slightly over the speed limit, anxious to get home.

Allan looked out the window. "I can't believe this. When you told me on the phone this morning that

Everett had overdosed, you could have knocked me over with a feather. I still can't believe it." He shook his head.

"Neither can I." She got stuck behind someone who was barely doing the speed limit. Putting on her indicator, she looked over her shoulder and moved into the passing lane, moving past the slower car and getting ahead. "How did we miss this?"

"I don't know." In his voice, she heard the guilt she felt. They'd been pretty involved parents since day one, but to miss something as big as this felt like an indictment. It made her wonder what else was going on with her kids that she had no knowledge of. Was she that clueless? Or had trouble been floating along just below the radar?

"I know it's late, but I want to stop at the hospital. I want to see him," Allan said.

"Are you sure?" She looked over at him. He looked as if he'd aged considerably since that morning. But almost losing your child to a drug overdose would age anyone.

She exited the closest ramp to the hospital. When they arrived, Allan said, "Park right out front. No need to come in. I'll only pop in for a few minutes."

She nodded. She dropped Allan off at the front entrance and pulled up and parked in a no-parking zone.

Allan was back within fifteen minutes. As he slid into the seat, he said, "He was asleep, so I didn't wake him."

Maureen pulled out of the hospital and into traffic, eager to get home to bed.

"Hard to believe that kid in the hospital bed is the same kid who couldn't do anything without his blankie," Allan said.

She smiled at the memory of it. "He must have carried that blanket around until he was seven years old."

"It was pretty ratty by then."

They drove in silence the rest of the way home. The house was dark when they arrived. Allan flipped on the kitchen light as they entered.

"Your carry-on, it's still in the trunk." She turned to retrieve it.

"Leave it. There's nothing I need tonight, and it's not like I'm going to unpack it now."

Maureen locked the door. With a quick glance, she looked around the kitchen, relieved that no one had left her a mess to deal with. But then, her mother had been there. There were no dirty dishes in the sink, no empty pizza boxes on the counter, and not a crumb on the table or the countertops. Even the dishcloth was folded in half and lying over the side of the sink, just how she liked it.

She went to turn off the light, but Allan said, "Don't turn it off. I'm going to have a quick drink."

"Okay."

"Care to join me?" He pulled off his jacket and threw it over the arm of a kitchen chair, unbuttoning the top button on his shirt.

She shook her head. "I'm beat, I'm going up."

"I won't be long."

"Sure." She gave him a quick kiss on the cheek, and he pulled her into an embrace. His warmth and solidness were reassuring.

Maureen didn't bother washing her face. She peeled off her clothes, slipped on her nightgown, collapsed in a heap on the bed, and passed out from fatigue. But she awoke from a deep sleep an hour later, feeling as if she'd slept all night. Allan was not beside her in the bed. Getting up, she felt around the floor for her slippers and made her way back downstairs to make sure Allan hadn't fallen asleep on the couch. His back would be bothering him in the morning if he slept there all night.

He was right where she'd left him, sitting in his seat at the head of the kitchen table. In front of him was a tumbler half full of scotch.

Maureen frowned. "Have you been drinking all this time?"

"No. I poured it with good intentions but can't seem to get it down."

As she stepped closer, she realized her husband of almost twenty-five years had been crying.

Immediately, she went to him, standing behind him and wrapping her arms around him. "Oh, Allan," she whispered.

He placed a hand on her arm. "I can't believe this! Drugs. Drugs!"

Allan rarely cried. And when he did, you knew it was about something that had touched his core.

Maureen kissed the top of his head. "We'll get through this like we've gotten through everything else."

"Will we?" He sounded despondent.

"Of course." He was having a bit of a wobble; it was her turn to be strong and positive. It would do Everett no good for both his parents to give up hope that things could turn around.

"Come on, come to bed. Things will look better in the morning," she said, not sure she believed it herself.

"It's always darkest before the dawn," he said.

"Yes." Allan loved all those old cliché sayings and corny dad jokes, as his father had.

He stood and emptied his glass in one gulp. Maureen held out her hand, took the empty tumbler, and loaded it into the dishwasher.

The following day, Maureen and Allan met with the substance use counselor, a young woman named Naomi. She went over the various options for treatment for drug addiction: inpatient, outpatient, and residential rehab.

"Did you want a referral?" Naomi asked.

In unison, they said yes. They'd discussed it on the way to the hospital. They had no idea how long Everett had been using drugs. But they would have a conversation with him today about entering rehab.

She gave them a couple of brochures, and Maureen tucked them into her purse.

"Of course, it will depend on your insurance coverage and which facilities have a bed available," Naomi said.

Allan folded his arms across his chest, rocking back and forth on his heels. "If we have to, we'll pay out of pocket. Privately."

"That can get pricey."

He nodded his acknowledgment.

They headed up to Everett's room a short while later, stopping in the lobby to get coffee and donuts. In the back of her mind, Maureen remembered that both boys were due to return to college over the weekend. Everett would not be going anywhere. She'd have to make some phone calls the following day once she knew what the plan was. He might have to take a leave of absence. It didn't matter; college would always be there. The first priority was getting him off the drugs. And keeping him off of them.

Everett was awake, with a barely touched tray of scrambled eggs, toast, oatmeal, and yogurt in front of him.

Maureen held up the bag. "We brought donuts."

Everett replied with a nod. She set the bag down on his over-the-bed table and pushed the coffee cup toward him. Allan set the take-out tray on the table as well, and Maureen picked up her coffee and set it on the windowsill. She peered inside the donut bag and helped herself to a glazed one.

She took the one chair in the room and pulled it out from the back wall so she could see Everett better. She parked it next to the windowsill and sat down.

Allan stood on the other side of the bed, arms across his chest.

"How are you feeling?" he asked.

"Fine," Everett said.

"Everett, what's happening here? Have you taken drugs before this?" Allan asked.

Everett's voice was so low they barely heard him. "Yes."

Allan drew in a long, sharp breath. Maureen recognized this mode of her husband's. It was the "I'm going to get to the bottom of things so I can fix them" mode. If he hadn't been a dentist, he would have made a great detective, something she'd told him more than once over the course of their marriage. She sat back, sipped her coffee, and set it back down on the windowsill. She pulled off a piece of her glazed donut and stuffed it into her mouth. It was sticky and sweet.

"How long has this been going on?" Allan asked.

Everett shrugged. "I don't know."

Allan raised his eyebrows and his voice. "You don't know?"

Everett finally lifted his head to look at his father. "Dad, come on."

Maureen closed her eyes. These were trigger words for Allan.

"No, you come on," Allan said. "We almost lost you yesterday."

"You're blowing this out of proportion." There was a flash of anger in Everett's eyes.

Maureen didn't know why, but she'd assumed Everett would be contrite. She hadn't expected anger. This worried her.

Allan looked over at her. "Tell him what the doctor told you."

Everett did not look at his mother.

"The doctor said if we didn't find you until later, it would have been a different outcome," Maureen said. "You probably would have died." Those words sounded so surreal to her.

"They're trying to scare you," Everett said.

"We're already afraid," Maureen said. Her appetite had disappeared, and she tossed the other half of her donut into the plastic trash can beneath the television mounted high on the wall.

"And if you're not scared," Allan said, "you should be."

Everett did the smart thing and kept his mouth closed.

"The doctors said you're taking oxycodone," Allan continued. "Where are you getting that from? That's a prescription-only medication. Doctors don't give that out for the fun of it."

Everett avoided meeting his father's eyes as he spoke. "From a friend of a friend."

"Does this friend of a friend go to Michigan?" Allan asked.

Everett shook his head. "No, I met him at an off-campus house party."

"And he just handed you drugs, and you took them."

Everett made a *tsk* noise as if he was annoyed. "I tried it. I wanted to see what it was like. I wanted to experience it."

Maureen spoke up. "But you kept doing it."

Their son looked down at his hands in his lap. "Yes."

"Anyway, we've spoken to the discharge planner about rehab," Maureen continued.

Everett snorted. "I don't need rehab. It's not like I have a *problem*."

They stared at their oldest son, stunned.

"What do you suggest, hotshot?" Allan asked. Beneath his calm exterior, Maureen sensed anger duking it out with disbelief. She knew how he felt. "You've been taking this stuff for what, a year?"

"I don't know. Less than a year."

"More than six months?"

Everett hesitated. "Yes."

This was disheartening to Maureen. Again, how had they missed this? Granted, he'd been away from home, but he'd been back as recently as Christmas.

"Why?" she asked.

"I don't know." Everett shook his head. His attitude suggested he was fed up with all the questions.

"Your mother and I only want to help you, Everett," Allan said quietly. "We're concerned."

"Don't worry about it, Dad," Everett said. "I can quit anytime."

"That's great to hear. You can quit today."

"I already have," Everett lifted his chin and stared at his father, his attitude defiant.

"Is everything all right at school?" Maureen asked.

He was about to answer, but Allan interjected. "Tell us the truth."

"It's not going too good," Everett said.

"Are you failing?"

"Yes."

"All right, we'll deal with the issue of school later," Allan said. "Right now, I think our best bet is to get you into rehab. The discharge planner has given us a couple of names of treatment facilities for addiction issues."

Maureen pulled the brochures out of her purse and set them on the table in front of her son. "There are some nice places. They even have an inpatient program here at the hospital if you'd prefer that."

Allan spoke. "Look them over and think about where you want to go. All these places have beds available, but you'll have to decide today, because you'll probably be discharged soon."

Everett didn't even glance at the brochures. He looked at his parents and shook his head. "No, I'm not going to rehab. I don't need it. I can handle this myself, without anyone's help."

Chapter Nine

By the end of the week, Maureen tried to resume some normalcy. Allan had booked the time off work for the conference, so he would spend the day at the hospital. But she had two clients to meet, and she wanted to cook some dinner. They hadn't seen much of Lance and Ashley over the last few days, as all their time was spent up at the hospital. What was the saying? The child that was suffering the most got the most attention? Or there was the one about only being as happy as your unhappiest child. It seemed to her that both applied.

She'd made a ham for dinner with a candy glaze just like her mother used to make, using toothpicks to secure maraschino cherries and pineapple rings to the outside of the ham. There were mashed potatoes and green beans to go along with it.

The four of them sat down to dinner. Maureen hadn't realized how hungry she was until she put a forkful into her mouth. For the past three days, she hadn't had a proper meal.

"What's going to happen with Everett?" Ashley asked, cutting her ham into pieces.

"We're trying to convince him to go to rehab." Maureen helped herself to another spoonful of green beans. "But he's convinced he can do it himself. He'll probably come home here."

A cloud of silence fell over them for a few minutes, the only sounds being the noise of cutlery.

Allan looked at Lance and Ashley. "Are either one of you doing drugs? Be honest. Your mother and I would like to know."

Ashley was offended. "No, Dad!"

Lance looked up from his plate at his father. "No. Honest."

"That's a relief."

After the dishes were cleared, Maureen brought over a cheesecake she'd picked up at the supermarket and sliced it up, plating four pieces and passing them around. Seated, she forked off a piece and popped it into her mouth.

Looking over at Lance, she asked, "Are you going back on Saturday?" The plan for Lance's return to college had been vague at best.

He shrugged. "I think so."

She felt bad that she'd hardly spent any time with him during his spring break.

"It won't be long before finals," Allan said, scraping the last bit of cheesecake off his plate.

Lance looked up at the ceiling. "May sixteenth. My last final. Hallelujah."

"See, you got through your first year." Maureen smiled encouragingly at him. Lance had never been keen on school. "I told you the four years would fly by. They did for me."

"Sorry, Mom, but it's dragging for me."

"I can't wait to go away to college," Ashley said excitedly.

Lance rolled his eyes. "That's because you're weird."

Ashley stuck her tongue out at him.

"I rest my case." Lance put a forkful of cheesecake into his mouth.

Maureen took her plate of half-eaten dessert and handed it to Lance. "Pass this to your father." She'd eaten too much ham and mashed potatoes. Despite the lovely meal, worry began to sink in about Everett and what it would be like with him living at home.

Chapter Ten

On Saturday morning, Allan was called into work for a dental emergency. Some kid had gone down a slide at a playground and put his front teeth through his bottom lip. Maureen assured him that she'd be fine picking up Everett, who was being discharged later that morning now that his labs had come back normal. She contacted her mother, who readily agreed to go with her.

Lance was packing up his car to return to his dorm and Ashley was still upstairs, sleeping.

"We won't be long, I hope," Maureen told him. "Gram is going with me to the hospital, so I've got to pick her up and then we'll head over to get your brother. Will you please wait until we get home before you leave?"

"Sure thing." He stood there, hesitant, his hands in his pockets.

She eyed him curiously. "Everything all right?"

"I was hoping to talk to you before I left."

"Of course, honey. As soon as I get back, you and I will sit down and have a talk."

"Okay, thanks, Mom."

She picked up her purse, double-checking to make sure her phone was inside, and grabbed her keys from the table. "I'll see you later."

She drove over to Heather Lane, and when her mother didn't come out of the house right away, Maureen parked in the driveway, climbed the steps onto the small front porch, knocked on the door, and went inside.

"Mom?" she called.

"In the kitchen."

She found her mother pulling the bag of garbage out of the trash can, tying it up, and setting it aside to be taken out.

"I'm running a bit behind," Louise said.

"Don't worry about it. You know how long it takes to get discharged. I highly doubt he'll be sitting on the edge of the bed waiting to go home."

Louise pulled a new garbage liner from the bottom of the trash can. Also at the bottom was a liberal amount of potpourri she kept there to keep the garbage smelling "fresh," if that was possible. A Christmas potpourri was currently in use, leaving the trash can smelling of cinnamon and bayberry.

Louise straightened up and lifted the bag of trash. "I'll take this out and meet you out front."

Maureen took the bag from her. "I'll take this out. You wash your hands and get your coat."

"Okay, *Mom*," Louise said with a laugh.

"It's what happens when you're the eldest daughter and you've been taking care of everyone since you were young."

Louise didn't comment on that. "I'll be out in a jiffy," she said.

Maureen almost smiled at the use of the word "jiffy." Allan would love that.

After dumping the bag of trash in the wheelie bin behind the garage, Maureen headed to her car, where her mother was just getting in on the passenger side.

As soon as Maureen slid behind the wheel and buckled up, her mother asked, "What's wrong, other than the obvious? Has Everett had a setback?"

"No, but he's refusing to go to rehab. Says he can kick the drugs himself," Maureen muttered.

"What is he thinking?"

Maureen shook her head. "I don't know. Allan and I spoke to him about it until we were blue in the face, but he was adamant he's not going to an inpatient facility."

"So, what now?"

"He's going to take a leave of absence from school, come home, and do an outpatient program."

"That's better than nothing." Louise said.

Maureen leaned back and sighed. She wished she shared her mother's optimism.

"It's tough, finding out you have a child taking drugs," Louise said quietly.

Maureen grimaced. "There's something about it that seems so seedy to me."

"It's disappointing."

"I am so ashamed."

"Shame is a useless emotion," Louise said thoughtfully. "Besides, you have nothing to be ashamed about.

Things happen. Things go wrong. I'm sure it's natural to feel these emotions, but you need to focus on why he started taking drugs. Get to the bottom of it. When I think of drugs or cigarettes or booze, I think people are looking for an escape. Find out what's going on in his life and in his head that he felt the need to turn to drugs."

"I hope it's that simple."

"It's that simple and it's that hard."

They were quiet for a moment, until Louise asked, "Are we going to sit in the driveway all day or do you think you'll start the car, honey?"

Maureen laughed and pressed the keyless ignition. She supposed they looked ridiculous, sitting there parked in the driveway with their seatbelts on.

Everett wasn't discharged right away. They were made to wait. Louise sat in the only chair in the room, and Maureen leaned against the windowsill.

By early afternoon, when there was still no sign of the doctor, Maureen offered to drive Louise home, but she refused, saying she had no plans that day and didn't mind waiting. Finally, mid-afternoon, one of the nurses entered the room with the discharge paperwork.

Everett was silent on the way home, holding on to his backpack as if he might have to jump out of the car at a moment's notice. They dropped Louise off first, who made Everett get out of the car so she could kiss and hug him goodbye. When he returned to the back seat, Maureen looked in the rearview mirror at him. "You can sit up front, you know."

"I'm fine." He turned his head and stared out the window.

Maureen waved goodbye to her mother as she disappeared into her house. As she backed out of the driveway, she tried to lighten the mood by saying, "I feel like a taxi driver."

"Okay, Mom."

They only lived a few blocks from Louise and were home in five minutes. She hadn't even put the car in park when Everett jumped out of the back seat and ran into the house.

She stared after him for a few moments, wondering how they were going to proceed. What was he going to do? Would he lock himself up in his room, only coming out for meals? Would he continue to be sullen and surly? Would they have to walk on eggshells around him? This was way out of their league. Finally, she got out of the car and went inside. There was no sign of Everett; he and his backpack had disappeared.

There was also no sign of Lance, and she hadn't seen his car in the driveway. On the kitchen table was a yellow Post-it note with Lance's familiar scribble.

Sorry, Mom, had to leave. Talk soon.

Maureen pressed her lips together. He'd wanted to talk to her about something and she'd let him down. She sent off a text to him right away.

Sorry I missed you. Delayed at the hospital.

Thirty minutes later, he responded.

It's okay.

She typed quickly. *Will I call you tonight? We can talk then.*

Not that important was his reply.

Chapter Eleven

"Maureen, I love it!" Mrs. Whittaker gushed. "That orange is the perfect shade! It pulls the room together." The older woman was dressed in shorts and a short-sleeved T-shirt, as summer had arrived.

Months after Maureen had done her initial consult, Mrs. Whittaker's downstairs was finished. It was like a breath of fresh air. Gone were the dark paneling and the sculpted carpet. In their place were hardwood floors, a large area rug, white-painted woodwork, and navy walls. And throughout the living room were the orange accents: a tulip chair that complemented the new living room furniture. Throw cushions in crushed velvet.

Maureen stood in the middle of the room and smiled, satisfied.

Mrs. Whittaker sat down on her brand-new gray sofa, brushing her hand over the fabric of the seat cushion next to her. "I can't believe this is the same room!" She stared, her head swiveling around to look at everything, her mouth agape. "You know, I think Mr. Whittaker would have approved too." She hugged herself, a broad grin across her face. "I love it! I *really* love it."

She got up from her new sofa and beckoned Maureen to follow her back to the kitchen, where her brand-new white laminate cabinets gleamed in the sunlight streaming through the windows.

She pulled a checkbook out of her purse. "Can I make you a sandwich? Or how about a cup of tea?"

Maureen laughed. "No, thank you."

Her client rummaged through a drawer, finally pulling out a pen. She was halfway through writing on the old-style green check when she paused, pen in hand, and looked up at Maureen. "How's Everett doing?"

This question blindsided Maureen. She hadn't expected it. Hadn't known that her client was aware of her family's problems. She stuttered, "He's all right."

If Mrs. Whittaker sensed Maureen's discomfort, she didn't let on, bending her head to finish writing out the check. "I was sorry to hear about his troubles. What a shame." Her lips compressed into a grim smile, and she shook her head. "It just goes to show you that it could happen to anyone."

She signed her name with a flourish and tore the check carefully from the book, handing it to Maureen. "Again, I can't thank you enough," she said.

With a shaky hand, Maureen tucked the check into a side pocket in her purse. With the mention of Everett, she was anxious to get out of there.

"Are you sure you won't have a cup of tea?" Mrs. Whittaker asked.

Maureen shook her head. "I have an appointment," she lied.

"Another time."

"Yes, another time," Maureen repeated.

Mrs. Whittaker walked her to the door and waved her off. As Maureen reached her car, the older woman called out behind her, "I'll be praying for Everett!"

"Thank you."

Maureen's neck disappeared into her shoulders as she looked up and down the street to make sure no one else was present. The street appeared empty, but people could have their windows open.

She unlocked her car, slid in, buckled up, and drove away.

Far too many people in town knew of Everett's overdose. Well-meaning people approached her all the time to ask after him and offer unsolicited advice. She understood the dynamics of a small town such as Lavender Bay, but she didn't feel that her son was communal property. Or that it was anyone's business.

It had been almost three months since his overdose, and they were tooling along. Ashley had graduated from high school, and they'd had a small party for her at the Annacotty Room. Lance had returned from his dorm and had gotten a job with a landscaping firm, working six days a week from dawn to dusk. He seemed to enjoy it, but she didn't see that much of him.

And Everett was back to living at home. He was looking for a job but had had no luck. She understood why people were hesitant to hire him. The only job offer he'd received was from Angie, who said he could work part time in the kitchen, and she would train him herself.

But Maureen had nixed that idea. She didn't want any trouble between her and her sister.

She and Allan kept an eagle eye on Everett, looking for any tell-tale signs of a relapse. And they kept him busy. He had a once-a-week meeting with an outpatient counselor, and Allan insisted he attend Narcotics Anonymous meetings, which meant he was driving all over the place, sometimes outside Lavender Bay. But Maureen wondered if it was doing any good. He never spoke about the meetings, and she didn't pry, although she wanted to ask questions: Did he contribute? Did he speak up? Did he get anything out of the meetings, or did he sit quietly like a bump on a log?

But their oldest son continued to reassure them that he was fine. Promised them he wasn't taking drugs. And they had no choice but to believe him. To prove it to them, he was up early every day and did everything that was asked of him. When their cleaner, Amy, took a week off to go to Florida, Maureen tasked him with washing the floors and dusting and vacuuming. He did this without complaint. Allan kept him busy for another week moving the dental practice to a new office.

Things seemed to be going well, but Maureen continued to hold her breath. Allan had mentioned the previous evening about going away for a weekend, but she had been unenthused. She was afraid if they left, everything would fall apart. As of yet, she wasn't totally convinced Everett would be able to stay clean. But she was hopeful.

Once home from her visit to Mrs. Whittaker, she poured herself a cup of coffee and sat down at the kitchen table. Roger the cat appeared and wound his way around her legs, purring.

"It's too early for dinner, Roger. You know that." She sipped her coffee and reveled in the quiet of the house. Today was Tuesday, and Everett had driven all the way to Cheever for an NA meeting. Lance was working, and Ashley had gone to the beach with Emma, who was home from college for the summer.

Roger, upon seeing that no dinner was forthcoming, trounced off to the family room.

Maureen finished her coffee and decided she'd do some laundry. She needed to keep up on Lance's work clothes: By the end of his workday, his clothes were stained with grass, mud, and sweat, and he went through a fresh T-shirt and pair of cargo shorts every day.

Balancing a laundry basket on her hip, she walked up the stairs and emptied the laundry hampers in hers and Allan's bathroom and in the main bathroom. As she turned to head downstairs, she peeked into Everett's room. The made bed was a good sign. She used to have to nag him to do it. His room was pretty clean: no used dishes piled on the floor, no dirty laundry thrown around the place. The drapes were open, and there wasn't so much as a speck of dust on the furniture.

Satisfied, she walked past his room but stopped dead in her tracks when she reached the top of the staircase. Backtracking, she stood in Everett's doorway and looked around again. Narrowing her eyes, she thought, *It's almost too perfect.*

God help her, she stepped inside his room and did something she'd never done before: she began to search it. She glanced at his bedside clock. His NA meeting was beginning in five minutes up in Cheever.

She started with the obvious, first the dresser drawers, rifling through each one and feeling around beneath piles of clothes for any drug contraband. She didn't even know what she was looking for, but she would know it when she saw it.

After the dresser, she looked through every drawer in his desk, even checking behind it and feeling around beneath the center drawer for an envelope or a packet or anything.

Still with no success, she rummaged through his closet, taking the chair from his desk and going through everything on the top shelf. The longer she looked and found nothing, the better she began to feel. But guilt crept in; she had no business going through his personal things. She told herself it was for his own good. When she was finished going through every shoe in his closet, she got down on all fours, lifted the bedspread, and searched beneath it. It was clear.

Finished, she sat on his bed, crossed her arms over her chest, and bit her lip. She hated to think Everett was lying to them and using again, but her gut told her there was something to be found in this room. Suddenly exhausted, she lay back, putting her head on his pillow. She closed her eyes for a moment and exhaled loudly. She rolled on her side and put her hand beneath the pillow to pull it tighter to her.

That's when she felt something. A plastic bag. Maureen shot up as if she'd been burnt, pulling out the package. It was a small baggie, and it was full of little white pills. She stared at it and burst into tears.

Chapter Twelve

After a few minutes, Maureen pulled herself together and got up, taking the baggie with her and putting it in a safe place in her bedroom. She had to get to work. She forced herself to compartmentalize what was happening, at least until later, because she had an appointment with a client. Once the washing machine was started, she headed out of the house for her next meeting.

When she returned home later that afternoon, Lance and Allan had beaten her home, Lance already showered and downstairs, looking for dinner. Ashley was already seated at the table, waiting to eat.

"Is Everett home?" Maureen asked.

"No, I don't think so," Allan said. He looked at Lance, who shrugged.

She pulled her wallet out of her purse and plucked some twenties from it, handing them to Lance.

"Do me a favor and take Ash out for dinner."

Lance frowned. "What? Why?"

Ashley sat there, unsure.

Even Allan looked puzzled.

"Your father and I have to have a chat with Everett, and we'll need some privacy. Can you disappear for a while?"

Understanding, Lance said quietly, "Sure, Mom."

"Is he using again?" Ashley asked, a hurt expression on her face.

"Honestly, I don't know. I hope not, but we need to talk to him."

Lance turned to his sister. "Where do you want to go for dinner, Ash?"

"Thai or sushi."

"Yeah, okay. Either one sounds good. Let's go."

As soon as the two of them closed the door, Allan turned to Maureen and asked, "What's this about?"

"One moment. I need to run upstairs and get something." In her bedroom, she retrieved Everett's baggie of pills that she'd hidden. When she returned to the kitchen she was about to show it to Allan, but she heard the door opening, and quickly stuffed the baggie into her pocket just as Everett came into view.

"We're eating in five minutes," she said.

"Great, I'm starving. I'll be down in five minutes." Everett's footfall was heavy on the staircase as he disappeared.

As Maureen hurriedly put some leftover beef stroganoff in a glass bowl and put it in the microwave, Allan asked, "Do you want to tell me what's going on?"

Looking over her shoulder to make sure they were alone, she pulled out the baggie. "I found this today in Everett's room."

Allan's shoulders sagged, and he leaned against the counter for support. "Oh no."

As the beef stroganoff reheated in the microwave, Maureen set the table for three, and Allan poured water into the glasses.

When the microwave pinged, she grabbed an oven mitt and pulled out the bowl. With a large spoon, she stirred everything around before dividing it up between three plates.

She carried two plates over to the table and set one down in front of her husband and one at Everett's place.

She grabbed her own plate and was just about to call Everett when there was a thunderous roar of footsteps on the staircase, followed by Everett barreling into the kitchen. Maureen took her seat at the table and placed her napkin in her lap.

"Mom, have you been in my room?" Everett demanded. He remained standing, his hands gripping the back of his chair.

"Sit down, Everett, and eat your dinner," Maureen said quietly.

Everett pointed at his mother and raised his voice. "Answer my question."

Allan interrupted. "Hey, hey, please don't use that tone with your mother, and whatever you do, don't point your finger at her."

Maureen pulled the baggie of pills from the front pocket of her jeans. "Look what I found! Is this what you're so angry about? That I found your stash?"

Everett reached for it, but Maureen kept it out of his reach.

Very quietly, Allan asked, "Everett, are those yours?"

"Yes, and I want them back." He tried to reach for them again.

Allan held out his hand to Maureen, who gave him the baggie, relieved to be rid of it.

"Is this oxycodone?" Allan's voice remained disturbingly quiet. There was no anger, which surprised Maureen.

"Yes," Everett answered.

"Where did you get them?" Allan asked.

Everett remained silent. Their dinners sat on the table, uneaten, growing cold.

"I asked you a question," Allan said.

Everett shrugged and said casually, "A friend."

Allan sighed. "You gave us your word that you would quit. You said you didn't need rehab. Remember?"

"It's not like I've been taking a lot of them since I came home."

"But you have been taking them," Allan said.

"Yes."

Allan leveled a glare at him. "Doesn't your word mean anything to you? You promised us you'd stop taking drugs, but you're doing it right under our roof."

There was no apology. "They're only pills," Everett muttered.

"And they're ruining your life!" Allan shouted. "You're exhibiting drug-seeking behavior and you aren't even aware of it. You had to take a leave of absence from college."

Maureen interrupted. "Everett, you need to go to a facility for rehab."

Her son narrowed his eyes at her. "Everything was going fine until you went snooping in my room."

Maureen looked at him in disbelief. "You're angry because you got caught?"

He ignored that comment. "I'm not going to rehab. I don't need it."

It dawned on Maureen and Allan that there was no point in arguing with him.

"Here's how it's going to be," Allan said. Maureen raised her eyebrows. This was Allan getting ready to lay down the law. "You can't stay here if you're going to continue to use drugs."

Everett went pale beneath his look of incredulity. "You're kicking me out?"

"No, I'm giving you choices. You can decide. Stop using and go into an inpatient rehabilitation center or you'll have to find someplace else to live."

"I don't believe this!" Everett said. "So much for unconditional love."

"I'm sorry, but it has to be this way."

Sheer panic filled Maureen. She didn't approve of these options, and she wished Allan had discussed them with her before he said anything. Images of Everett living with a houseful of drug addicts—or, worse, living on the streets with a shopping cart full of his belongings—filled her head. She felt sick to her stomach. But she and Allan didn't contradict each other in front of the kids. That was the way it had always been. A united front. So even though she disagreed, she kept quiet. She would talk to him about it later.

"I'll give you until tomorrow to figure it out," Allan said.

Everett didn't say anything at first. He looked at Allan and held out his hand. "Can I have it back?"

It was Allan's turn to look incredulous. "You can't be serious."

When he realized he was, Allan said gravely, "I'm sorry, but I'm not giving them back. I won't allow it." He paused and looked at his son. "There are rules that have to be followed here by all of us. There can be no exceptions to these rules. It isn't fair to Lance and Ashley to have to live with all this turmoil."

Everett muttered a few choice expletives beneath his breath and stormed out of the room.

Later, when they were alone, things were tense between Maureen and Allan. She'd been stunned that her husband had issued such an ultimatum to Everett, and she was afraid of what choice her oldest son would make.

She carried a basket of clean laundry upstairs and dumped it on her bed, folding the clothes haphazardly.

Allan entered their bedroom. "I suppose you think I'm wrong."

"I wish you would have discussed it with me first before you gave him that ultimatum," she said tightly. "I feel out of the loop."

"How do you think I feel? It didn't take long for him to start using again. How do we know he hasn't been doing it the whole time? He won't go to rehab, and if he stays here, what does that make us? Enablers?"

"How about loving and supportive parents?" she said, shaking out a T-shirt that had been left in the dryer too long. It was so wrinkled it begged for the iron, but she didn't care. She folded it quickly and placed it on top of the pile.

"I've been giving him cash for helping me with moving the office," Allan said. "I suppose he used it to buy oxycodone."

Through clenched teeth, she said, "Kicking him out on the street isn't the answer." She had a feeling that Everett would leave. And then not only would she have to worry about his drug problem, she'd also have to worry about his living arrangements—who he was living with and whether he was eating properly. He was already too thin.

"Don't say that." Allan's voice was sharp. "I'm not kicking him out on the street. I'm giving him choices, hoping he chooses the right option."

"And if he doesn't? Where will he go? Where will he live?" She glared at her husband.

Allan heaved a sigh. "As long as he's using, he can't live here. What about Lance and Ash? It won't be long before he starts stealing from us."

Maureen's voice shook. "How dare you. He's addicted to drugs, he's not a thief."

"Wake up, Maureen. Drug seeking can lead to stealing. He's not working, he has no income, where's he going to get the money to buy drugs?"

"He was raised better than that," she cried.

"Yes, he was, but we raised him to just say no to drugs, and look where we are. So stealing isn't outside the realm of possibilities."

Maureen started to cry.

Allan softened his tone. "Look, honey, I'm not saying he's a bad kid, because he isn't. He's a great kid, but the drugs are going to cloud his judgment and he's going to make poor choices."

Maureen nodded quickly, swiped at her eyes, and sniffled. "I know."

She took the last item off the bed, folded it, and stacked all the laundry into the basket. Maureen took in a deep breath, feeling anxious. "Let's let things settle tonight, and we'll discuss it again with him in the morning." It was like her mother always said: everything looked better in the morning.

"Okay," Allan said, and left the room.

She couldn't remember the last time she and Allan had had a fight like this. Raised voices. They had plenty of disagreements, but they were always done in a civilized manner.

When they woke up in the morning, Everett was gone.

Chapter Thirteen

Maureen took in a deep breath and exhaled slowly.

Everett was still in Lavender Bay. There had been two sightings. Angie was clearing a table when she spotted him across the street, but when she went outside, he was gone. And Aunt Gail had seen him turning the corner at Oak and Vine, a takeout bag in his hand. But when she turned the corner to follow him, he disappeared between two houses, and her last glimpse showed him hopping the fence in the back.

Maureen hadn't had a good night's sleep since he disappeared two months ago. Like most mornings lately, she was up earlier than necessary. Lying in bed trying to sleep was a futile exercise. She made her way downstairs to the kitchen, followed by Roger, who meowed all the way until she fed him.

The house was quiet. She closed her eyes and listened to the silence.

Opening her eyes, she lifted her phone from the kitchen table, momentarily ignoring the fact that the tabletop was covered with toast crumbs. She didn't have the energy to wipe it off, much less care about it.

A quick glance out the window showed it wasn't raining. She scribbled a quick note for Allan, letting him know she'd gone for a walk.

She grabbed her keys and sunglasses from the table and glanced into the family room, where Roger sat on the back of the sofa, his tail moving slowly as he looked out the window to the backyard, his interest keen on the birds at the feeder.

She exited, pulling the door closed softly behind her so as not to wake anyone up. Outside, she tucked the keys in her pocket. The morning sun was strong and bright, and she immediately put on her sunglasses. The street was quiet, as most people weren't up yet, and she headed in the direction of the beach. It was such a beautiful morning that the lake beckoned.

This early in the morning, there was hardly anyone on the beach. A lone jogger ran past her, the back of his T-shirt soaked with sweat.

She'd forgotten how much she loved being at the beach at this time in the morning, when it was all but deserted.

As she strolled along, her gaze swung across the shoreline and out over the lake, which appeared green and gray this morning, with foamy surf at the shore. The sand was damp and flat, which made it easier to walk on. The air was always a little cooler near the water, as the lake wouldn't warm up properly until later in the summer.

For as far as she could see, the backs of the houses that lined Pearl Street ran parallel to the beach. In the distance, she saw her sister Nadine's house. Nadine had turned the house into an inn after her marriage ended, and things seemed to be going pretty well for her. Maureen was pleased about that. Everyone deserved peace and happiness. Sometimes, it was hard-fought and hard-earned.

She was glad Nadine had returned to the area to live. That made three out of the four sisters living in Lavender Bay. If only they could convince their youngest sister, DeeDee, to move back home. But at least she seemed happy in Florida.

The beach was littered with shells, stones, and beach glass in shades of brown, white, and bottle green. Though she appreciated the colors and textures, she was not a collector of any of it. She thought of it like décor for the beach itself and liked to look at it scattered across the sand the way nature had placed it.

She wondered if she should get a dog she could take for walks on the beach, but she quickly dismissed that idea, thinking there was a lot of work involved in owning a dog. Cats were so much more independent. Besides, if she truly had the urge to walk a dog, she could borrow Nadine's dog, Herman, and that would scratch that itch.

Something caught her eye, and she stopped in her tracks. There among a pile of shells, stones, and a couple of pieces of beach glass, the sun bounced off something metallic. At first, she thought it was foil paper or a candy wrapper as it was a dull gold. But as she neared it, she realized it was a disc or a coin of some sort. Bending over, she plucked it from where it lay half-buried in the sand.

She wiped it against her jeans to get rid of the small particles of sand that clung to it. It appeared to be some sort of religious medal, as it bore the impression of a saint. Narrowing her eyes, she examined it, but the writing was faded, some of the letters worn off. Nevertheless, she managed to figure out that it was a St. Anthony medal.

As much as she wasn't one to pick things up off the beach, she would keep this. It looked old, and she wondered how it was lost and what the story was behind it. She wiped it off some more and stuffed it into her pocket. She'd comb the lost-and-found column of *The Lavender Bay Chronicles* to see if anyone was looking for it.

But she soon forgot the medal, her thoughts drifting back to Everett and how she could help him. Her heart hurt.

PART TWO

Laura

Chapter Fourteen

New Year's Eve 1933

Laura Wainwright stood in front of the cheval mirror in her bedroom and cast an admiring glance at her reflection. Her blond hair had been cut in a blunt bob, and she wore her favorite dress. The periwinkle blue accentuated her eyes. She'd dabbed a little rouge on her cheeks and put on some lipstick. She had a kohl pencil but skipped it, knowing her father would disapprove.

She was anxious to get out and be with her friends. For almost two months, since the death of her sister Lenore's husband, John Hadley, the house had been like a tomb. She hadn't seen Lenore since the funeral. Her older sister wasn't speaking to her, she needed time. She couldn't stay angry with her forever. Since the funeral, Laura had been holed up in her bedroom, avoiding people. Not that that was necessary, as hardly anyone ever visited the house anymore. But after a dreary Christmas, she decided she was no longer going to sit home. It was time to get out and mingle. She'd overheard the new housekeeper, Joan, saying that Margo Miller was throwing a New Year's Eve party to ring in 1934, and Laura decided she would go.

Margo's parties were the bee's knees. Laura's parents must have intercepted her invitation and withheld it from her. That was most likely the case, as they had advised her to lie low until things blew over. A new year was just what she needed, if only to put this last ghastly year behind her.

She debated between wearing her good, sensible winter coat or borrowing her mother's fox stole. It was old, but it still looked divine. But a glance out the window at the falling snow made her decide in favor of the winter coat. Returning her attention to the mirror, she adjusted her brand-new cloche hat, careful not to ruin her crimped hair.

Humming, she spritzed on some perfume and placed two bangles on her left wrist, grabbed her purse, and headed down the stairs.

Her parents, seated next to each other on the sofa in the parlor, looked up at her as she approached.

Eleanor Wainwright frowned. "Where are you going?"

"Margo Miller is having a New Year's Eve party tonight," Laura said.

Her parents looked dumbfounded.

"Were you invited?" her father asked.

Laura looked closely at her father for some sign of pretense, but she saw none. "Maybe my invitation got lost in the mail." She pulled on her gloves. "Margo and I were the best of chums in high school."

"I think you should reconsider," Mrs. Wainwright warned.

"Oh, Mother, really."

"Do you think it's good form to go over there uninvited?" Laura's father asked.

Tired of the circular conversation, Laura rolled her eyes. "Like I said, I'm sure my invitation went astray."

"I would advise you to take your mother's advice." The Honorable Leo Wainwright was using his stern voice, the one he used when he expected to be obeyed.

But Laura was twenty-one, old enough to decide for herself. With a lift of her chin, she said, "I won't be late."

It was a two-block walk to Margo's house. It took longer than usual because she wore heels, and the sidewalks were slick with fresh-fallen snow. Chilled, she pulled her coat closer around her, grateful she'd skipped the fox stole. A smile spread across her face. It would be good to get back out in circulation and see the old gang.

As she approached the two-story Miller house, she stepped up her pace in anticipation. The house was ablaze with lights, every window illuminated, and from the street she could hear the music from the Victrola, which she knew to be on a table behind the sofa.

She rang the doorbell and stomped her feet to get the snow off her shoes, not wanting to track it into the house. The noise level increased as the door swung open, and the light became brighter, spilling out onto the porch, almost like a spotlight on Laura. She was greeted by Margo's older brother, Jim, whose big smile quickly disappeared from his face.

"Hello, Jim! How are you?" Laura stepped inside the brightly lit front hall.

Jim Miller said nothing, not welcoming her and not offering to take her coat. The music blared from the living room, and a light haze of cigarette smoke filled the air. The house was packed with people, most of whom she recognized as she'd gone to school with them.

"I'll see if I can find Margo," Jim said, and disappeared into the crowd. She wondered what had gotten into him. He was usually pretty chatty and friendly. At one time, he'd even harbored a crush on her. Must have had a bad day.

She looked quickly around the hall for a place to lay her coat, but without success. A couple of people turned to look her way as she hovered in the doorway of the parlor, and she smiled and lifted her hand in greeting, but they turned their backs on her.

The music of the Victrola ceased. The loud voices stilled, and an uncomfortable, charged silence filled the air. No one approached her. She swallowed hard.

Margo finally appeared, coming down the hall. Laura turned away from the parlor and smiled.

Margo's expression was cool, and she abstained from reaching for Laura and kissing her on each cheek, as was their custom.

Quietly, Laura said, "Hello, Margo. It looks like a swell party." Her voice shook as she spoke.

Margo's mouth looked tight, stern. "I'm surprised you're here, Laura."

"I figured my invitation got lost in the mail," Laura said weakly.

"No, I didn't send you an invitation."

Laura felt the heat rise up her neck and travel to her face.

"With all the scandal with your boyfriend," Margo said, "I wouldn't have thought you'd have the nerve to show your face in public."

Back in the spring of 1932, Laura had fallen under the spell—that was the only way she could explain it—of a handsome ne'er-do-well named Horace Howard. It ended when Horace shot and killed her sister's husband, the local chief of police. Horace had been running bootleg liquor in from Canada, and John had been killed over it, only weeks before Prohibition was repealed. Horace was currently in jail, waiting for his trial, and would likely be sent to the electric chair.

Laura started to say something, opening her mouth to protest and say it hadn't been her fault. *She* hadn't killed John Hadley. But she realized it would be a futile argument.

Tilting her head slightly, she said quietly, "I apologize for intruding. I won't stay." She turned on her heel and walked toward the front door. No one tried to stop her. Perspiration broke out on her brow, and she felt overheated in her heavy winter coat. Nausea and lightheadedness gripped her. That walk to the Millers' front door was the longest one she'd ever taken. As she passed the entrance to the parlor, she could hear the whispers and the twitters.

As soon as she closed the door behind her, she sagged against it and gasped. Her eyes filled, and she was all but blinded by tears, but she had to get off that porch and away from the Miller house. A couple was walking up the pathway, arm in arm. Laura lowered her head and brushed past them, walking quickly, needing to put distance between herself and the party.

She did not go directly home but chose instead to keep walking. She couldn't face her parents just yet.

She hadn't been invited! She, Laura Wainwright, one of the most popular and pretty girls in Lavender Bay, had been excluded. Not wanted. That had never happened before. It shook her to her core. Thankful for the darkness, she cried with abandon. Her parents had warned her, but she hadn't believed them. She couldn't quite wrap her head around the fact that other people would blame her for what happened to Lenore's husband. Guilt by association, her mother had said more than once.

The night was cold, and the sky was inky black. The moon peeked in and out behind passing cloud cover. As she walked the streets of Lavender Bay, merriment spilled out of the lit-up houses as people welcomed in the new year. But that feeling of festivity fell short of reaching Laura, and she feared she would be left behind with the awful events of 1933.

Without realizing it, she found herself on Pearl Street. She paused in front of Lenore's house, the only one on the street not lit up like a Christmas tree. It was shrouded in darkness. It looked lifeless.

She stood there for a long time, until she could no longer feel her toes. Behind those darkened windows was her sister. If only she could see her and say she was sorry. Lenore was due with a baby any day; it should have been a happy time for her.

Snow swirled around Laura. Into the darkness, she whispered, "What have I done?"

The first morning of the new year was bright and sunny and beautiful. The snowscape glittered, and the sky was a clear blue. Laura tried to see it as a portent of better days, but that was difficult in light of the events of the previous evening.

She'd waited to return home until she was sure her parents had gone to bed. They'd kept lights on for her on the front porch and in the parlor.

Now it was mid-morning, and she figured she better head downstairs for breakfast before her mother came looking for her.

Her parents were speaking quietly to each other but stopped when she entered the dining room.

"Happy New Year, Laura," her mother and father said together.

"Happy New Year."

Her mother scrutinized her. "How was the party? You didn't stay late."

Laura shook her head and pulled out a chair to sit down. She looked at the breakfast dishes but didn't feel hungry. She reached for a piece of toast, figuring she'd be able to get that down. "No, it was kind of a bust. And I was tired, so I left early."

There was no way she'd tell them of her humiliation at the hands of people who had once been her friends. Especially after they'd warned her not to go.

"Were there a lot of young people there?" her father asked.

She nodded, taking a bite of toast. She chewed and swallowed, then took a sip of tea. "The usual crowd. People I went to school with."

Her parents didn't ask any more questions, and she was grateful for that. She continued to eat her breakfast in silence.

When Leo was out of earshot, Laura's mother poured more tea into their cups. "I suspect it didn't go as well as you've led us to believe," she remarked.

Ashamed of being caught in a lie, Laura bowed her head. "No," she admitted, and poured out the whole humiliating story.

Her mother sighed. "It was as I thought."

"I was foolish to go over there."

"Yes, but you'll learn. It's not all about you all the time, Laura."

She looked at her mother. Those were harsh words. She and her mother had always been close. They liked the same things. They were two peas in the same pod, as her mother liked to say.

"I know that," Laura said. But did she really?

"Sometimes I wonder if you do. What has happened is a great tragedy, and whether it's right or wrong, people are going to paint you with the same brush as Horace Howard."

Laura almost winced at the mention of his name. How one person could cause so much damage was beyond her. And she'd been a party to it, finding him exciting at the time.

"Laura, it's important that I say a few things to you. And they may be difficult to hear, but you must hear them nonetheless."

She'd never seen her mother so serious.

"For good or bad," Eleanor said, "I've coddled you all your life. You and I have an extremely close bond. It's been like that ever since you were born, in the same way Lenore gravitated toward your father. It's just the way it is."

This warmed Laura. Despite everything that had happened, her mother still loved her. That was a relief.

Eleanor went on. "But sometimes, I have not been as firm with you in the discipline department as I probably should have. And there are times when you are a very selfish individual."

If her mother intended to shock or hurt her, she'd hit the target.

"That's a mean thing to say, Mother."

"Sometimes the truth hurts."

Laura didn't know what to say to that. She looked at her teacup, the tea growing cold.

"But it's not too late for you to turn yourself around and become a better person."

"Gee, Mother, you make it sound like I'm destined for prison." This was a distressing conversation. Laura Wainwright needed to be rehabilitated? *Gosh*.

The severity of her mother's expression softened. "Oh goodness, no. But think about the way you were treated last night at Margo Miller's house."

Laura shuddered; she'd prefer never to repeat that experience.

"If you keep on making mistakes in your personal life by picking men who are no good, you will be treated like that for the rest of your life."

Laura snorted. "How do you know I won't be treated like this for the rest of my life anyway?" She couldn't see people ever welcoming her anywhere again.

"You won't be. It seems impossible right now but with time, memories of the events will fade, and people will forget or move on."

Laura looked down, fingering the hem of the tablecloth. "I am so sorry for all the pain I've caused Lenore. I wish I could go back and do everything over."

Eleanor sighed. "Your sister is going through a terrible time right now. It's awful what has happened."

Laura felt the tears welling up but pulled herself together. "But will she ever forgive me? Ever talk to me again?" She couldn't imagine spending the rest of her life not talking to her sister. She'd never have thought she'd miss her as much as she did. She ached to see her, and she wanted to see her new baby when it was born. She wondered if she'd be allowed, but she dared not voice that. Not yet.

"Again, she'll need time. But your sister isn't the type to hold a grudge. Not even over this."

Laura digested what her mother had said and decided to try and listen for once.

"Now," Eleanor said, "on to other things. I'm going to take the train to see Aunt Millicent next week. Would you like to go with me?"

Aunt Millicent was her mother's older sister, who lived outside of Cleveland. "Yes, please. How long are we going for?"

"A week. Aunt Millicent would like to see you."

To get away from Lavender Bay for a week would be good. And the fact that there was someone out there who wanted her company lifted Laura's spirits slightly.

Chapter Fifteen

January 1935

Laura waited for the man from Hooper's Garage to arrive to repair a puncture in the tire of the car. Her father was in bed with a terrible cold and had asked her to answer the door for the mechanic. As she had nothing else to do, she waited in the front hall, sitting on a side chair as her mother and Joan ran up and down the stairs with tea with lemon and honey and bowls of chicken soup.

There were some decisions to be made about her future. In the last year, she'd gone four times to Ohio to stay with her Aunt Millicent. Sometimes she took the train by herself. On her last visit, before Christmas, her aunt had suggested she come to live with her in her house, which was located outside of Cleveland. At first, Laura thought it was a ridiculous idea, but then a few days into the new year, her aunt had sent her a letter saying she could get her a position in the local bank. That's when Laura gave serious consideration to her aunt's suggestion. It might be nice to go and live somewhere where no one knew her. Where no one knew of what had happened. And if it had to be another state, then so be it. It had been more than a year since John Hadley's death and the townspeople, although no longer crossing the street to get out of her way, remained cool. Little Johnny, her nephew, had just had his first birthday party, and she'd been sure Lenore would extend an olive branch and invite her, but no invitation was forthcoming. It broke her heart. In the past, she'd thought her older sister was such a drudge, but she missed her.

The sound of a vehicle pulling up to the house forced Laura to her feet. Peering out one of the windows that flanked the front door, she spotted a tow truck with the words "Hooper's Garage" on it, parked at the curb.

Laura threw open the door and grabbed her coat off the tree stand, prepared to walk with the mechanic to the car.

A man not much older than herself jumped up onto the porch. He was dressed in black coveralls, and over his left breast was a white patch with red lettering that read "Edwin."

"Tire puncture?" he asked.

She nodded, slipping on her coat. "I'll walk you over."

He frowned. "Not necessary. It's too cold outside. You should wait inside where it's warm."

She laughed. "It's all right. You're not even wearing a coat."

"I'm a man."

Now she chortled, and they both laughed. Pulling the door closed behind her, she stepped out onto the porch into the frigid January air. She pulled gloves out of her pockets and tugged them on. They walked side by side down the driveway and along the snow-covered sidewalk.

Edwin whistled a merry tune as they strolled together. Although he was pale—weren't they all; it was winter—he had the brightest green eyes and nice auburn-colored hair. A smattering of freckles across his nose made him look young, but the fine lines at the corners of his eyes said otherwise. He had a long, narrow nose and broad cheekbones. Overall, she found him very handsome. It had been a long time since she'd been in the company of a man her age. It'd been a while since she'd even thought about a man. The business with Horace had cured her of that.

When they reached the car, Edwin removed the spare tire from the back end of the car and rolled it around to the side of the flat.

"I'll change it for you in a jiffy."

"Thank you."

She remained on the sidewalk and stamped her feet to stave off the cold. The man whistled as he worked, locating the spare and wheeling it around to the side of the car with the flat. He made easy work of it.

When he was finished, he pulled a rag from his side pocket and wiped his hands. "You're all set now, miss." He glanced with a nod at the punctured tire he'd thrown on the snow-covered verge. "That can't be repaired. Mr. Wainwright will need to purchase a new tire."

"I'll be sure to tell him."

As she began to walk away, he thumbed over his shoulder and half turned, looking at the car. "Don't you want to drive it back?"

She shook her head. "I don't drive."

"You don't? Why not?"

She responded with a shrug, "I don't know. I never learned." There had never been a reason to. Someone else had always driven her around.

He regarded her, narrowing his eyes slightly, but there was no animosity behind them, only puzzlement. Finally, he said, "Do you have the key? I'll drive it back to your house."

"I'm sorry, I didn't think to bring it."

"No problem. We'll walk back for it."

"Thank you so much." It was refreshing to talk to someone her age without the air around them being loaded with her past.

He acknowledged her gratitude with a slight nod.

Grateful for conversation, she wasn't in a hurry to let him go. "Are you new in town?"

"I am. I came up from Pennsylvania to work in my uncle's garage."

She'd seen the truck around town at different times but had never paid any attention to it. But she would now.

"I'm Edwin Knickerbocker. I'd shake your hand but mine are covered in grease." He held out his hands to illustrate his point.

She smiled at him. "Laura. Laura Wainwright."

"Pretty name for a pretty girl."

She blushed. It had been a long time since anyone had paid her a compliment.

They arrived back at the house, and Laura ran inside to retrieve the car key. She returned to where Edwin waited at the end of the driveway.

"I'll only be a second," he said. He ran back to the car, surefooted through the slush and snow.

Edwin drove the car carefully and parked it behind his tow truck. He got out and dashed up the driveway toward her, whistling. He handed the key back to her.

"Look, Laura, would you be interested in going to see a picture with me?" His eyes never left her face, and he seemed to be holding his breath.

The words were hardly out of his mouth before she found herself nodding and thinking she'd like very much to go see a movie with this Edwin Knickerbocker with the bright green eyes.

With her reply, he smiled broadly and told her he'd pick her up the following evening at seven.

She couldn't wait.

Laura was beyond excited. She spent extra, careful time on her hair and applied a light amount of cosmetics to her face. From her closet, she chose her best and favorite dress. She liked this Edwin Knickerbocker, and she wasn't sure of the reason yet. Was it because he knew nothing of her past, or was it because he was interested? She'd almost forgotten what that felt like.

Her parents were unusually quiet as she waited for Edwin to arrive. Her father chomped on an unlit cigar, the newspaper in his hands. Their reticence was not without reason. They were skeptical of her choice. Was every beau to be colored with the Horace Howard brush? This guy seemed decent, or at least she thought so. But then, could she trust her own judgement? Her excitement faltered. What if she'd gotten this wrong too? But then she reminded herself that she'd be moving to Ohio soon. She was going to enjoy herself that evening.

When the clock struck the hour, the doorbell rang.

From behind his newspaper, her father spoke. "At least he's punctual."

She practically ran to the door, opening it wide to allow him in. He looked different from when she'd met him the previous day, when he wore grease-stained coveralls. Today he wore a fedora and a suit, and he'd shaved.

Suddenly, Laura felt shy. But she did manage to get out, "Come in, Edwin." As he stepped into the front hall, he removed his hat. She led him into the parlor, where her mother's hands sat idle in her lap, her needlepoint momentarily forgotten. Her father had put the newspaper down to inspect Laura's date.

Edwin walked purposefully toward her parents, his hand outstretched. "Mr. and Mrs. Wainwright. Edwin Knickerbocker. It's a pleasure to meet you both."

Leo Wainwright stood and shook Edwin's hand. Edwin turned slightly and leaned down to shake Eleanor's hand.

"I understand you're from Pennsylvania," Mr. Wainwright said.

Edwin did not shrink or back down under his scrutinous glare.

"That's right, sir. I came up to give my uncle a hand in his garage."

"Bert Hooper is your uncle?"

"That's right."

Mr. Wainwright nodded approvingly. "I know Bert. And is it your intention to become a mechanic?"

"Yes, sir. I'm doing an apprenticeship with my uncle. He has no sons, and he hopes to leave the garage to me someday."

"So, you like fixing cars?"

Edwin's face brightened. "I do. I find everything about them fascinating."

"They are fascinating, that's for sure," Eleanor chimed in.

Laura edged closer to Edwin. "We should get going, Edwin, we don't want to be late."

He smiled at her. "I'm sorry, Laura. Once I get started talking about cars, I lose all track of time. But you'll keep me on the straight and narrow, I suspect."

She lowered her head and blushed. His comment implied that she'd see him again.

The feature playing that evening was *Times Square Lady* with Robert Taylor, and as they walked toward the ticket seller, Edwin tucked her arm in his and said, "I hope this is all right."

"It's fine." She didn't care what they saw; she was enjoying being out of the house for an evening.

When they stepped up to purchase their tickets, the expression of the woman behind the counter soured as she spotted Laura. Edwin pulled out his wallet and asked for two tickets.

The woman handed them over without another word, and Edwin looked over at the line for the popcorn vendor on the sidewalk. "How about some popcorn, Laura?"

"Sure, that would be lovely."

They stood in the line for the vendor behind two other couples. The couples ahead of them turned and when they spotted Laura, they quickly bent their heads together in a flurry of whispers.

Laura felt the heat creep up to her cheeks and averted her eyes. If Edwin noticed what was going on, he didn't comment on it. When it was their turn, he asked for two bags. The vendor scooped up the popcorn, handing a bag to each of them.

As they made their way into the movie theater, heads turned to look at Laura. She wanted to crawl out of there and go home. This had been a bad idea. Edwin pointed to an empty row of seats and asked her if it was all right. She nodded quickly, anxious to slide down into her seat. Luckily, as she sat down, the red velvet drapes parted, revealing the large screen, and the lights dimmed until the interior of the theater was dark. She'd never been so grateful for a darkened room. As the black-and-white newsreel began, the whispers abated, and Laura settled down in her seat.

"Have you seen this movie before?" Edwin leaned over to her. He smelled nice. He tossed a handful of popcorn into his mouth.

"No, I haven't," she said, taking the opportunity to study his profile in the darkness. It was strong, and it looked honest. She concluded that he was no Horace Howard. By the end of the movie, a sadness settled over her like a blanket as she realized that this wouldn't last.

It couldn't. Eventually, he'd find out about her past and he'd dump her so fast her head would spin.

The walk home was quiet.

"Didn't you like the picture?" he asked. He scratched behind his ear.

"Yes, I did," she reassured him.

"You're awfully quiet."

"It's nothing. Seriously."

"A penny for your thoughts," he said.

She laughed. She liked him.

Avoiding his comment, she asked, "Did you enjoy the movie?"

"Yeah, it was swell."

When they'd reached the Wainwright house on Bluebell Lane, Edwin stood on the sidewalk with his hands in his pockets and stared at it. Finally, he pronounced, "It's a fine house."

"Thank you."

He turned to face her. "Can I see you tomorrow night?"

She ignored the little voice in her head that told her not to pursue this, to end it before she inevitably got hurt. She nodded. "I'd like that."

"Good. Come on, I'll walk you to your door."

At the front door, they said goodnight. He did not try to kiss her, and in a way, she was relieved. In the past, she'd have been offended if a suitor didn't try to kiss her. Although some took it too far and it ended up practically being a wrestling match. Tonight, she was not upset that he didn't try.

He saw her the following three evenings. Each time, Laura begged off going out, instead inviting him to stay and play cards or a board game. She didn't think she could handle the stares and whispers out in public. By the fourth evening, her parents had warmed up to him and engaged in small talk before leaving the two of them alone.

As they cleaned up the card table, putting the board game away and getting the glasses to take to the kitchen, Edwin asked, "Would you like to go for a bite to eat tomorrow night?"

Laura panicked. A restaurant wouldn't provide the sheltering darkness of a movie theater. Sooner or later, someone would confront her, and how would she explain that to Edwin?

"I don't know," she replied. She carried the empty soda bottles into the kitchen and returned to Edwin in the parlor.

"Dinner? Tomorrow night?" he pressed.

"I don't think so," she said. "Why don't you come here, and we can listen to the radio."

He frowned.

As her posture sagged, Laura realized she would have to tell him the truth. It had been a wonderful few days in his company and she'd love to see more of him, but honesty was called for. It wasn't fair to keep him in the dark. She wondered what Lenore would do in a situation like this.

Summoning some inner courage she didn't know she had, she approached him and took his hand. When he held her hand, she felt safe and protected.

She led him over to the sofa and sat, patting the space on the cushion next to her.

"I need to talk to you about something, Edwin," she started softly.

"Is this the part where you tell me you never want to see me again?" he teased with a grin.

With a smile, she said, "Not at all." Butterflies flew around in her stomach. "But I do need to talk about something serious."

She drew in a deep breath, steadying herself. Edwin raised one eyebrow in response.

Without stopping, she poured forth her whole story. When she finished, she looked at him. At first, he didn't say anything, and her heart sank as she wondered if he was going to bolt for the door. But he surprised her by reaching out and taking her hand in his.

"I'm sure it was very difficult for you to share this, Laura, but I can't tell you how much I appreciate your honesty."

"You're not mad?"

Confusion clouded his features. "Mad? Why would I be mad?"

She wanted to say *because everyone else is*, and opened her mouth, but then closed it.

"It was a terrible tragedy," he said, "but it wasn't your fault. You only had the misfortune of introducing the man to your family."

She didn't say anything. She couldn't, because she was too overwhelmed with emotion.

Edwin leaned back against the sofa. "I suppose this hasn't been easy, living in a small town like this."

Often as she walked through town, she felt like a modern-day Hester Prynne, as if she had some kind of invisible brand across her forehead, condemning her. "No, it hasn't," she admitted. "People blame me, and I suppose I can't fault them. *I* blame me. I was headstrong and wouldn't listen to anyone about Horace."

"Is that why you don't want to go out anywhere?"

"Yes. I'm thinking of moving to Ohio to live with my aunt," she said. Her voice wobbled.

"Come here," he beckoned. He laid his arm across the back of the sofa.

Laura shifted and scooted over closer to him, but sat upright, almost rigid.

He patted the back of the sofa. "Come on, sit back."

She leaned back but stayed out of reach of Edwin, feeling shy.

He laughed. "You're a funny little bird, Laura." He moved closer and put his arm around her, pulling her to him, placing a kiss at her temple. Of all the kisses she'd gotten over her lifetime, she regarded this one as the nicest of them all. "Now, I hope you don't move to

Ohio just yet, as I've only just met you and I'd like to get to know you better."

She was at a loss for words and found she could only nod. He'd discovered the absolute worst about her, and he still wanted to get to know her better. It was almost too good to be true.

He crossed one leg over the other, his arm still wrapped around her. "Tomorrow's Saturday. What will we do? If you don't mind the long drive, we could go up to Cheever for dinner."

Laura nodded enthusiastically. No one knew her up there. "I'd like that." Hurriedly, she added, "As long as you don't mind."

Edwin grinned. "I don't mind at all."

She laughed. It had been a long time since she'd felt this light.

Chapter Sixteen

1942

Rain pelted against the windows of the house Laura and Edwin had rented after they were married. May, usually a portent of summer sunshine, was looking like a complete washout. It seemed as if it would never stop raining. The dampness was worse than the cold, and Laura wore a heavy cardigan over her apron and dress.

She looked up briefly from her *Photoplay* magazine and thought, *I wish it would snow, if only for something different.*

This was her favorite part of the day, when the girls were down for their nap. Three-year-old Edna and two-year-old Edith were sound asleep upstairs. Both were generally good nappers, and thank God for small favors. Having two babies back-to-back had exhausted her.

She would have loved to put the radio on, but she would never risk waking the girls. The two hours of peace and quiet in the afternoon were too important to her to chance it.

She flipped through the magazine again, not having much else to do. Their house was small: two bedrooms upstairs with a bathroom and a kitchen and parlor downstairs. It was easy to keep clean, especially since Lenore had passed along her old vacuum cleaner when she'd purchased a new one. Two bills had come in the mail, but Laura had set them aside for her husband; he took care of all that. On the menu tonight was chicken and mashed potatoes, but she'd already done all the preparation. She only had to cook it.

Although she wasn't much of a cook, she did try. With the war on, rationing had begun, and she'd saved up the butter rations because Edwin loved buttery mashed potatoes. Sometimes, she wished she'd spent more time in the kitchen with Lenore and their original housekeeper, Hilda, when she was growing up. Lenore had come over a couple of times to teach Laura how to make some basic dishes. The sisters had been on better terms ever since Lenore showed up unexpectedly on Laura and Edwin's wedding day. It had been the best gift they had received.

A wail from upstairs interrupted Laura's peaceful afternoon. She glanced at her wristwatch.

"Drat!"

One of the girls was awake a half hour early. That first wail was joined by a second, and Laura knew they wouldn't be going back to sleep. She put the magazine up on the top shelf of the cabinet so the girls wouldn't get a hold of it. They'd torn the last one to pieces. She ran up the stairs to get them.

Edwin was quiet all through dinner that evening. Despite being busy with getting the girls fed, Laura had noticed his lack of chattiness. Edna was a good eater and loved chicken and mashed potatoes, just like her father, but Edith could be fussy and required a lot of coaxing. Finally, Edwin pushed his chair back from the table and stood. He picked Edith up and sat again, setting their younger daughter on his knee. He put a little bit of mashed potato on his fork and swooped it away from himself and then back to his mouth with exaggerated motions, making noises like an airplane. He swirled the fork in front of his face and finally landed it in his mouth and clamped his lips shut, announcing, "Mmm. Yummy!"

He repeated this performance until Edith clapped her hands and said, "Me, me!"

With a nod, Edwin indicated to Laura that she should pass Edith's plate down to him. It became a game. Two bites for Edwin and one for Edith.

"You're going to spoil her," Laura complained.

"Ah, she's only a baby. You can't spoil them."

"She's not a baby."

"Can I sit on Daddy's lap?" asked Edna, all smiles.

"No," Laura said.

Edna sank in her chair, put her fork down, and rested the side of her head on her hand.

"Come on, Edna." Edwin turned slightly toward his oldest daughter and patted his vacant knee.

Edna bounded out of her chair and jumped up onto her father's lap. With his right hand, he pulled her plate over and announced, "We're all going to eat our dinner."

Laura stood up from the table and put her hands on her hips. "Really, Edwin, you spoil them both."

He grinned at her. "You were spoiled, and you turned out all right."

"Sort of," she said, suppressing a smile.

"I've got plenty of room if you want to sit on my knee too." Over the heads of their daughters, he winked at her.

She shook her head but couldn't help but laugh. "I give up."

The three of them cleaned their plates and when they were finished, Laura excused the girls, and they toddled off.

She made two cups of tea and set them on the table, rejoining her husband. He'd gone quiet again.

"What's wrong?" she asked. "Did something happen at work?"

"No," he said. He brushed the back of his neck with his hand. He left his tea untouched.

After being married for a few years, she knew to wait. It had been a lesson in patience for Laura. He was gathering his thoughts and when he was ready, he would share what was bothering him. As she waited, her mind drifted to other things. What she would cook for dinner tomorrow. Also tomorrow was wash day. She hated wrestling with that wringer washing machine out back.

"I joined up." Edwin said it so suddenly she wasn't sure she'd heard him correctly.

"What did you say?"

"I joined up today."

"The Army?" She blinked several times in succession. "But you don't have to go. You're a married man with dependents."

"But I *do* have to go, sweetheart."

Laura sat there with her mouth open, incredulous. "Edwin, why? Don't you love us?" She knew that was a selfish thing to say, but it was what popped out of her mouth.

He burst out laughing. "Of course I love you and the girls. That's why I'm going."

That made absolutely zero sense to her.

"Why would you think I didn't?" he asked.

"Oh, I don't know, because you're running off to war?"

"Honey." He leaned across the table, reaching for her, but she pulled back and crossed her arms over her chest. "I'm not going to war to get away from you and the girls, I'm going because it's my duty. I can't expect other men to go off and fight while I stay behind."

"But what about us?" she asked, her voice shrill.

"I've thought about that. You can go stay with your parents."

She didn't want to do that. She liked the four of them together in their own house. But if he did go off to war, she'd have no choice. Edwin took care of her and the girls, and she wouldn't be able to manage without him.

"How long have you been thinking about this?" she asked.

"Honestly? Since Pearl," he replied.

It had been a little more than five months since the surprise attack on Pearl Harbor. Every evening after dinner, Edwin pulled up a chair right next to the radio in the parlor and listened, anxious for any news at all about the war. And although he mentioned from time to time that he'd go off and fight in a heartbeat, Laura had paid no attention, thinking it was a man's wishful thinking, that where there was a fight, it was their natural inclination to want to be a part of it.

"What about the garage? What about Uncle Bert?" she asked, hoping to make him see some sense. Uncle Bert wasn't getting any younger, and one of his mechanics had left last week for boot camp. He couldn't do it all by himself. Edwin was very fond of his uncle; she couldn't believe he'd leave him in the lurch.

"I've talked it over with him."

Laura felt wounded. "You talked it over with Uncle Bert? What about me?"

"Honey, it was a man-to-man talk."

Abruptly, she stood up, the chair scraping against the floor. "Thanks a lot. I'm your wife. You should have discussed it with me *first*."

"You would have tried to talk me out of it," he said, opening his hands to her, palms out.

"Of course I would. But I would have liked to be included in the discussion."

She walked over to the sink full of dirty dishes. She eyed the black enamel roasting pan that would need to be scoured, and the urge to throw it out the window was strong. Tears filled her eyes. A gamut of emotions coursed through her. She was angry. She was sad. And most of all, she was afraid. He wasn't going off to summer camp; he was going off to war. Men got wounded. Men got killed. A knot formed in her stomach. She picked up the dishcloth, threw it back down, and covered her face with her hands and sobbed.

Immediately, Edwin came up behind her and placed his hands on her shoulders, murmuring, "Shh-shh."

She pulled her hankie from the pocket of her apron and wiped her nose. Edwin turned her around and placed his hands on her upper arms. His voice was low when he spoke. "Laura, honey, don't cry. I have a job to do, like most American men. I can't be over there worrying about you."

She nodded quickly and gave her eyes a wipe with the handkerchief. "I'm afraid, Edwin. Afraid for you."

"Don't be. I can take care of myself."

She looked around the kitchen, her eyes wet, and in the background, she could hear the girls chattering in the other room. "But what will I do? I don't know how to do anything."

He was quick to disabuse her of that notion. "That's not true, Laura. You can do a lot of things."

She tilted her head and smirked, looking up at him. "Like what? Read *Photoplay*?"

He laughed. "And that too. Before I leave, I'll show you some things, like how to write a check, for instance, and what bills need to be paid when. And how to secure the lids on the garbage cans so the cats don't get into them." His thumbs made slow circular motions on her upper arms. "Besides, this war will be over quick. I'll probably be home in time for Christmas dinner."

She leaned into him, wrapping her arms around him. She didn't want to learn to do those things. Edwin took care of all that. She whispered against his shoulder, "Please don't leave me."

"You're going to be fine, honey."

With his hands cradling her face, he leaned in and kissed her forehead. Laura closed her eyes, loving the feel of his warm, strong hands. He wrapped her in a hug, and she wished they could stay like that forever.

She loved Edwin with all her heart, but sometimes she wished he wasn't so noble and good-hearted.

Chapter Seventeen

June 1943

Laura sat slumped in an armchair near one of the front windows in the parlor, gazing out on Bluebell Lane, a recent letter from Edwin in her hand. At her feet, the girls played together quietly with their dolls, getting along for a change. Her mother and father had gone up for their afternoon naps. All the windows in the house were thrown open. The sky was overcast, but it was warm and humid. Her clothes stuck to her. The air was filled with the cloying scent of the hyacinths bunched in a vase on the coffee table.

Absentmindedly, she turned the envelope in her hand, tapping its corners against her thigh. She missed Edwin terribly, and she missed the home they'd created together. Although they had only been there a few years, that home had been a safe haven for her. At Edwin's insistence, she'd moved back to her parents' house with the girls, and she felt adrift. Her identity had been thrown into question. She felt like teenaged Laura again instead of the wife and mother role she'd grown accustomed to.

She pulled Edwin's letter out from the envelope again. Even though the missive had arrived earlier that morning, she already had it memorized. Edwin wrote regularly, and she saved all his letters, tying the bundle with a blue ribbon and tucking it safely in an old hatbox beneath the bed. When he first left for the war, she'd written him every day, but that had quickly gotten expensive, so every night before she went to bed, she sat at the little writing desk in her room and jotted down the day's events, whether it was something the girls had done or visitors they'd had or some kind of funny anecdote. Her mother had given her some good advice: to make sure all her letters were positive and cheerful. He had enough to do fighting Nazis, and he didn't need to be worrying about what was going on back home. At the end of each week, she folded her daily letters, gave them a spritz of her perfume (his favorite), tucked them into an envelope, and walked them down to the post office to mail.

As much as she relished his letters—and truth be told, they were the highlight of her week—they were a poor substitute for Edwin himself. She found herself sniffing them, seeing if she could get a trace of his masculine soap-and-shaving-cream scent, but they smelled of nothing.

How she wished this war would end so they could go back to the way things used to be! If only she could have gone with him. But deep down, she knew that was a nonsensical thought. She'd probably only get in the way.

With a sigh, she continued to stare out the window, her gaze landing on the two automobiles parked in front of the house, one belonging to her father and the other to her and Edwin. If she'd ever bothered to learn how to drive, she'd at least be able to take the girls and go places, even if it was just for a car ride. Maybe Edwin should have taught her to drive before he left instead of how to write a check.

Fingering one of her curls, she continued to stare at the cars. Her finger paused mid-twirl. Why couldn't she learn to drive? She knew the perfect person to teach her.

Tucking the letter between the cushion and side of the armchair, she leaned forward and smiled. "Girls, how about we walk over and see Aunt Lenore?"

Edna jumped up. "And Johnny too?"

Laura nodded and stood up from the chair.

Edith shrieked with delight, and Laura put her finger to her lips. "Remember, Grandma and Grandpa are resting upstairs," she whispered. "No screaming."

Edna nodded knowingly. "Because they're so old."

Laura gave her oldest daughter's hair a quick tousle, reminding herself to watch what she said in front of the girls.

Holding each girl by the hand, she walked over with them to her sister's house on Pearl Street. She'd always thought two children were perfect, one for each hand. And although she hadn't told Edwin, she'd decided she wanted no more. She knew he longed for a son, but who knew when he'd be home, and she didn't want to start all over again with babies and bottles and diapers.

Lenore was out back with Johnny, bent over the Victory garden she'd planted the previous month. Seeds of carrots, onions, radishes, and beets had been sowed in the four by six plot. Off to the side was a small pile of discarded weeds.

The girls ran to Johnny, jumping up and down.

Lenore straightened and smiled. "Laura! This is a surprise. Hello, girls!"

Edna and Edith continued to jump up and down, smiling broadly.

With a nod to the swing set at the back of the yard, Lenore said to her son, "Why don't you push the girls on the swings? But be careful. Remember, they're little."

She hadn't finished her sentence before the girls were running toward the swings, beckoning Johnny to follow them.

Once they were out of earshot, Laura got to the point. "Lenore, I have a favor to ask of you. Will you teach me how to drive?"

Lenore smiled. "I'd be happy to."

Laura collapsed onto the sofa, tuckered out. The girls were already in bed, fast asleep, and her parents had gone upstairs early, citing fatigue. They'd all spent a nice afternoon at the beach and after supper, she'd taken the girls for an ice cream cone.

Learning to drive had been one of the best things she'd done for herself. She'd had no idea of the freedom and independence to be found with driving a car. To get behind the wheel any time and go anywhere you wanted was a thrill, although she had to be mindful because gasoline was rationed. When she'd written to Edwin and told him that Lenore had taught her to drive, she'd skipped the part about how it had taken her a month to learn properly. The main thing was that she had got the hang of it. Driving tests had been suspended because of the war, so she wouldn't have to worry about that until the war was over, and she was now driving all over town with the girls in tow.

A yawn escaped her, and she supposed she should head up to bed, but she was too tired to stand. Reaching over, she picked up an edition of *The Saturday*

Evening Post that had been lying around for a couple of months. It was creased and wrinkled from being thumbed through. On the cover was an illustration by Norman Rockwell of Rosie the Riveter. His version depicted a plump woman wearing a kerchief, goggles, and coveralls, eating a sandwich while a rivet gun lay in her lap. The image had horrified Laura's mother, who felt that fashion had plummeted to abhorrent depths since her own Edwardian heyday, with modern-day women dressing like dock workers. In the past, Laura would have agreed. To her it had always seemed important for a woman to retain her femininity. For herself, she felt it was one of her strong suits. However, even she realized that in a factory, wearing a dress and heels might be impractical.

After a quick study of the cover, she flipped through the pages, saw nothing of interest, and tossed the magazine aside. She picked up her mother's magazine, *Woman's Home Companion*, and rifled through it, looking for something interesting to read. She yawned again and was about to close the magazine when something caught her eye, and she turned back to the previous page.

There was a big box advertisement at the bottom of the page, calling for housewives to work at a factory up in Cheever, New York, twenty miles north of Lavender Bay. It was an aviation plant making cargo planes for the war. She read it again and again. The ad said everyone had to do their part. Said that the wage was good and that there'd be open recruitment the following week, with an immediate start.

Setting the magazine aside, she stared at the wall across from her and thought about this. Opening the magazine again, she read it one more time, and finally tore the page out, folded it neatly, and stuck it into the pocket of her dress. Suddenly feeling energetic, she jumped up and headed upstairs to get ready for bed.

The more times she reread the ad looking for factory workers, the more excited and determined Laura became. With just enough gasoline in the car to get back and forth, she drove over to Cheever, telling no one where she was going. She did not want anyone to try and talk her out of it. And try they would. She simply told her parents she had a few errands to attend to.

To say she was nervous would be putting it mildly. In her thirty years, she'd never worked at a job outside the home. She'd always been taken care of, whether by her father or by Edwin. In school, she had not set the world on fire with her grades; she'd been an average student. Women like Laura got by on their beauty. It carried a girl places. But looks could only take you so far, and they certainly didn't last forever. Since she'd had children, her figure wasn't as firm and toned as it used to be. And to her dismay, she'd found her first gray hair the other day.

She was gone longer than she'd anticipated. Twenty miles was farther than she thought, and it turned into an all-day affair. There was a large crowd of women, including a few she recognized from Lavender Bay. After she filled out an application, there'd been a lengthy interview where they asked about her education, her background, and her work experience. The lack of a work history frightened her somewhat, as she had none and couldn't see how that wouldn't put them off. But finally, they told her she could report for work in two weeks' time and to make a stop on the way out for her security badge.

She couldn't quite believe it; she'd secured a job. And at an aviation plant making airplanes no less! These were certainly strange times.

At home, she parked her car by the curb and ran into the house.

Her mother met her at the front door. "Where have you been, Laura? We've been worried sick about you!"

Laura leaned forward, placing her hands on her mother's upper arms, and laid a quick kiss on her cheek. "I'm so sorry, Mother, I got detained and there was nothing I could do about it."

"Detained? Doing what?"

Edna and Edith were at her side, clamoring for her attention, each girl trying to talk over the other. Laura dropped down on her knees and gave them a quick, reassuring hug. "It's all right. I'm home. Did you wash your hands? It's almost time for supper."

The girls stopped talking and ran off to wash their hands.

"Laura?"

"Mother, I'm sorry, I promise I'll tell you all about it at supper," she said. She ran up the stairs to use the bathroom, her bladder never having quite recovered from her pregnancies.

As soon as she landed in the upstairs hall, she ran into her father, who was on his way down.

"Well, if it isn't the return of the prodigal daughter," he said.

"Oh, Dad, do you always have to call me that?" she huffed. Edwin used to tell her to ignore it, but sometimes it annoyed her. "I'll be down in five minutes with the girls."

Not waiting for his reply, she dashed off to the bathroom.

Chapter Eighteen

Eleanor Wainwright gripped the armrests of her chair, her mouth slightly open. Leo leaned back and sighed, closing his eyes.

More or less, Laura had expected this reaction.

Her mother spoke first. "When Lenore opened her home to transients, I didn't think it could get any worse. But it appears I was wrong."

Laura did not point out that her sister's so-called transients weren't that; they were boarders who were all employed. She held her tongue.

Mr. Wainwright was unusually quiet, which scared Laura even more. Her father always had something to say about everything. Why should this be any different?

"Have you lost your mind?" her mother pressed.

Laura lifted her head. Her mind was made up. She was going to do this.

"A boarding house is one thing," Eleanor stammered. "But this . . . this . . . working in a factory? Making planes, of all things? This is something else. I'm flabbergasted."

Laura turned in her father's direction, feeling the heat of his scrutiny.

"Is this an impulsive decision, Laura?" he asked, his thumbs hooked into the pockets of his vest.

"No," she said, her voice barely above a whisper. It was true that her nature had always tended toward impulsive. But as a mother of two young girls with a husband off fighting in the war, she could no longer afford that luxury.

Eleanor looked over at her husband. "I don't know what to say."

"Hmm," was Leo's response.

When they both went quiet, Laura spoke. "I've given this a lot of thought. I want to do this." She *had* to do this. Her darling Edwin was off fighting somewhere in Europe, enduring God knew what conditions. Sometimes, she feared he'd be killed as a sort of retribution for Lenore losing her husband. That thought kept her awake at night.

"I forbid it!" her mother announced. "No daughter of mine is doing factory work."

Laura protested. "But I want to do my part!"

"Then why don't you roll bandages with me at the ladies' auxiliary or sell war bonds or help out with the various drives?" her mother said. She looked to her husband for support.

Leo lowered his head and sighed. Finally, he spoke. "It's no secret that they are actively recruiting women to work in the defense industry. All the men went off to war, and if we want to win it and bring the boys home, someone has to build the planes and guns."

Eleanor stared at him, blinking several times. It was not the answer she'd wanted from her husband. "But it doesn't have to be our daughter."

Leo replied, "It will have to be someone's daughter."

"What about Edna and Edith?" Eleanor asked.

Laura's girls were now four and three, and that was the thought that worried her the most. Who would watch them while she was doing shiftwork? She couldn't ask her parents to do it. Not every day. Their health was failing, which alarmed her. It was difficult to watch them struggling, her father with gout and emphysema and her mother with terrible arthritis. No, she couldn't expect them to chase after a pair of lively girls. But she was not to be deterred. She was going to do this. She'd figure it out, and she had two weeks to do it.

As if on cue, Edna and Edith came running into the parlor, both crying and squealing. They landed at Laura's legs, and Edna pointed to her younger sister. "She bit me!" She lifted up the sleeve of her dress to show a half-moon-shaped, purple-colored bite.

Laura chastised the younger girl. "No biting, Edith. And the two of you, *please*, stop fighting!"

"Come on, girls, let's go to the kitchen and see what Joan has for us," Eleanor said, slowly standing from her chair. She grimaced as she straightened up, then took each girl by the hand and carted them off to the kitchen.

Alone with her father, Laura thought of following her mother. As she went to stand, her father said, "You're serious about this."

Laura nodded, sitting back down. "I am."

"Why? I understand that you want to do your part, like everyone else. That's a given. But is there something else?"

It was a fair question, and she thought for a moment before answering. "I spend all my days worrying over Edwin." She looked down at her lap. "I miss him. I pray for him constantly. And I'm lonely. The people of Lavender Bay have never completely forgiven me for John Hadley's death." She looked up but avoided her father's gaze, choosing instead to look out the window. "It's true that I want to do my part, and I'd also like to go somewhere where no one would know me."

"I see. And do you think you would stick it out?" He regarded his youngest daughter solemnly.

She bristled at what he was suggesting and squared her shoulders. "I'll stick it out."

Her father lowered his head, his jowls expanding around the lower perimeter of his face. "Leave it with me, Laura. I'll talk to your mother."

Her posture relaxed and her shoulders sagged.

Two days later, Lenore arrived at the Wainwright house with Johnny. He was almost nine. With a smile, Laura ruffled his hair and kissed him on the forehead before he ran off to play with the girls.

Lenore looked well. It had taken a long time—John had been dead almost ten years—but she seemed to have gotten some of her pep back.

They sat in the kitchen, enjoying a cup of tea. Joan had gone to town to do the shopping.

"Dad tells me you're going to work in the factory over in Cheever where they build the C-46s," Lenore said.

Hesitant, as she didn't know what kind of reaction Lenore would have, Laura said, "I'd like to. If I can manage to get someone to look after the girls."

Lenore reached over and patted her knee. "Look no further. I'll take care of the girls while you're at work. I think this is a great idea for you."

Surprised, Laura said, "You do?"

Lenore nodded. "Yes. If I wasn't running a boarding house, I'd go with you."

"Thank you, Lenore, that means a lot to me."

"I think watching the girls full time would be too much for Mother and Dad."

"I agree."

They both went quiet for a moment in the uncomfortable realization that their parents were getting older.

"Are you sure you don't mind?" Laura asked. It was a big task to take on. The girls could be a handful on the best of days.

"Not at all. I'd love to have them."

Chapter Nineteen

Despite the straight run up the highway, the twenty-mile ride back and forth between Cheever and Lavender Bay six days a week was going to be a long trek. Laura posted an ad in *The Lavender Bay Chronicles* looking for others to carpool with. She also tacked up an index card with her name and phone number on the corkboard at the back of the post office. There were no responses to either. Because she was now considered an essential worker, she was able to secure extra gasoline rations, but she would have preferred to share the drive with other women, if only for some conversation.

Going in alone on her first day, she had no idea what to expect. She'd never worked in her life. Shaking, she took a deep breath and followed the crowd of women walking through the factory doors. Immediately, she was directed to a side room where she was given standard-issue coveralls and a pair of shoes for the plant. Next, she was assigned a locker. When she'd changed into her coveralls, she thought she looked ridiculous, but she supposed it didn't matter what she looked like.

Posters were plastered all over the walls. *Loose Lips Might Sink Ships. We Can Do It*—this one depicted a Rosie the Riveter type flexing her muscle. And then there were numerous slogans encouraging them to buy war bonds.

The women were divided into groups, and she found herself in a group of twenty, directed to a room where a projector had been set up between two rows of wooden benches. She slid onto a bench and scooted over when another woman followed her in, giving Laura a brief smile.

A man stood at the front of the room, hands on his hips, his right hand holding a clipboard. "Come on, ladies, take your seats and settle down."

He was about Laura's age, maybe a little older. There was no wedding ring on his finger, and her first thought was *Why aren't you off fighting*? He was of average height with thinning hair and sharp gray eyes that were too close together. His top lip was so thin it didn't look like he had one.

Once everyone hushed, he spoke. "I'm Les Stockton, I'm the assistant to the foreman. If you have questions about anything, you come to me. This group has been selected to train as riveters." A murmur rippled through the crowd of women. "You'll be drilling the rivets into the planes. Each plane contains thousands of them, and I cannot emphasize enough how important this job is. The last thing our fellas need is for their plane to fall apart mid-air because we didn't put it together properly."

Laura shuddered; she certainly didn't want that.

"You'll work with a partner, which I'll assign to you, and training is six weeks. Now, I've got a short film for you to watch about the different types of flush riveting." He pointed to a woman in the back row. "You, with the bright red hair—yes, you—flip that light switch off."

The room went dark, and the assistant foreman started the projector. The reel spun, and the machine made a clickety noise. As she watched the film, Laura began to doubt she could do the job. There seemed to be a lot of math involved: the diameter of the rivets, the degree of the countersunk head, and then there were the varying thicknesses of the metal sheets you were drilling into. Her heart began to sink. She'd never been any good at math in school. How was she supposed to figure all this out? More than once, she was tempted to raise her hand and excuse herself.

The film was only about fifteen minutes long. When it ended, the woman next to her whispered, "Yikes!" That made Laura feel somewhat better, that she wasn't alone in her confusion. When the overhead lights went back on, she glanced around the room as unobtrusively as possible to look at the other women. It was a mixed bag: some stared blankly at the screen, some wore frowns, and one or two had their mouth hanging open. But the consensus was the same; they looked as confused and doubtful as she felt.

But she carried on. Every day, she showed up and every day, it became slightly better. She only wobbled during those times when she was arriving or leaving and spotted groups of three or four women either climbing out of cars or piling into them. Some she recognized from Lavender Bay. Although some nodded their acknowledgement, others pretended not to know her. Luckily, she was so busy focusing on what she had to learn for her job as a riveter that she didn't have time to let it upset her too much.

For the training period, she'd been paired with a riveter who'd been working at the plant for ten months. A woman named Millie who had five kids and whose husband was in North Africa. When Millie handled that air gun, she made it look like she'd been using it all her life. Laura doubted she'd ever look that adept and skillful.

At the end of the second week, Les approached her to check her work. She stopped the rivet gun and lifted up her goggles. Millie held the bucking bar in her hand.

He examined her work and nodded, giving her a smile that revealed his tobacco-stained teeth. "You're getting the hang of it, Laura." He gave her shoulder a squeeze, his fingers lingering a little bit longer than necessary over the strap of her brassiere.

At the end of the training, she was assigned a partner, a woman named Antoinette but who preferred to be called Toni. They worked together on the cargo planes, one drilling in the rivets and the other holding the bucking bar on the other side of the hull against the drill. It was hard work. The drill was heavy, and the bucking bar was something else. You had to hold it steady, and the constant vibration of the drill against the bar made your wrists ache.

Toni lived in a suburb outside of Cheever. She was the same height as Laura, and like most of the women in the factory, she wore her brown hair covered with a kerchief. She had bright hazel eyes and a heart-shaped face, and whenever the drill was silent or when they were on their breaks, she was friendly and chatty, and Laura relished the work relationship with the other woman.

One morning, Laura arrived late, as the fog was heavy coming in from Lavender Bay. She punched in, slammed her locker shut, and ran all the way to her plane, where she found Les huddled with Toni. He was rubbing her shoulder as he spoke to her, his fingers going around in a circular motion. Toni stood frozen, her expression blank.

Laura stepped up her pace. "I'm sorry I'm late. The fog was terrible."

Immediately, Les removed his hand from Toni's shoulder, and she quickly took three steps away from him. She replied, "Everyone was late this morning."

Les looked at the watch on his wrist. "You better get started, girls. We need to keep the production up." Turning on his heel, he walked swiftly away.

"Creepy Les," Laura remarked, not taking her eyes off of him.

Beside her, Toni agreed. "You got that right."

Chapter Twenty

One afternoon, Laura and Toni sat on upturned crates for their break, chatting. Laura rubbed her aching arms.

"If I have to drink any more watered-down coffee, I'm going to cry," Toni said, crossing one leg over the other.

"Have you tried Postum?" Laura asked. Although she liked coffee and tea, she didn't care for the chicory substitute or for the war-time practice of reusing coffee grounds. She'd tried Postum and found she liked it.

"I have, but I didn't care for it."

Before Laura could comment, they spotted Les giving a young woman a tour of the plant. She was taller than Les by about an inch. She was also very pretty, with long hair the color of honey, which she wore parted on one side. Her neck was swanlike, and she had a beautiful pair of gams. She held a handbag in front of her.

"Look, he's cornered a new recruit," Toni noted.

"Ugh. It's a curse to be pretty here."

"Wait for it," Toni said as they kept their eyes glued to Les and the innocent-looking girl with the great legs.

"Coming up next, the shoulder squeeze," Laura announced in a deep voice.

And sure enough, Creepy Les rested his hand on the girl's shoulder as he swept his other hand around the plant, whispering something to her. The girl had a look of consternation on her face as she glanced at the unwelcome hand on her shoulder. Removing his hand, he placed it on the small of her back and led her away. She tried to step away to the side to put distance between them, but he kept the grip on her back firm.

"How does he get away with this? Why doesn't Mr. Treadwell do anything? It's a distraction." Toni's voice was tight with anger.

"Does Mr. Treadwell even know?" Laura wondered.

Toni sighed. "Good question, but if he doesn't, he should. Come on, let's get back to work. Breaktime is over."

Within half an hour of resuming their drilling of rivets into the cockpit, Laura's bladder became uncomfortable. She turned off the drill gun and rapped on the cockpit window. Toni lowered the bucking bar and lifted her goggles. "What's wrong?"

"I'm sorry, Toni, I can't hold it. I've got to run to the bathroom."

Toni laughed. "Wasn't pregnancy fun? To be left with all these problems we never had to deal with before: weak bladders, stretch marks, droopy bellies . . ."

"Uh-huh," Laura said as she made a run for it. The restroom was empty as they hadn't broken for lunch yet, and she used the toilet quickly and washed her hands before leaving.

As she exited the restroom, she ran into Les and the young woman, the former trying to escort the latter into an unused office. Laura had heard rumors about this office and the things Les attempted on poor, unsuspecting women. She'd always managed to avoid him, going the other way whenever she saw him coming.

"Oh hey, how are you?" she said loudly as Les opened the door to the darkened office.

The girl, startled, turned to look at her. She remained mute, staring at Laura with a look of confusion on her face. But Laura kept talking, closing the distance between them.

"Gosh, I haven't seen you in a dog's age. How's your mother?" Laura asked.

Now the girl looked frightened. Les didn't look too happy at being interrupted.

"Get back to work, Knickerbocker," he said.

Good-naturedly, she said, "Come on, Mr. Stockton, it's been so long since I've seen my friend."

At that moment an alarm went off somewhere in the plant, and Les looked in the direction of it, clearly unhappy. To the young woman he said, "I'll catch up with you later."

When he was out of earshot, the young woman asked, "Do I know you?" Up close, she was even prettier. Her looks were almost sultry and her soft, quiet voice added to the intrigue.

"No, you don't." Laura held out her hand, and the younger woman shook it. "Laura Knickerbocker."

"Diana Quinn."

Laura pulled the door closed on the office. "Look, we call him Creepy Les."

The girl's eyes widened.

"Here's a piece of advice. Whatever you do, don't be alone with him. And no matter what, don't go into this room with him."

Diana swallowed hard. "Gee, thanks for looking out for me."

Laura gave her a reassuring smile. "Don't mention it. Just be careful around him."

Wide-eyed, Diana asked, "Are all the men like that here?"

Laura shook her head. "Nope. Some will whistle at you, but that's as far as it goes."

Soon it became Laura's mission to warn every new girl about the assistant foreman, ending with the caveat that they too should warn others coming in after them. The work was hard enough and important enough without having to deal with the likes of Les.

Chapter Twenty-One

A month later, Laura had just parked her car in parking lot of Cheever Aviation when she spotted Diana getting out of the passenger side of the car in front of hers. The driver was a short woman, no more than five feet tall, with thick, dark curly hair and dark eyebrows. Although Laura didn't know her, she'd seen her around the plant. She got out of her car and made sure it was locked.

Diana threw her hand up in a wave and smiled. "Hi, Laura!"

"Hi!" she said, joining the two women.

"This is my friend Joy Ruggiero," Diana said. "And Joy, this is Laura Knickerbocker, the woman I was telling you about."

"Right." Joy nodded, appraising Laura with her lively dark brown eyes. "I heard you warned her off Creepy Les."

"All women coming into the plant need to be warned," Laura said evenly.

"That's for sure." With a nod toward Laura's car, Joy asked, "Do you drive alone?"

"I do," Laura said. "I couldn't find anyone to carpool with."

"Where do you live?"

"Lavender Bay."

Diana grinned. "I live in Lavender Bay too."

Laura's eyebrows lifted. She'd never seen her around Lavender Bay, and it wasn't that big a place.

"I'm over on Peony," Diana explained. "We just moved there two years ago. Came up from Pennsylvania. My mother inherited the house from her aunt."

"That's not far from me at all. I'm on Bluebell Lane," Laura said.

Joy chimed in. "I pick up Diana on my way in and it'd be no problem to pick you up as well. I mean, if you want to carpool with us."

"I meet Joy at the Gibson's Grape Jelly factory," Diana explained. "Mr. Gibson lets those of us who carpool to the Cheever plant park there."

Laura couldn't believe her luck. "That'd be great! I could even pick you up and we could meet Joy at the factory."

The three of them spoke for a few more minutes before heading inside. Laura thought they must have looked quite the trio, one very tall—because Diana was close to five ten—Joy petite, with Laura in between. But the three of them really seemed to click.

They all worked swing shift together, and for their first week carpooling, they were assigned the night shift. Joy worked in a department soldering cables for the planes, and Diana worked with the buffers. Laura didn't like working nights. She had no problem staying awake but no matter how much sleep she got, she never felt rested.

On their first drive to Cheever, the three of them were quite chatty.

"I got a letter from my Sam today," Joy said as she drove along the highway. She sat on several cushions to see over the steering wheel. "I thought when he went away, the letters would be all romance."

"And they're not?" Diana asked, surprised.

"Nope. Today's letter reminded me to get the oil changed on the car. Then he waxed poetic about my lasagna and my eggplant parmigiana saying he couldn't decide what he'd eat first when he came home."

Laura sat in the back seat and almost laughed when she spotted the look on Diana's face. Diana was younger than the two of them and was in the beginning stages of a romance with a sailor fighting in the Pacific, who was still writing letters about his undying love and devotion.

The time passed quickly, and before they knew it, they were pulling into the entrance for the plant. Joy rolled the car through the gate, and the guard, old enough to be their grandfather but pretty spry, came out of the security hut. He motioned for Joy to roll down the window. "Badges, girls."

As soon as the three of them clocked in, their conversation ceased, and they headed off to their respective jobs.

The ride home in the morning was nothing like the ride in. Gone was the nonstop chatter. The main goal was to stay awake, Laura thought, and more importantly, to make sure Joy didn't fall asleep at the wheel. Once Joy started yawning, Laura followed suit, but she kept an eagle eye on her. Meanwhile, Diana had climbed into the backseat and was out cold as soon as the car pulled out of the gate.

One down, Laura thought, glancing over her shoulder at the sleeping Diana. The younger woman reminded her of the film star Veronica Lake.

Laura spoke to Joy to prevent either of them from drifting off. "I don't know about you, but I'm not crazy about nights."

Joy tilted her head, not taking her eyes off the road. "I know, I feel like something the cat dragged home." She let out a big yawn. "At least it's not permanent."

They were to rotate between all three shifts, six days a week.

As they neared Lavender Bay, Laura began to nod off but shifted in her seat several times in an effort to remain alert. Her eyes burned. She felt slightly queasy, and she couldn't determine if it was because of hunger or fatigue or both.

As Joy pulled into the vast parking lot of Gibson's Grape Jelly, she perked up. She pulled up behind Laura's car, looked over her shoulder, and said, "Diana, wake up, we're here."

"Huh." Diana bounced up, her hair smashed against one side of her head.

Laura and Joy laughed.

As Laura and Diana got out of the car, Laura said to Joy, "We can take turns driving to Cheever so it doesn't all fall on you."

Joy nodded, yawning. "Sure thing, kid."

"And you have my phone number if you need to reach me."

"Yes. Lavender Bay 4362," Joy rattled off.

"See you tonight." Laura smiled and closed the door.

With a tired smile and a wave, Joy drove off.

Diana lived over on Peony Lane, which wasn't far from Bluebell Lane. It was only after Laura dropped her off at her house that she became super sleepy and had to fight to keep her eyes open for the two-block ride home.

The house was quiet; she'd almost forgotten that the girls were over at Lenore's. Her parents were in the dining room, eating breakfast. Both looked up when she entered, and both spoke at once.

Her father beamed. "There's our working girl."

"Laura, you look exhausted," her mother said.

"How did it go?" her father asked. As she'd been at the job for three months, she guessed her father was impressed that she'd lasted that long. Admittedly, so was she.

"Fine." She said with a nod, and looked at the breakfast spread out on the table. Her stomach growled.

"Why don't you have something to eat," her mother suggested.

She slid into the chair. "I think I will." A yawn escaped as she piled scrambled eggs onto her plate.

"How do you manage to stay awake all night?" Leo Wainwright asked.

"I was so busy I didn't have time to think." That was true. Plus, she was so afraid of making a mistake that she paid close attention. The men fighting the war depended on high-quality goods, and she was resolved to do the best job she could.

"You'll go to bed for a little while?" Eleanor asked.

"I will. Did Lenore say what time she'd bring the girls home?"

"Sometime after lunch."

Thank you, Lenore. That would give her a good chunk of time to sleep. She ate quickly, scraping her fork against the plate as she gathered the little bits of scrambled egg and put them into her mouth. She washed it all down with a glass of orange juice, which she drank in one gulp.

"Laura!" Eleanor said.

Leo butted in. "Mother, leave her be. She's a working girl now, and she no longer has time for a leisurely breakfast."

"Thanks, Dad," Laura said. "I'm sorry, Mother, I'm in a hurry. I want to get to bed." She piled her silverware on her empty plate, stood, and pushed her chair in. "I'll see you later."

In her bedroom, she peeled off her clothes and threw on the bathrobe that hung on the back of the bedroom door. She used the bathroom to brush her teeth and wash her face. Looking in the mirror, she winced. The bandanna had done no favors for her hair. It was flattened against her head. Not caring, she padded back to her room, shut the door, closed the drapes, and crawled into bed. By the time her head hit the pillow, she was fast asleep.

The sound of the girls shrieking woke her with a start. She rolled onto her side, blinking, and looked at the bedside clock, which ticked quietly next to her. It was almost two in the afternoon. She'd slept for five hours but felt as if she could sleep another five.

As the volume of her daughters' voices rose higher, Laura sighed and rolled over. She pulled herself up to a sitting position and swung her legs over the side of the bed and yawned. A cup of tea and a sandwich would be nice. Slowly, she got out of bed, made her way to the bathroom, and got dressed.

As soon as she appeared downstairs, the girls rushed her. She crouched down and held her arms open for them, enveloping them in a hug. They were warm and smelled of fresh air. They were adjusting to their mother being gone long hours. Going to Lenore's helped tremendously because the girls loved it over there.

"Were you good for Auntie Lenore?" she asked, eyeing them.

Immediately, they went quiet and nodded. She lifted an eyebrow at Edna, who put her finger against her teeth.

"Are we going to Auntie Lenore's tonight?" Edna asked.

"Yes. Mommy has to go to work again," she explained.

"That's okay," Edith said. "Hilda gave us molasses cookies last night." Hilda had once worked for the Wainwrights but had now been keeping house for Lenore for many years.

"That was nice."

Edna concurred. "They were yummy."

Chapter Twenty-Two

Laura, Joy, and Diana settled nicely into a routine—and a friendship. They'd requested management to schedule them on the same shifts as they were carpooling together, and knowing that gasoline was being rationed, the foreman, George Treadwell, was more than accommodating, nodding and making a note on his clipboard with a pencil he kept tucked behind his ear. Although Laura didn't think she'd ever get used to nights, which left her feeling groggy and slightly sick to her stomach, she made the most of it. On occasion, a fourth girl rode with them, a young woman named Betty who rarely stopped talking and had an opinion on everything.

Laura and Joy took turns driving each week. The latter admitted that her legs and back sometimes ached by the time she got home, from stretching to reach the gas pedals.

They were on their fourth night of nights. *Two more, then a day off,* Laura thought as she hunched over the steering wheel. Rain blasted against the windshield, leaving her no choice but to drive at a snail's pace.

"Can you go faster?" Betty asked from the back seat. "We're going to be late."

In a clipped voice, Laura replied, "I'm going as fast as I can for the conditions. I can't see past the front of the car." The current blackout status didn't help. She continued to crawl along the highway, trying to increase her speed in increments. She didn't want to be late either, but she didn't want to risk getting into an accident.

Diana, sitting next to Betty in the back seat, spoke up. "Did you hear about Grace Gibson?"

Everyone in Lavender Bay knew who Grace Gibson was. The only child of the owner of Gibson's Grape Jelly, she'd led a privileged life in a mansion at the top of the only hill in town. Laura wondered if the war affected people like the Gibsons. Were they removed from all the nastiness? Had money bought them a pass?

Next to her, Joy turned around to face Diana. "No, what about her?"

"She's gone off and become a Red Cross worker. She shipped off to the Pacific last week."

"Now why would she do a thing like that?" Joy asked.

"Probably got sick and tired of eating all that grape jam and jelly," Betty quipped.

That resulted in a round of giggles among the women.

When the laughter died down, Diana added, "Apparently her father threw a fit. But she told him if he prevented her from going, she'd run away and join the circus or something like that, and he'd never see her again."

"She has everything! Why go off to a war zone?" Joy asked.

"Probably the same reason as the rest of us, tired of waiting and anxious to do something meaningful to help out," Laura said.

The waiting was the worst thing. Waiting for the war to be over. Waiting for the men to come home on leave. Waiting for them to come home for good. Waiting for things to go back to the way they were, for the blackout to lift, for the rationing to end, for butter to appear back on the shelves. Waiting, waiting, waiting. Sometimes, Laura thought it would drive her right around the bend.

It was one of the many reasons she was grateful for the job. It helped pass the time. Not to mention the money. Seventy cents an hour was more money than she could possibly have dreamed of. She'd opened a bank account and had her own checkbook. No more asking Edwin for money to buy something. Not that he minded, he was such a sweetheart. But she liked this bit of independence. She helped with some of the household bills and had tried to pass off money to Lenore, who'd refused, horrified. Laura got around it by arranging to have groceries sent to Lenore's house. Her whole life, she'd been dependent on other people; this was a new role she relished. It made her feel good to be generous to someone else.

She understood Grace's desire to do something. She was sure they all felt it. It was hard to sit home, idle, while the men were off fighting in horrific conditions. Only the other day, the town had received word that Billy Stodges had been killed in action. The plane he was in was on a bombing run to Germany when it was shot down over the English Channel. Years ago, when Billy was younger, he used to steal pies and cakes from the Wainwrights' kitchen windowsill, with either Lenore or Hilda chasing him with a broom and he, running off with his loot, laughing his head off, knowing they'd never catch up with him. Upon hearing the news, Lenore and Hilda had cried.

As they neared Cheever, the rain abated but the pavement was still wet, and Laura increased her speed slightly.

Betty spoke up. "I had a run-in with Creepy Les yesterday. I hope he isn't there tonight."

"Ugh," Laura said. Their assistant foreman was an ongoing problem.

"What happened?" Diana asked.

"The usual. Hand on my shoulder, fingers practically playing with the strap of my brassiere." Betty's tone was one of disgust.

"What did you do?" Laura asked.

Betty laughed. "I told him my big brother was due home on leave and if he didn't remove his hand from my shoulder, my brother would remove it permanently." She guffawed. "You should have seen the look on his face."

Joy piped in. "I don't know how he gets any work done with the way he harasses everyone."

Laura sighed. The mood became serious, but Diana broke it and started singing. She was a big fan of the Andrews Sisters and started with "Don't Sit Under the Apple Tree." Soon all four of them were singing along with her.

Laura parked the car in the employee lot, and they all hurried to the main door with only three minutes to punch in. Looking around at the stampede of women heading for the time clock, it was obvious that the torrential rain had delayed most everyone.

She was breathless by the time she punched her timecard. The company was strict. If you were late, you were docked pay. And she worked too hard to hand it back to them.

They stored their belongings in the locker room, and Laura, Joy, Diana, and Betty continued to talk amongst themselves as they hurriedly changed into their coveralls, lacing up their boots and applying their headscarves.

As Laura tucked her hair beneath her scarf, they were approached by Stella, a woman who'd been working at the factory since long before they started. Stella was a big, burly girl. Laura wasn't sure where she was originally from, but she'd never seen her around Lavender Bay.

Stella was tall—not as tall as Diana, but her burly physique gave her an intimidating look. Her eyes were dark, and her face was weathered and lined, whether from being outdoors or personal circumstances, Laura did not know.

"Come on, we better get going," Joy said, slamming her locker shut.

Diana turned, tying her headscarf at the base of her neck so that her long locks hung down her back.

"Where are you going?" Stella asked Joy, hands on her hips, her stance wide.

Joy looked from Laura to Diana as if she didn't understand the question.

"I'm going out on the line to do my shift."

"Uh-uh," Stella said with a shake of her head. She looked at Laura and Diana and said, "You two can skedaddle along."

Diana looked over at Laura, uncertain.

Laura planted her feet. "No, we'll wait. But we have to hurry; we don't want to be late."

Not taking her eyes off of Joy, Stella said, "Italians are our enemy."

Not this again.

Since they'd started working at the plant, Joy had been badgered on occasion about her Italian heritage. Despite her short stature, she stood her ground. There was a steely glint in her eyes, and she never broke eye contact with Stella, even though she had to look up at her. "First of all, I am an American, born in this country just like you. Second, my parents are Americans, also born here. I'm here to serve my country the same as you are."

When Stella continued to stare her down, Joy said with a lift of her chin, "Now step aside so we can get to work."

Stella wore an amused expression, as if she were merely toying with Joy.

"Come on, girls, let's go." Joy turned to step away.

Stella threw an arm against the wall, blocking her.

But Joy was too quick and used her short stature to her advantage, easily ducking beneath Stella's arm and exiting the room with Laura and Diana in tow.

Laura thought her friend was very brave, and told her so as they practically trotted to their workstations.

"It's not that I'm brave," Joy explained. "It's just that I'm sick of it. I'm as American as everyone else. And isn't my Sam fighting for the United States? He's not fighting for Italy."

"I don't think I'd be as brave," Diana said.

Joy stopped and looked at her. "Sometimes, you have to. You have no choice but to stand up for yourself. If I don't stand up to these bullies, it will be ten times worse, and they'll make my life more miserable than it already is. I'm not quitting this job, and no one will force me out. The work here is too important. Now, come on!"

Laura admired her friend for her conviction and her courage.

At the main hallway, they parted ways. Laura hurried to her plane, where Toni and her rivet gun waited.

Sometimes she wished she could do something else, but no matter what job they put you on, there was always going to be a downside. With any of the jobs, tedium was the greatest enemy. Doing the same thing over and over, day in and day out, could be wearying. To fight, she had to constantly remind herself that if her work kept Edwin safe, then she could do it. It never failed to give her a renewed sense of purpose.

Chapter Twenty-Three

1944

Laura paced the platform, wringing her gloved hands. Edwin was due home on leave, only the second one he'd had since joining up. She missed him so much that sometimes her body and heart ached for him. She'd been able to get a few days off from work so they could spend the time together.

The weather was damp, and a fine mist hung in the air. February had been milder than expected with some days hitting almost sixty degrees.

She'd done her hair in the popular Victory rolls style, glad to be rid of the kerchief, and had applied some red lipstick. She didn't want Edwin coming home to a drudge. She had on her best shirtdress and her most comfortable pair of shoes that still had a bit of a heel on them.

She felt the vibration and heard the whistle of the approaching train before she saw it. When it finally came into view and rumbled into the station, her breath caught in her throat. She was so excited she thought she might faint.

It came to a stop with a final *whoosh*, and within seconds, the doors were thrown open and passengers disembarked. As the platform became crowded, Laura stood on her tiptoes to get a better view. There weren't many servicemen on this train. Over the heads of the crowd, she spotted him before he saw her, and she lifted a gloved hand and cried out, "Edwin!"

The crowd, sensing a reunion, parted, and there he was.

He raced toward her, his duffel bag over his shoulder, and Laura broke into a run. He dropped his bag as he reached her, and she jumped into his arms, hugging him tight as he lifted her off the ground and kissed her.

"Oh, Edwin! How I've missed you!" she said as he set her down.

"Not as much as I've missed you," he said with a laugh. "How are you? You're looking as beautiful as ever, I see!"

She reached up and placed her hand on the side of his face. "I'm so happy to see you."

He smiled and looked around. "Come on, let's get out of here." He wrapped his arm around her and leaned in to kiss her again. "Just as I remember!"

She elbowed him with a laugh. "Let's go, the car is out front."

With their arms linked, they walked through the small train station to the parking lot out front, and he threw his bag into the back seat.

Both of them went for the driver's side. Laura laughed and said, "You're on leave, honey. I'll drive."

"Swell," Edwin said with a grin.

She got into the car, thinking that while he was home, she wanted him to relax and take it easy. His furlough was only fifteen days, and she knew they would fly by. In no time, she'd be bringing him back to the station. Immediately, she pushed that thought out of her mind. Right then, at that moment, Edwin was there with her, and that was all that mattered.

"It's great to be home!" he said as he got into the car.

As Laura drove out of the parking lot, he looked over at her and winked. "I could get used to this." And to prove his point, he leaned back and lowered his Army garrison cap over his eyes, folded his arms across his chest, and feigned sleep.

"Don't you dare fall asleep on me, Edwin Knickerbocker!"

Immediately, he pushed his cap back onto his head and sat up. "How are the girls?" he asked.

"They're fine. They're shooting up like sprouts."

He looked out the window, his smile faltering. "I hope they remember me."

Laura took her eyes off the road for a moment to look at him. "Of course they do! They've got your picture next to their beds, and Edna keeps your letters tucked under her pillow."

This resulted in a laugh from her husband.

"So, what's new in Lavender Bay?" he asked.

"Not much. Lenore's got a full house over on Pearl Street. Mother and Dad are fine, although Dad is struggling with some gout." She thought for a moment. "The cinema closed down."

"That's a shame. Why?"

"The owner is sick, and his son is off in Africa."

"There's a lot of that," Edwin mused. "That cinema is where we had our first date."

"I remember," she said.

"How's Uncle Bert?" he asked.

"Like a new man since his operation. The garage is up and running again, and I think he's happy to be back at work. The girls and I visited him last week on my day off."

"Good."

When Laura pulled up to the house and parked the car, the front door burst open and both girls rushed out, hopping down the steps and yelling, "Daddy!" Behind them, Leo and Eleanor stood on the porch and waved. Mr. Wainwright moved slowly, leaning on a wooden cane.

Edwin had no sooner got out of the car than Edna lunged at him.

"Daddy!"

Edith followed suit, and Edwin scooped them up, planting one on each shoulder. "How are my best girls?"

Edna wrapped her thin arms around her father's neck and kissed his cheek. This resulted in laughter from Edwin. "I missed you, Daddy!"

"I missed you both! So much!" He carried them up to the porch, where Laura's parents waited to greet him.

Laura pulled out his duffel bag from the back seat.

Edwin turned around and said, "Aw, honey, leave it. I'll get it later."

"I don't mind."

Edwin set the girls down on the porch to shake Leo's hand. "Sir, it's good to see you."

"And you," Leo said. "You certainly are a sight for sore eyes." He put his hand up alongside his mouth and joked, "It'll be nice to have another man in the house. I'm outnumbered here."

Edwin threw back his head and laughed.

Eleanor laid a hand on his arm. "You must be hungry. We've got a nice luncheon prepared for you, and Lenore has made some of that delicious war cake of hers."

Lenore was always testing new recipes with the limited ingredients available. This one was eggless and had an abundance of raisins and spices: nutmeg, cinnamon, and cloves. Laura liked this one, although it would have been better with a spread of butter. Sometimes, she wondered if the old staples like butter and sugar would ever be as readily available as they used to be.

They gathered around the table. Laura had put the girls on either side of their father. She'd learned a long time ago that they couldn't be seated next to each other, because they always started fighting.

Once all the platters and bowls were on the table, she sat on the other side of Edith.

The girls took turns telling their father all their news. Edna crowed about how she was learning to read, and Edith showed her father her new bow. Edna favored her father with her auburn hair and green eyes, and Edith was the image of Laura: blond and blue-eyed.

"Girls, let your father eat his lunch in peace," Eleanor pleaded.

"I don't mind, Mrs. Wainwright," Edwin said. "I've missed them."

"Of course you have," Laura said. He looked at her and grinned and winked.

"Edwin, when are you going to start calling me Eleanor? You've been in this family for almost ten years now."

"Old habits die hard, Mrs. Wainwright."

It was good to see that Edwin had an appetite. He shoveled the food into his mouth as if they were going to take his plate out from under him any minute. Happily, Mrs. Wainwright filled his plate with seconds, and he didn't refuse. He looked thinner than when he was last home, Laura thought. How could they fight a war if they were hungry?

When they were finished, Laura helped Joan clear the table, and her parents retreated upstairs for their afternoon nap. Edwin changed his clothes and took the girls outside. Laura had splurged and bought two second-hand bicycles for them, and Edwin promised the girls that by the time his leave was over, they'd both know how to ride them.

After the dining room was cleaned up, chairs pushed in, and the linen tablecloth given a good shakeout over the side porch rail, Laura joined Edward and the girls outside. She sat on the top step of the porch, watching as he held the back of Edna's seat as the girl pedaled, a bit wobbly. Edith, being a year younger, struggled to keep her balance. When it was her turn, Edwin held on to the back of her seat and the handlebars as well.

As Laura watched them, the girls laughing and shouting, she wished it could always be like this. Just the four of them. When Edwin wasn't there, things felt flat. She and the girls were like a three-legged chair; they simply didn't work properly without him. She said a silent prayer, like she had so many times before, that he would make it safely home from the war.

When they had enough of the bikes, the four of them took a stroll around Lavender Bay, neighbors coming out to say hello. Laura and Edwin walked arm in arm, with the girls running on ahead of them.

"You should have kept your uniform on," she said.

"It feels good to get back into my regular clothes."

She didn't point out that they were practically hanging off of him.

By evening, the girls were tuckered out, and fell fast asleep on the sofa in the parlor. Edwin carried them up to bed.

Later that night, Laura slept with Edwin's arms around her, and again, she thought, if it could only be like this all the time.

The following night, they went out dancing. They met up with Diana and Betty, as Laura was eager for Edwin to meet them. Joy had planned to come out as well, but one of her kids was sick and she decided to stay home.

They danced all night, rarely sitting down. They jitterbugged to Glen Miller's "In the Mood," and when the orchestra played "Begin the Beguine," Edwin held her close, his hand folded over hers against his chest.

Diana and Betty didn't stay late as they were on the morning shift, but Laura and Edwin stayed long after they left. They practically had to be kicked out of the place, stumbling out in the early hours of the morning, Edwin's right arm slung around her shoulders, a lit cigarette in his other hand. The cool air was a welcome relief. They were sweaty from all the dancing, and Laura's hair was damp and clung to the nape of her neck.

"The fresh air feels good," Edwin said.

"It sure does. I can't remember the last time I danced like that."

"I don't think we've ever danced like that."

"No, we haven't." Impulsively, she reached for his hand and kissed his knuckles.

"You've got nice friends, Laura. I'm glad."

"I wish you could have met Joy. She is one top-notch gal."

"Where's her husband?"

"He's in Europe as well."

They walked two blocks in silence with only the moonlight to guide their way, due to blackout restrictions, Laura simply enjoying being in his company.

"Do you ever get lonely, Laura?" he asked.

She snorted. "Every night when I go to bed by myself."

"No, seriously."

His mood had shifted. She'd noticed that the last time he was home. Suddenly he would become very somber. He could be in the middle of laughing and yukking it up, and then he'd go quiet, as if someone had flipped a switch.

Laura's left hand held on to his right hand, which was slung around her shoulder, and she slid her free hand around his waist.

"Edwin, where do you go when you go quiet?"

"Huh?"

"Where are you right now?"

He took a long drag on his cigarette and flicked the elongated ash onto the sidewalk. "I don't know. I think of what's going on over there and all the guys I've left behind, and I don't know if I should be here."

She stopped walking and frowned. "What do you mean? Do you not want to be home with us?"

"More than anything, sweetheart. But last week, we lost five guys in our unit." He shook his head, his eyes narrowing as cigarette smoke drifted in front of his face.

They turned to face each other, and Edwin went on. "As much as I love coming home—and it's the only thing that keeps me going, knowing that I have you and the girls waiting for me—there's a part of me that feels guilty for enjoying myself when I'm here. Especially when so many men, some a lot younger than me, will no longer enjoy anything."

Laura took both his hands. "Oh, Edwin." She knew something about guilt and how it could eat you up inside. It had almost destroyed her life, but then he'd come along with his cheery countenance, his practicality, and his positive outlook, and showed her that she could move on and be happy.

She stepped closer and lifted one hand to trace it along the side of his face. She felt so much love for this man that to know he suffered broke her heart. It was unfair. He was too good.

"I wish I could take the pain away from you," she said in a low whisper.

"I know, Laura. I appreciate that. Sometimes I wonder what I ever did to deserve someone as wonderful as you," he said.

Smiling, she asked, "Do you want to know what you did?" She turned and walked slowly backwards, facing him. "You loved me for me!"

"It was easy, honey," he replied.

"Come on, I'll race you!" Laura laughed and she turned on her heel, and broke into a run, heading into the darkness toward Bluebell Lane.

They didn't stop until they reached the house, stumbling at times, and it was a miracle that neither had fallen along the way. Laura reached the house first with Edwin behind her and they collapsed on the porch steps to catch their breath, still laughing.

Chapter Twenty-Four

The night before Edwin's departure, the two of them sat alone in the parlor. The Wainwrights had retired early, citing fatigue, but Laura knew better. Her parents were allowing them to be alone. She'd made an effort to remain cheerful, doing her hair, putting on a little lipstick, and making sure he had a good dinner: roast turkey, with an apple pie for dessert. She would not think about tomorrow and how bereft she would feel when he boarded that train with his duffel bag slung over his shoulder.

They'd had a busy day. All the days had been busy, Edwin preferring to do as much as possible in the short time he had. In the evenings they visited family, and one evening they had his Uncle Bert and Lenore and Johnny for dinner. Neighbors would drop in unannounced.

Everyone clamored to see him, but Laura liked it best when they were alone in the bedroom at night and she had him all to herself.

The only sound was the ticking of the grandfather clock in the corner. Laura picked up the newspapers from the floor, folded them neatly and set them on the needlepoint stool. Finished, she leaned against the back of the sofa.

Edwin put an arm around her. "You've changed, Laura."

She looked up at him. The war hadn't dimmed the sparkle in his bright green eyes, and she was glad of that. "Have I? In what way?"

For a moment she thought he would remark on her appearance. She was no longer the young girl he'd met almost ten years ago. Raising their two children and working at the plant hadn't been easy. When she looked in the mirror, she thought she was beginning to see lines on her face.

"You're more confident," he said.

She hadn't expected that. "I am?"

He leaned in and kissed the side of her head. "Yes, you are. You're more independent, doing things you never used to do."

"Like what?"

"Working, for one. Paying all the bills. Driving. Making unilateral decisions."

That much was true. The other day, Edna's bike had a flat tire, and Laura went ahead and took care of it, using an air pump for the first time without even thinking to ask Edwin.

"Oh." Had she changed? She supposed she had. But then she didn't have a choice, did she, with circumstances such as they were.

Was he angry? Was he disappointed? Did he feel left out? Was he going to expect her to go back to the way she was? She didn't think she could. She no longer recognized that girl from so long ago. Before the war, she could have guessed Edwin's reaction to a multitude of things. But now, she wasn't sure how the war had affected him. The other women at the plant spoke openly about their husbands when they returned from leave. For most, the reunions had been joyous but for some, the husbands came back brooding or angry or both.

"How's the job?" he asked.

She nodded. "Good. Hard, and the hours are long, but I don't mind."

"Are there men there who work at the plant?" Edwin asked. He'd gone quiet.

"Yes, but it's mostly women."

"And how do they treat you?"

"Well, there are a few women from Lavender Bay, and they do nod hello and all that, but for the most part no one knows about my past scandal." It was sweet of him to ask, she thought.

Edwin shook his head. "No, not that. I meant the men. Are they giving you a hard time? You're very pretty, you know."

She gave him her best smile. "Thank you." But the first thing that came to mind was Creepy Les. During her last shift, he'd caught up with her, walking by her side, clipboard in his left hand and his right hand on the small of her back, his fingers moving in a slow, circular motion. Laura had been unnerved. When they were out of earshot from other people, he'd asked her in a whisper if she was lonely and if there was anything he could do.

The whole incident made her feel like she needed to take a bath.

But she'd never tell Edwin about any of this. First, he'd want to go and punch his lights out, and she didn't want her husband getting into trouble over that jerk. And second, he'd soon be thousands of miles away again, and he'd worry.

"For the most part, pretty good. But you know, you still have a few who'll whistle as you walk past."

Edwin smiled. "Honey, they're always going to whistle at you."

They were quiet for a moment before he circled back to the previous subject.

"Like I said, you're a completely different person to the one I left behind. You're more of a take-charge type now."

When she finally spoke, she stammered. "Um, well, I just do things. You know, what needs to be done."

He laughed, and her posture relaxed.

"I see that. I hardly recognize you anymore." Absentmindedly, he rubbed her back.

"I'm still the same person," she assured him.

Would he no longer love her if she was too different? She didn't think she could bear that.

"When I first met you, and even when we were first married," he said, "I got the distinct impression that you were someone who needed looking after."

She winced. Although what he said was true, it made her sound like she had needed adult supervision. Now here she was, a decade later, drilling rivets into planes. It was stranger than fiction.

Reaching for his hand, she whispered, "Maybe I grew up."

"You sure did."

She looked up at him. "What do you think of the new, improved version of me?"

"It'll take some getting used to."

Her smile faltered. "You don't like it?"

"I didn't say that. You're different, that's all."

She leaned closer to him. "Maybe I am different. Maybe I've grown up and matured or whatever you want to call it, but how I feel about you has never changed. It will never change. I love you, Edwin, please know that."

He laughed and pulled her to him and kissed her. Against her lips, he murmured, "All right, you've convinced me."

In a mocking tone, Laura said, "Whew, you scared me."

He kissed her once more. "You know, your confidence is very sexy," he whispered.

"Tell me more!"

Chapter Twenty-Five

Toni banged on the hull of the plane. Laura couldn't hear her workmate over the noise of the drill, so she shut it off.

"What?" she asked. But before Toni could answer, Laura became aware of the alarms going off in the plant. Her stomach knotted. Alarms going off in that number and intensity meant there was a big problem somewhere, possibly an accident. Two weeks before, a young girl had suffered a terrible burn to her right arm. She hadn't been back since. Laura had learned very quickly that it could be a dangerous place to work.

All work up and down the line came to a grinding halt. It was a different place without all the noise of the machinery. But there was still the sound of the alarms reverberating through the cavernous space, echoing.

She set her drill down and sat on one of two upturned crates. Toni joined her. Work would be halted until the problem was fixed, whatever it was. Sometimes that happened quickly, even just a few minutes if the alarms had gone off accidentally. Other times, they could be sitting around for hours, waiting for the all clear.

"I love that headscarf you're wearing," Laura said. Her workmate wore a dusky blue scarf with the word "Victory" printed all over it, the capital "V" stylized in red and blue.

Toni touched it. "Isn't it swell? My cousin sent me this from Canada. She's working at an aircraft plant in Hamilton."

"It's nice."

"I've got an extra at home, I'll bring it in for you."

"That'd be great."

The conversation stopped when Joy came running toward them. Laura jumped up off her crate. "What's wrong?"

Although breathless from her long run, Joy managed to get out, "It's Diana! She's gone and got her hair caught in the buffer."

The three of them took off in a run. All Laura could think about was Diana's beautiful hair. Hopefully, it wouldn't be too bad.

Like everywhere else in the plant, the machinery in Diana's section was silent, but they could hear their friend screaming and wailing. They approached the crowd gathered around one of the machines, And Laura elbowed her way through, anxious to get to her friend. When the other women saw them, they parted like the Red Sea to allow them through, knowing they were Diana's friends.

Laura saw many things at once when she finally reached the center of the circle. A substantial lock of Diana's golden hair wound around the buffer machine, having been torn from her head, and to Laura's horror, she realized that there was blood and pieces of skin at the end of it. Her stomach roiled and she gagged, but she did not want to alarm her friend and with every bit of strength within her, she tamped it down and forced herself to look at Diana, who was supine on the floor, her long legs stretched out. The plant manager and foreman were crouched, hovering over her.

Laura pushed forward and knelt down next to the foreman, Joy doing the same on her other side.

What she saw would be an image Laura would carry with her for the rest of her life. Not only was a large chunk of Diana's hair missing, but part of the scalp was gone as well, leaving the left side of her head looking like raw meat. Laura's stomach somersaulted. She looked at Joy and knew she mirrored the way she looked. Pale as a ghost. Even Joy's lips had gone white. Both of them reached forward at the same time and held Diana's hands.

"We're here, Diana," Joy said.

Diana looked at them through her tears. "Is it bad?" she wailed.

"It's going to be fine," Laura said, having no idea if that was true.

"You'll be fine, honey," Joy said, "but we need to get you to the hospital."

The foreman and the manager stood. Behind them, there were gasps and even a scream at the sight of Diana's injury. Quickly, Laura removed her headscarf and laid it gently over the wound. Diana yelped in pain.

"Sorry, Diana," Laura whispered.

The ambulance crew arrived and moved Diana onto a stretcher. Laura and Joy stood, following closely. As they passed Creepy Les, Laura asked, "Can we go with her to the hospital?" Even though she'd lose a day's pay, she didn't care.

"Not on your life," was his answer.

Mr. Treadwell, standing next to him, frowned. Laura looked to him, and he nodded. "Yeah, go on, get out of here."

As they walked away, following the stretcher, Les said to someone, "Get that scalp out of here and throw it in the incinerator. Get this place cleaned up as soon as possible so we can get back to work."

It was then that Laura started crying.

―――ele―――

They followed the ambulance in Joy's car.

On the ride over, Joy kept muttering and crossing herself and lifting the religious medal that hung around her neck and kissing it.

Laura looked over at her. "Are you all right? Did you want me to drive?"

Joy shook her head, continuing to whisper some prayer.

When the hospital was in sight, Joy, still pale, asked, "How are they going to fix that?"

Laura had been thinking the same thing, wondering if it *could* be fixed. "I don't know." She put her elbow on the door and placed her hand on her forehead, trying to process all that had happened.

She dropped her hand. "Gosh, we should call her mother."

"As soon as we get to the hospital."

Laura patted her pockets. "I left everything at work. I don't think I have a nickel."

"Don't worry, I've got some change in my pocket."

The ambulance drove right up to the hospital entrance. Joy looked around for a parking spot and eventually found one quite a distance from the entrance. It was a few minutes before the two of them rushed through the front doors.

They were greeted by an elderly nun. The sister was tall and garbed in the traditional habit of her order: a black tunic that fell to the ground and a black head covering with a white wimple.

"Can I help you?" she asked.

Laura nodded. "Our friend Diana Quinn was just brought in from the Cheever Aviation plant. She was in an accident."

"Most unfortunate." The nun gave them directions to the waiting room.

As they stepped away, Laura turned and asked, "Is there a payphone?"

The nun pointed a crooked finger. "Right around the corner."

"Thank you, sister," Joy said.

The phone box was a wooden one with a small bench. The two of them crowded inside. Joy dug around in her pockets and pulled out a small amount of change, sorted it with her finger, plucked a nickel out, and handed it to Laura.

Laura put the nickel in the slot and dialed the number for Diana's home.

As she dialed, dread settled around her. It was a phone call she didn't like making.

She covered the mouthpiece with her hand and said to Joy, "What do I say to her?"

"Keep it simple. You don't want to upset her too much." Joy advised.

"Hello?"

"Mrs. Quinn? It's Laura Knickerbocker, Diana's friend."

"Is everything all right?"

"That's why I'm calling. Diana had an accident at the plant, and Joy and I are at the hospital in Cheever with her. Would you be able to come over?"

"Is she, is she . . . dead?" Mrs. Quinn's voice was shaky.

"Oh goodness, no."

The older woman's relief was palpable across the phone line. "I'll see if my neighbor can drive me over," she said, and hung up the phone.

Laura and Joy sat next to each other in a small waiting room. They had no idea where Diana actually was in the hospital. Hopefully, someone would come out to them. Within the hour, Mrs. Quinn arrived. Laura and Joy stood and hugged her.

Like her daughter, Mrs. Quinn was a tall woman. She had fine bone structure and her hair, though silvery gray, was thick. She was a handsome woman.

"Now tell me, girls, what happened?" she said when they pulled apart. She held their hands in hers.

"I don't know the specifics, but her hair got caught in one of the buffers," Joy explained.

Mrs. Quinn gasped, covering her mouth with her hand. Then she asked, "How bad is it?"

Laura looked at Joy before answering, "It looked pretty bad."

No one was sure what condition Diana would be in, but at least she was alive. It made Laura think of her sister's friend, Alistair Young. He'd gone off to war and lost his leg. His wife, Harriet, had said that at the time: that she didn't care, she was just glad he was alive. Laura had to agree, because there was no coming back from death.

They waited many hours. In the meantime, Laura managed to get change for Joy's dime so they could each make a phone call to their families to let them know where they were and that they'd be late coming home. Laura's mother was horrified at the news, but there was an undercurrent of relief in her voice that it hadn't been her daughter.

A nun came into the waiting room, made eye contact, and approached them. She was short and stick thin, but instead of being overwhelmed by her habit, she owned it. Hands tucked into her sleeves, she walked—or rather, glided—toward the trio. The three of them stood up, Mrs. Quinn in the middle with Laura and Joy on either side like two bookends.

"Are you the family of Diana Quinn?" The nun wore a small smile. "You can see her now."

"Is she all right?" Mrs. Quinn's voice shook.

The nun tilted her head and gave a slight nod, still smiling. "The doctor will explain everything to you. Follow me."

Never in her life had Laura met anyone with such presence and grace. The woman was not much taller than Joy, and yet her aura suggested she was meant to be obeyed. Laura thought it was a mistake to hide a person like this in a hospital; she should be over on the front lines, defeating Hitler.

Mrs. Quinn followed directly behind the nun, and Laura and Joy brought up the rear. Their footsteps echoed off the industrial linoleum floor. There was a faint smell of bleach, and Laura looked around. There were no scuff marks on the walls, no dust on the baseboards, and the freshly waxed floor shone to within an inch of its life. There were statues of Jesus and Mary, and crucifixes hung on the wall. Although she wasn't Catholic, Laura found it oddly comforting.

Diana was in a ward in an iron-framed hospital bed. Her eyes were closed. A thick white bandage completely circled her head. On the right side, her long hair trailed out from beneath the bandages. But the other side was devoid of hair.

A doctor stood at the foot of the bed, writing something on a clipboard. When the three visitors approached, he put the clipboard in its holder at the foot of the bed frame and tucked his pen into the front pocket of his white coat.

Mrs. Quinn went to her daughter and took her hand. "Diana." Her voice was low. There was no response. Diana appeared to be in a deep sleep. Laura and Joy went around to the other side of the bed.

"Are you the girl's mother?" the doctor asked.

Mrs. Quinn nodded, and he looked over at Laura and Joy.

"We're her friends," Laura said.

"I'm Dr. Pellman." He paused for a moment before continuing. "Diana has suffered a serious injury."

"How bad is it?" Mrs. Quinn asked.

"The force of the machine pulled out part of her scalp."

Mrs. Quinn's shoulders shook as she cried. Joy placed an arm around the older woman and gave her a reassuring squeeze.

"As awful as it sounds, Mrs. Quinn," Dr. Pellman said, "it could have been a lot worse. Your daughter was lucky. She could have been killed."

Mrs. Quinn put her hand to her mouth and gasped. Laura thought that comment put things in perspective.

"We've just brought her out of surgery. We went in to repair as much of the scalp as we could. We've sedated her because she's in a lot of pain and she needs to rest to heal."

As Mrs. Quinn continued to sob, Laura asked, "Will she be okay?"

"Eventually. She's lost a lot of blood and needed a transfusion. We're concerned about infection."

"Will her hair grow back?" Joy asked.

Dr. Pellman shook his head, his expression grave. "No. There's no way for the hair to grow back without the scalp."

Mrs. Quinn cried, "She'll be disfigured?"

Laura swallowed hard. It was too awful to bear.

Dr. Pellman pressed his lips together, rolling them inward. His silence answered the question for them.

Joy rubbed Mrs. Quinn's back. "She can wear headscarves or wigs. It'll be okay, you'll see." But it sounded like she was trying to convince herself as well.

They visited Diana as often as they could, but Diana had nothing to say, and would sometimes just lie there staring at the ceiling as Laura and Joy looked on in dismay. They tried to cheer her up, but to no avail.

Mrs. Quinn had told them that when the doctor removed the bandages and Diana took a look at herself in the mirror, she leaned over the side of the bed and vomited onto the floor. And then didn't eat for two days.

Joy shook her head as they drove away from the hospital. "That poor kid."

"I feel so helpless," Laura said. "Helpless and useless."

Chapter Twenty-Six

Laura walked over to Lenore's house to pick up the girls. She'd been on the night shift for the past week, and the girls had been staying over at her sister's house.

The house on Pearl Street looked well. It appeared bright and pretty with a profusion of red and pink flowers out front. She glimpsed the lake beyond the house and thought briefly she might take the girls and Johnny to the beach over the weekend on her day off, maybe even splurge on an ice cream for them. It was the least she could do since poor Johnny always had the job of keeping the girls entertained.

She knocked on the front door.

Through the window, she spied Lenore walking from the kitchen. When her sister saw her, she waved her in.

"Laura, how many times do I have to tell you that you don't have to knock, just come in," Lenore said as Laura entered.

"I know. But I can't help it."

"Try. Come on back to the kitchen, I'm making tea. Would you like a cup?"

"If it's not too much trouble."

Laura followed her sister back to the kitchen. Lenore provided a dinner for all her boarders every day, so it was no surprise that there was a pot on every burner of the stove. Laura didn't know how she managed; she didn't think she'd like to cook for that many people. It was a lot of potatoes and carrots to peel.

"How were the girls last night?" she asked, half dreading the impending reply. It could go either way.

"Fine. We did some baking until bedtime, and that seemed to keep them busy."

"Thank you," Laura said with a sigh. Her sister was doing her a huge favor, and she wanted her daughters to be as good as gold for their aunt, which didn't always happen. But it seemed Lenore and Johnny had a good grip on the situation.

"Where are they now?" she asked. Lenore handed her a cup of tea. "Thanks."

She'd finally gotten used to drinking it without sugar, but she poured a liberal amount of milk from the little jug into her cup.

"Johnny took them for a walk. They were starting to get antsy." Lenore joined her at the table and asked, "How are Mother and Dad?"

"Fine. Mother is thinking of taking the train to see Aunt Millicent."

Lenore looked worried. "Is that a good idea? For her to be traveling alone?"

Laura sighed. "Probably not. But you know Dad won't go, and Aunt Millicent isn't in the best of health."

"I know."

"Where's Hilda?"

"She's gone to town to get a few items."

"How's she doing?"

"Slowing down, like everyone else." Lenore picked up her teacup and took a sip. "I'm sorry I have no biscuits. Would you like a piece of cake?"

Laura shook her head. "No thanks, I'll eat before I go to work."

"How's your friend Diana?"

"The same. Depressed. But home now."

"Hopefully she'll do better at home," Lenore said.

"Hopefully."

"How's work going at the plant?"

"You know, okay."

Lenore smiled. "Mother and Dad are very proud of you."

This came as a shock to Laura. "They are?"

"Of course. We all are. Doing your part for the war and doing a man's job at that!"

Laura fumbled with her answer, still shocked to hear this news. "I needed to do something."

"And you have. So good for you!"

This was high praise coming from her sister, and Laura was secretly pleased. Lenore, the sister who had done everything right and never put a foot wrong, who was loaded with common sense where sometimes Laura felt she herself was in short supply of it, was proud of her.

"Can I talk to you about something?" she asked.

"Of course. Anything."

It was rare to find Lenore alone in the house, but Laura was glad of it. There was so much she needed to discuss.

"I need some advice about what's going on at work."

"It sounds serious."

"It is." She gathered her thoughts. She placed her elbow on the table and leaned her cheek against her fist. Lenore stood and poured more water into the teapot.

"All of us women are glad to be there at the plant, for the most part. We all have an important job to do."

"You sure do." After Lenore sat down, she said, "What's going on?"

First, Laura told her of the abuse Joy had endured at the hands of some of the other workers because of her Italian heritage.

Lenore was appalled. "That's awful. We're all in this together."

"I know that, and you know that. But some people out there apparently have some awful ideas."

"And she continues to work there."

Laura smiled. She admired Joy greatly. "If anything, it makes her more determined to stick it out."

"Good for her!"

"But I have a problem."

"Are you being harassed by those women too?" Lenore leaned slightly forward.

"No, not the women. One of the men."

Her sister leaned back in her chair, her eyes widening. "Oh."

"Yeah, oh."

"What's going on?"

"There's a guy at work. We call him Creepy Les. He makes all sorts of lewd comments to us under his breath, so no one else can hear, and he can't have a conversation without touching you." The memory of the discomfort caused her to squirm in her seat.

Lenore blanched. "Touching you? How?"

"He likes to touch your shoulder, right over your bra strap. I'm not the only one he does it to. We all try to avoid him because he's such a creep." Laura's anger rose within her. "But it's hard. Sometimes, he coerces women into this unused office across from the restroom. We all try to warn the new girls coming in not to be alone with him."

Lenore scowled. "That's awful. How old is this guy?"

"Around thirty or so. My age."

"And he's not off fighting?"

Laura shrugged. "He's got a concave chest or something, I don't know. The other day I was coming out of the restroom and a woman was leaving that office in tears."

"What about the management?"

Laura scoffed. "He is the management. He's the assistant to the foreman." The plant manager was only concerned about production and meeting quotas. And although the foreman, Mr. Treadwell, was a peach and the father of four daughters, he was under too much pressure already. She didn't think he'd want to have to deal with the interpersonal relationships of the workers, and she told her sister as much.

Lenore looked horrified. "Are you sure about that? He should make it his business."

"Anyway, what do I do?" Laura asked, hopeful that Lenore would have the answer.

"For one thing, don't ever let him see that you're afraid of him." Lenore paused. "There are a few options. First you have to stand up to him, somehow. I can imagine how hard that is, but it might be the only way to get him to leave you alone."

"What if it gets worse?" Laura asked.

"Then you'll have no choice but to report him or you'll have to quit. You can't work under those conditions."

Laura sighed. She couldn't tattle. She wasn't a squealer. *Snitches get stitches*—that's what the girls said at work. Some who had gone to management with other complaints had found their work lives miserable. Besides, who were they going to believe, her or him? He was her boss. And she certainly didn't want to quit. She resented Les for putting her and all the other women in this predicament.

Before they could say anything else, Johnny appeared with the girls, who looked tired and worn out and had some sun on their faces.

Chapter Twenty-Seven

When Laura returned to work, she had her sister's advice planted firmly in her head. She hoped she didn't crumble when it came down to it. It was easy to sit in her sister's kitchen, drinking tea and being galvanized into action. It was a whole different thing to actually stand up for yourself, especially against someone who wielded some power. She didn't have to wait long for a confrontation.

Les approached her as soon as she picked up her drill.

"A word, Laura," he said, flipping through some pages on his clipboard. He performed this action all the time. She thought it made him feel important to have paperwork.

"Yes?"

She was aware of Toni behind her, getting ready for the day's work, trying not to listen. She was glad she was not alone. She hoped whatever Les had to say was work-related.

"Let's go somewhere where we can talk privately." His tone suggested that he expected to be obeyed.

Laura planted her feet. It felt a little unladylike, but she stood firm. "We can talk right here, Les."

He glared at her. "I prefer to go somewhere private."

"And I prefer to hear what you have to say right here."

He rounded on her. "Mrs. Knickerbocker, you don't get to prefer anything. You do as you're told."

Laura felt the heat creep up her neck and fan out along her face.

Toni was at her side. "Come on, Laura, you can't stand here all day chit-chatting. We've got to get to work. Remember what Mr. Treadwell told us yesterday? If we don't pick up our speed, we're canned." She looked pointedly at Les. "We don't want to get fired."

Everything Toni said was a lie, and Laura knew she wouldn't always be around to save her but this time, she'd dodged a bullet.

Les's eyes swept down the length of Laura's body and then back up, resting on her breasts.

"We will have this chat, Laura. Someday. At my choosing." He turned and walked away, carrying his all-important clipboard at his side.

Beside her, Toni said, "You need eyes in the back of your head with him. He's a snake."

"That's for sure. Come on, we better get to work. These rivets aren't going to get drilled in themselves."

Toni laughed.

For the next few weeks, Laura was careful, making sure she was never alone. But it was tiring trying to keep a constant watch out for Les. If she saw him coming, she cut through other departments, taking the long way around to her plane. Or she disappeared, making an excuse to use the restroom. At times, her bladder felt ready to explode as she held it until she spotted him so she could run to use the facilities and bide her time. She knew this wasn't exactly what Lenore had in mind, but she hoped he'd forget about her and leave her alone. But that would mean he would move on to someone else.

But fate caught up with her one afternoon as rain pounded on the rooftop of the plant, adding another layer of noise to the already considerable cacophony. As she was coming out of the restroom, the whistle sounded signifying the end of the lunch break, and she ran straight into Les. Before she could think, he grabbed her by the elbow and hustled her into the office across from the restroom, closing the door behind them. The room was dark, and the blinds were drawn. Outside the window, she heard the parade of mostly female workers heading back to their stations.

In the dark, his eyes glittered. He set the clipboard down on a desk.

Now she was afraid.

"I keep trying to talk to you, but you keep avoiding me," he said, approaching her.

With each step he took, Laura took a step back, trying to stay out of his reach. As he neared, there was a whiff of body odor emanating off of him, and in the faint light of the room and up this close, she could see a fine sheen of perspiration along his upper lip.

"I have to get back to work," Laura said firmly, trying to control the tremor in her voice. Lenore had advised her not to show fear, but it was proving to be difficult in reality. "Mr. Treadwell will be mad."

"I'll put in a good word with the boss, don't worry." His eyes settled on her breasts, and she hated the way that made her feel. Minimized. Objectified. Without averting his gaze from her bosom, he said, his voice thick, "You know, Laura, you're probably the prettiest girl in the plant here."

This was one time she didn't say "thank you" for the compliment.

Taking another step back, she hit the back wall of the small office. He closed the gap with two steps, lifted his arm, and placed his hand on the wall next to her.

"If you play nice," he said, "I can make sure you get the cushy jobs. No more drilling rivets. Maybe you'd like one of the positions where you can sit down. No more standing all shift on your feet." His voice dropped to a whisper as he leaned in. "Would you like that, Laura?" His breath smelled of onions.

"No, I'm fine where I'm at. I like my job." Sure, she'd like a job where she had the chance to sit down, but she knew there'd be a high price to pay with Les.

Enough was enough.

"I have to go," she said sharply. She placed her hands on his chest and pushed him away. But just as quickly, he grabbed her by the wrists and forced her back against the wall.

"You will play nice, Mrs. Knickerbocker." He bent his head, his mouth against her ear. His breath was hot on her neck.

Laura's breath became quick and shallow. She was afraid she might start to hyperventilate. "No."

He ignored her. "You must be lonely with your husband so far away for so long." His body was so close to hers that you wouldn't have been able to slide a sheet of paper between them.

Outside, she could hear all the machines. Her screams would get lost in the din.

She started to wriggle. "Get off of me."

"I don't think you mean that." Les's tone was low, barely above a whisper. Intimate.

He released one of her wrists and she tried to push him away, but he pressed against her. She was no match for his strength. As hard as she pushed, he didn't budge. He placed his hand on her waist, sliding it up toward her breast and groping it.

A combination of panic, fear, and anger overtook her. This was not going to happen. No one touched her like that except Edwin. She'd heard other girls talking about "kneeing" a man, but she didn't think she could do it. She lifted her leg slightly and with her work boot, kicked him in the shin.

"Ow!" He let go of her and hunched over and she kicked him again. Harder. He staggered back, giving her enough room to slip away from him and make a run for it.

She had just reached the door when she felt him behind her, grabbing the waistband of her coveralls. Her fingertips grazed the doorknob, but he pulled her back into the room. She brushed past the desk and reached out, her hand sliding along the top of it until it landed on the stapler. She grabbed it, and when he turned her around and tried to press her up against the desk, she raised her arm and brought the stapler down hard against his forehead, drawing blood, hitting him again and again until he finally staggered back, muttering expletives and holding his hand to his head. Blood gushed through his fingers.

Dropping the stapler, she ran out of the room, not looking back to see if he was following her. All she cared about was getting back to the main thoroughfare of the plant where there were plenty of people around.

She wanted to put some distance between herself and Les and the unused office, so she headed to the restroom on the other side of the plant. Toni was probably wondering what had happened to her, but there was no way she'd be able to drill in the rivets with shaky hands. She needed to pull herself together. The restroom was empty, and Laura collapsed against the tiled wall, leaning forward, hands on her knees, and drew in some deep breaths. Tears stung her eyes, but she refused to give in to them. Finally, when her breathing had returned to normal and the shaking stopped, she stood and went over to the sink to splash cold water on her face. She pulled off her kerchief and patted her face dry. As she refixed her scarf over her head, tucking in her hair, she noticed a splatter of blood across her neck and the top of her coveralls. Although her coveralls were dark, the splotches were large and unmistakable.

She heaved a sigh, splashed some water on her neck, and rubbed away the blood spatter.

Placing both hands on the edge of the porcelain sink, she stared at the floor. Lenore had told her she had two options.

It was time to pick one.

Summoning her inner Lenore, imagining her horror and hearing her voice urging her to do what needed to be done, Laura finally composed herself and walked out of the restroom.

With legs that felt like jelly, she walked toward the middle of the factory where the elevated platform with all the offices was located. She took hold of the rail and climbed the metal stairs, her boots clunking against the steps. Her body buzzed with anxiety, and bile rose in her throat, the taste of acid strong.

The management offices were at the top, three stories up, with windows all the way around overlooking the factory floor. As Laura climbed the three flights, the pit of dread in her stomach grew larger with each advancing step.

She'd been up here once before, at the start, to fill out paperwork. She spotted Mr. Treadwell through the glass window, his bald head bent over papers spread out on his desk.

The shaking started again, but she forced herself to knock on the door. The first knock was so weak he didn't even hear it over the noise in the plant. Stilling her body, she rapped a second time, this time with more force. The foreman lifted his head and waved her in.

As she stepped into the office, she realized she hadn't prepared what she was going to say, and there was a momentary sense of panic, a feeling that she should flee and go home and never return. Her hands were damp, and there was a fine sheen of perspiration beginning to form on her forehead, just below her headscarf.

She was not asked to sit down, so she stood in front of Mr. Treadwell's desk. Out the windows was a bird's-eye view of the plant. All those planes and the different departments. All that metal and grayness dotted with a variety of colorful headscarves.

"Mrs. Knickerbocker, what can I do for you?" he asked. He was always a pleasant man. Firm, but there was no nonsense from him. His open expression soon morphed into a frown, and he leaned forward, elbows on his desk. "Is that blood on your coveralls? Has there been an accident? Why are there no alarms going off?" He glanced out the window.

"No and yes," Laura stammered. She squeezed her eyes shut. "I mean, yes, it's blood, but there wasn't an accident."

With a sober expression, he asked, "Care to explain how you got blood on your coveralls?"

Still stammering, she said, "Yes. I will. Of course."

Calm down and get it out.

Although Mr. Treadwell wasn't smiling, there was a hint of kindness in his eyes. It was rumored he had four daughters and six granddaughters. She couldn't look at him or she'd start crying. She fixed her gaze on the wall just behind him and forced herself to control the tremor in her voice.

"Les Stockton made an unwanted advance and touched me"—swallowing hard, she waved her hand in the general direction of her breast—"so I clocked him in the head with a stapler."

"That's a serious accusation to make against the assistant foreman," Mr. Treadwell said gravely.

"I know. But it's the truth," she replied.

He leaned back in his chair, processing what she was telling him. "There's never been a complaint against him."

That was the problem.

"Maybe so," she said, "but I'm afraid I'm going to have to quit because I can't—can't—work under these conditions."

Before Mr. Treadwell could reply, there was a sharp knock on the door, which caused Laura to jump. In came Les Stockton holding a blood-soaked towel to his head.

Laura felt herself get lightheaded to the point she feared she might faint.

"George, do you want to see Mrs. Knickerbocker's handiwork?" Les raged.

Mr. Treadwell put up his hand. "I can see quite enough from here. Mrs. Knickerbocker claims you made unwanted advances."

Les snorted, still holding the towel to the wound on his forehead. "She's lying. She's unhappy with her job and wants a desk job, and when I said no can do, she hauled off and hit me with the stapler!"

Laura's mouth fell open and her eyes widened at his blatant lie.

"I've never said anything about a desk job, Mr. Treadwell," Laura said. "Mr. Stockton is always making inappropriate comments and looking at parts of my body he shouldn't be looking at. I'm sick of it."

"Did anyone else see what happened?" Mr. Treadwell demanded.

"No, he's too slick for that."

Mr. Treadwell coughed, cleared his throat, and looked over at Les for an explanation. Creepy Les leaned against the credenza behind him. "None of this is true, George. You know how hysterical these females get."

To his credit, the foreman did not respond to Les's comment.

Les straightened and spoke, his face reddening, spittle forming in the corner of his mouth. "George, you need to fire her! She's a menace—"

Mr. Treadwell held up his hand to Les, who shut his mouth. "Hold on a minute, Les. Go to the hospital and get some stitches. Leave Mrs. Knickerbocker to me."

Reluctantly, Les moved past Laura, exiting the office, but not before he leveled a glare at her.

Laura wanted to wrap this up and go home. "As I said, Mr. Treadwell, I think it's best if I quit."

"Don't do anything hasty, Mrs. Knickerbocker. Go home, take tomorrow off, and report back to work the day after unless you hear from me."

She stared at him, saying nothing.

"Understood?"

She nodded, eyes not blinking.

On unsteady feet, Laura left the office, made her way down the three flights of stairs, and walked in the direction of the locker room. She was thinking she should head to her plane and let Toni know she was leaving. But Toni intercepted her halfway.

"I've been looking all over for you, Laura. Where've you been?" Her eyebrows knitted together. "Is that blood?"

Laura gave Toni the abbreviated version of the story, telling her about the incident, the stapler, and then Les blaming the whole thing on her. Toni's response fluctuated between disbelief, bewilderment, and downright rage.

Wearily, Laura told her, "Anyway, I'm going home. I'm to stay home tomorrow and come back the next day. If he doesn't fire me."

Toni gave her a reassuring smile and reached over and rubbed the top part of her arm. "You won't be fired. I can almost guarantee that."

Laura's smile was small. Even if she didn't get fired, how could she continue to work in the same place as Creepy Les?

Toni was still speaking. "If you were going to be fired, he would have done it today."

"You think so?" Uncertainty filled Laura. Would he drag her into work after a day off only to fire her? It didn't make sense. But a lot of things didn't.

"That Les is something else," Toni muttered. "That no-good—"

"Forget about it, Toni," Laura said wearily.

"No, I won't. Wait until everyone finds out about this."

"Look, I'm sorry to leave you in the lurch," Laura said.

"Don't worry about it, kiddo. See you when you come back."

Chapter Twenty-Eight

On her day off, Laura found herself walking over to her sister's house on Pearl Street. She wanted a distraction to take her mind off of Les and his lies. Her parents were feeling good that day and had taken the girls for a drive. Although she missed her girls, she was looking forward to having some time for herself. As she walked, her thoughts turned, as they often did, to Edwin. Rumors abounded that the war was winding down. She wouldn't believe anything until Edwin was discharged from the military, but she was hopeful. Some days she missed him so much she wanted to cry.

Remembering her sister's instructions, she let herself into Lenore's house, and was met with the clean-smelling fragrance of Murphy Oil Soap and the sound of Big Band playing on the radio: Benny Goodman's "String of Pearls."

She called out. "Lenore?"

"Hello, Laura," her sister called. "Come on back, we're in the kitchen."

Laura followed the sound of amiable chatter coming from the kitchen. Hilda and Lenore stood at the sink. Hilda was washing the dishes, and she looked over her shoulder at Laura and smiled. "Hello, Laura, how are you?"

"Good, you?"

"Fine. How are your mother and father?"

"Good. They took the girls for a drive."

Lenore stood next to Hilda, drying the dishes after Hilda washed and rinsed them.

"Do you have an extra towel?" Laura asked. She didn't feel like drying dishes, but she also didn't feel like sitting around and watching Lenore and Hilda work.

"Almost finished." Lenore's smile was bright. "Sit down and I'll put on the kettle. Did you want some toast and jam?"

Laura shook her head. "No thanks." She looked around. "Where's Johnny?"

"Over at a friend's house."

"And your boarders?"

"Everyone went out," Lenore replied.

"It's nice when the house is quiet," Hilda added, rinsing a plate and laying it on the drainboard.

Lenore set her towel down and turned on the kettle. She pulled three cups down from the cabinet.

"I'll get another chair." Laura stood and went to the dining room.

Once the dishes were dried and put away, the three of them sat down to have tea.

"How's work going?" Lenore asked.

Laura laughed but it wasn't funny. "Not good. I'm probably going to lose my job."

Lenore could not hide her surprise. "What? What do you mean?"

"Why would you think that?" Hilda asked.

In between sips of tea, Laura relayed the whole sorry tale.

Lenore and Hilda were outraged.

"He deserves more than a few stitches," Hilda said. "If butter wasn't rationed, you could have put a block of it in a sock and given him a few belts."

Laura wanted to laugh, but then she saw that Hilda was serious.

Lenore sighed. "I know you like your job, but you did the right thing in reporting him to the boss. You can't work under those conditions."

"I see that now."

Lenore gave her sister a sympathetic smile. "I know how much this job means to you, but if your safety is at risk, you're better off without it. If Les gets away with this, and it sounds like he might, you could be in even more danger. Who knows what he'll do, now that he knows he has carte blanche."

"It's awful." Hilda shook her head. She picked up her teacup and drained it.

Laura hadn't given that thought consideration: that now Les might ramp up his advances. That thought made bile rise in her throat. What she had endured that day had been terrible, and she never wanted to go through something like that—or worse—again.

"I'm glad you told your boss what happened. It's unfortunate that Les lied, but at least you spoke up. That's the most important thing."

Hilda agreed. "You were very brave."

Laura didn't feel brave at all. She was scared and worried. And she felt helpless and powerless. She might have to give up a job she liked, all because of some man who couldn't keep his hands to himself.

Chapter Twenty-Nine

When Laura returned home, her parents were still out with the girls. As soon as she stepped through the front door, the phone began to ring.

"I'll get it, Joan," she called back to the kitchen.

She picked up the handset and answered. "Hello?"

"May I speak with Mrs. Knickerbocker?" asked a male voice. Immediately, Laura recognized it as Mr. Treadwell and felt her stomach constrict.

"This is she."

"This is Mr. Treadwell from Cheever Aviation."

"Hello, Mr. Treadwell."

She picked up the base of the rotary phone and, stretching the cord, carried it to a side chair in the front hall so she could sit down.

The foreman continued. "I wanted to call you and confirm that you'll be here for work tomorrow morning."

As much as Laura wanted the job, she couldn't work with Les Stockton. There'd be no going back. She had to stand firm.

"Mr. Treadwell, I'll remind you that I wanted to quit the other day before I left," she said gently.

"Never mind that," he said. "I'll expect you here for your shift tomorrow."

"I'm sorry, but I wouldn't be able to work with Les Stockton."

"Mr. Stockton will no longer be working here," Mr. Treadwell told her in a tone that invited no questions.

Laura was speechless. In all the realm of possibilities, she'd never entertained this one.

"Oh," she finally managed to get out.

"Will you reconsider your resignation?" he asked.

Smiling, she said, "I'll be there tomorrow, sir, for my shift."

"That's great news. Thank you, Mrs. Knickerbocker," he said, and hung up.

Laura sat there for a few minutes, processing everything and reveling in the knowledge that she'd be working at a place where there was no Les Stockton.

―⁓―

Joy drove the following day, full of news on the ride into work.

"After you left work the other day, word spread pretty quickly about what happened. For the rest of the shift, other women left their stations and went upstairs to complain to Mr. Treadwell about Les and his harassment The line was so long down the stairs that he had to stay late to deal with it. And he wasn't happy about it."

Laura couldn't believe it. Although there was some gratification that he was gone, it bothered her that so many women had fallen victim to Les and that he'd gotten away with that behavior for so long.

"Anyway, yesterday morning, Mr. Treadwell came in early and fired Les as soon as he arrived," Joy crowed. "Mr. Treadwell called him up to the office and security escorted him out. Everyone was clapping and cheering as he left." Joy's smile stretched across her face. "Mr.

Treadwell held a general meeting and said there was too much important work to be done to allow a distraction like Les. Said morale was lagging among the workers, and he couldn't tolerate that."

It was a relief, that was for sure.

"If they hadn't fired him, I was going to bring my rolling pin in this morning and give him a few whacks on your behalf," Joy said.

Laura couldn't help but smile at her friend. "You're pretty fierce, Joy."

Joy winked. "Dynamite comes in small packages."

As they walked through the doors of the plant, Joy linked her arm through Laura's, and they walked together to the locker rooms to change and punch in.

There were a few women in the locker room, and they congratulated Laura, some patting her on the back.

Soon, she and Joy walked out and headed to their departments. With her stomach in knots, Laura made her way through the plant, toward her station. As usual, the floor was packed with women either finishing or starting their shift. But when she was spotted, the crowd separated, forming two lines of women in coveralls and headscarves on either side of her. She frowned, unsure what was going on.

Then the clapping started, and Laura blushed. All the women on both sides of the line clapped and cheered her on, some even stepping out of line to pat her on the back or shake her hand.

At the end of the line, near her plane, stood Toni, smiling broadly and clapping along with the other women.

Laura smiled. She was so happy she was shaking.

Laughing, Toni said, "Thank you, Laura!"

Laura was buoyed by the change in things. More than ever, she was excited about her work. "Come on, Toni, let's get this plane put together for our boys."

"You got it!"

Creepy Les was replaced by a young man named Buster Rolle. Buster had worked in almost every department in the factory since he was eighteen. Unable to go to war because he'd had polio as a child, leaving one leg shorter than the other, he knew how to build a plane inside and out. He was fair, and he treated everyone professionally. And most of all, he kept his hands to himself.

Chapter Thirty

Laura and Joy stood on the front porch of Diana's house. Their friend had been discharged from the hospital and was recuperating at home.

The Quinns lived in a little cottage on Peony Lane. Betty had decided not to join them, saying she wouldn't be able to look at Diana. This angered Laura. Diana was their friend, and she needed them.

Lenore had given her a war cake to take over. And Joy had brought some homemade biscotti, which Laura was addicted to. On the way over, they'd stopped at the magazine stand and picked up a few movie magazines.

Joy pressed the doorbell, and they waited. Laura stood ramrod straight, holding the loaf of war cake in one hand.

Mrs. Quinn answered the door. "Hello, girls."

"Hello, Mrs. Quinn," Laura said. "We were hoping to visit Diana."

The woman looked from one to the other. She hesitated before speaking. "I don't know if she wants to see anyone, but I'll ask." She held open the door and invited them in. The house was warm and smelled of boiled cabbage. Laura and Joy stepped into a parlor that, although small, was minimally but tastefully decorated with neutral wallpaper and a matching easy chair and sofa with cream lace antimacassars over the arms and backs.

"Diana could do with some company. One minute. Let me check." The older woman disappeared down a narrow hall, and Joy looked at Laura and shrugged as if to say, *What can you do?*

Mrs. Quinn reappeared and beckoned to them. Laura and Joy followed her through the parlor and then down the hallway. Diana's bedroom was the last one on the right.

Diana was tucked up in her bed beneath a quilt. Across from the maple bedframe was a matching five-drawer bureau, and a painting of a horse hung on the wall

When their friend looked up at them, Laura's heart went out to her. A scarf covered her head, but bandages were visible beneath. The left side of Diana's face was covered in black-and-blue bruises fading into a yellowish green. Her eyes were rimmed in red, and her nose was swollen.

Laura exchanged a glance with Joy, and they both approached Diana and hugged her.

There was one chair in the room, and Joy pulled it closer to the bed and offered it to Laura, who shook her head.

"Is it okay if I sit on the edge of the bed?" Laura asked. She didn't want to be presumptuous.

"Sure," Diana said.

Laura made herself comfortable at the end of the bed, near Diana's covered feet.

"How are you doing, kid?" Joy asked.

Diana shrugged. She lowered her head and swiped at her eyes with an embroidered handkerchief.

"Oh, Diana, it'll be all right," Joy said.

Laura hovered, unsure what to do but wanting to comfort her friend in some way.

Diana sniffled and wiped at her nose with her hankie. "I don't think it will. The doctor said the hair will never grow back because the scalp is gone, and hair can't grow back over scar tissue."

Laura felt slightly nauseous. Diana had had beautiful hair, just like a movie star. And she'd seen Diana's head at the time of the accident. It had been horrific. It was a sight she was never going to forget.

Joy fumbled to say something. "It's awful what happened to you, honey, but you can get around it. You can wear a wig or a hairpiece."

Laura jumped in. "Joy's right. There are lots of ways you can camouflage it."

Diana looked at them as if to say, *Really?*

"Where's Betty?" she asked.

Laura kept it vague. "She couldn't come."

Diana's shoulders slumped. "I suppose it's too much to ask of people. My friends will start dropping off."

"Not us!" Joy said. "We'll all still be friends."

"But I'm not coming back to the plant," Diana said.

"So what?" Laura asked. "And Joy's right, you've got us."

"I had a letter the other day from Preston," Diana said. "He's coming home on leave next month."

Laura didn't know what to say to this.

"Have you told him?" she asked.

Diana shook her head.

Joy leaned forward on her chair. "Don't worry, honey. You can tell him when he gets home."

"What if he breaks up with me?" Diana's voice was barely above a whisper, as if it was too terrible a thought to contemplate, much less voice. "You know, when he sees it." She glanced toward the side of her head.

Laura was quick to reassure her. "You're getting way ahead of yourself."

Joy jumped in. "Laura's right. Besides, any man worth his salt would know you're a gem. If this Preston is as nice as you say he is, you have nothing to worry about."

"Just because you're missing your—" Laura caught herself and clamped her mouth shut.

Diana looked at her with the first real smile since they'd arrived. "Just because I've got a large bald patch on the side of my head? You think he should overlook that?"

Laura and Joy went silent, but as soon as they realized Diana was being flip, they burst into giggles.

Once they stopped laughing, Laura spoke. "Yes. It should be overlooked."

"I agree," Joy said. "Diana, you have so many wonderful qualities and besides, haven't men come home missing arms and legs? Their girlfriends and wives didn't chuck them to the curb, did they?"

Laura was certain that somewhere in America, a poor GI who'd seen the wrong end of the war *had* got dumped, but said nothing. Because nothing was one hundred percent.

They stayed for another half an hour, bringing Diana up to date on all the gossip at work and having a cup of tea and a slice of war cake and some biscotti. By the time they left, Diana's spirits had improved.

"That poor kid." Joy shook her head as she drove her car in the direction of the Wainwright house.

"She's so worried about Preston." Laura was worried too. Not everyone would take up with someone who was disfigured. She chomped on her bottom lip, said a prayer for Diana, and hoped everything would turn out all right.

"If I didn't love my Sam so much, I'd let Diana have him. Sam doesn't care what you look like, as long as you can cook," Joy said, turning off of Peony Lane.

Laura laughed. "That can't be true! I'm sure he's nuts about you."

"Yeah, when I make a pan of lasagna or baked ziti," Joy deadpanned. "I'm telling you, Laura, all his letters are about food and how I should come over and cook for the front."

"That's a high compliment."

"It's hardly romantic, is it."

"Some men aren't romantic," Laura said. It was a gene that escaped some of them and seemed to be in overload in the women.

"What about Edwin? Is he romantic?" Joy asked.

Laura shifted uncomfortably in her seat. As much as she loved Joy, she didn't want to share intimate details of her and Edwin's relationship. She opted for vague. "Our letters are mostly about what's going on at home and with the girls."

But Joy pushed. "No romance?"

"Some, but not too much," Laura said. "He's not overly gushy. And I wouldn't like that anyway. His letters are . . . perfect, actually."

"Lucky. Sometimes I feel like I'm a waitress and Sam's sending in his order."

Laura snorted and quickly covered her mouth with her hand. "Joy, you are too much."

"I know, kiddo, that's why we get on so well."

Laura and Joy visited Diana a few times before her fiancé was due home, to keep her spirits up. They encouraged her and on the last visit, she removed her headscarf to show them her scar. Laura knew it was important not to make a big deal about it. But it looked worse than she'd anticipated. There was a large, scarred bald patch above Diana's left ear, extending up to the top of her head and forward to her temple. There'd be no way to conceal it with the hair she did have.

"I brought something," Joy said. She reached into the brown paper bag she'd brought and pulled out a wig of black hair.

Diana stared at it, blinking. Laura didn't know what to say.

"Now, I know it's not the same color as your own hair," Joy said, "but try it on. It belongs to my cousin Rosalie. She has thinning hair and wears wigs all the time. She said you could have this one."

Carefully, Diana took hold of the wig, flipped it around, and placed it on top of her head, wincing once when it touched the scarred bald spot.

Both Laura and Joy stared at her. *That won't do at all*, Laura thought. The straight dark hair of the wig fell to Diana's shoulders and was styled with severe bangs covering the forehead. Laura reached for a small mirror that sat atop the bureau and handed it to Diana.

Diana studied her reflection, turning her head this way and that to get a better view. She looked up at her friends, who waited with anticipation.

"I can't decide if I look like Cleopatra or Mata Hari." She tugged the wig off and handed it back. "I do appreciate it, Joy, please don't think I don't."

"It's okay, honey, you're not a brunette. The color does nothing for your complexion."

They all looked at each other and started to laugh.

Joy patted her arm. "See, you find you can laugh again."

"As long as I don't leave the house." There was bitterness in Diana's voice. She hung her head, and Laura recognized this as part of Diana's pattern: all was okay, and then something triggered a downward spiral. It could be days before she'd come out of it. She and Joy had compared notes with Mrs. Quinn, who was appreciative of their frequent visits.

"Don't say that." Laura hated seeing her friend like this. She knew too well what it felt like to have to hide away in your house. Small towns were wonderful but like anything, there were disadvantages.

She planted herself on the edge of Diana's bed. "I'm a living example that you can show yourself in public and go on."

Diana's eyes locked with hers, and Laura wondered if she already knew.

Joy's eyebrows knitted together. "What do you mean?"

Laura swallowed hard, reminding herself that these women were her friends and they'd been through a lot in a short period of time. Drawing in a sharp breath, she gathered her thoughts and poured forth her story regarding the death of her sister's husband and the grief and shame she'd brought down on her family.

"In the beginning, she said, "I was treated like I was invisible by everyone in town. I thought it would always be like that, that I'd have to hide out in my house and never leave it."

Joy and Diana appeared to digest what she had told them.

"I'm surprised neither one of you has heard the story before."

"Not me," Joy said. "But it doesn't matter anyway."

"I knew of it," Diana admitted.

"But you didn't say anything. And you became my friend." This surprised Laura. She realized that maybe some lingering aftereffects of that time in her life still clung to her.

Diana shrugged. "Someone mentioned it at some point. I don't remember. Anyway, like Joy says, it doesn't matter, does it?"

Maybe it didn't matter anymore. Or maybe the impact had lessened with time.

"The point is, when I met Edwin, I was honest with him and told him everything upfront, and he stuck with me," Laura said.

"I hope Preston will be like that," Diana fretted.

"Of course he will. It'll be fine," Joy said.

"Okay, so what do I do about this when Preston comes home?" Diana circled her finger around the side of her head.

"I could look around for a wig closer to your own hair color," Joy suggested.

"I can't have you do that," Diana said. "You're working six days a week. You've got children at home. No, the wig is out. Besides, the netting inside irritates my bald spot."

"What about colorful headscarves?" Laura asked.

Diana smirked. "You do see the irony in this, don't you? At the plant, I refused to wear a headscarf properly, and now I'll be wearing them for the rest of my life. God certainly has a cruel sense of humor."

"Don't think about that. Laura and I will get some nice scarves for you."

"We'll get ones to match the dresses you already have," Laura told her.

With a nod, Diana waved a hand toward the closet. "Take a look through my wardrobe."

They moved hangers down the rack. There were several dresses: a white floral, a green, and a navy dress with white polka dots.

"What will I do about stockings?" Diana moaned.

There was nothing that could be done about that. Nylon had been commandeered by the war department to make parachutes and other essential items for the war.

"Do you have a pair of the rayon or cotton?" Joy asked of the substitutes that some women used.

Diana grimaced. "I do, but they sag around the ankles and knees. I look like I have elephant legs with all the wrinkles."

Laura thought for a moment. "They've got leg make-up out there that supposedly lasts for a couple of days."

"I don't know," Diana said.

"Or you could wear ankle socks," Joy suggested.

"I'll look like I'm twelve again and at my height, it would be hard to pull off."

"Or we could draw a seam on the back of your legs with eyebrow pencil." Joy was excited about that one.

Laura had tried that once. Edwin had gotten a ruler and drawn a line down the back of her legs using a black eyebrow pencil. The memory of it brought a smile to her face. But she shook her head. "If it rains or you cross your legs, it rubs off and it's a mess."

They all thought for a moment.

"If you wore slacks," Laura said, "no one would know."

These days, more and more women were wearing slacks. Laura wore them too; they were much more comfortable than dresses.

Joy shook her head and disagreed. "No, that won't work. He's just spent lots of time cooped up with hundreds of men wearing pants. He's going to want to see her in a dress. He *deserves* to see her in one. Besides, she's got a great pair of gams. Like Betty Grable."

Laura folded her arms across her chest. "You're right."

Diana sighed. "Let me think about it."

They left her to mull it over. Her boyfriend wouldn't be home for a couple of weeks, so she didn't have to make a decision that day.

"Any word from Diana?" Joy asked as soon as Laura slid into the front seat. They were working the afternoon shift.

At least it wasn't the night shift. The thing Laura didn't like about working four to midnight was you were hanging around all day waiting to go to work. On the other hand, she did get a lot done around her parents' house before she left. They were definitely slowing down, and now she realized that it had been a good idea for her and the girls to move in with them while Edwin was overseas.

She shook her head and slammed the door. "Nope."

Diana's boyfriend had arrived home yesterday, but there'd been no word. Laura had been praying for her.

"Diana's a top-notch gal. I'd hate to see her get hurt," Joy said, echoing Laura's thoughts.

"You and me both."

"Let's cross our fingers and hope for the best."

Chapter Thirty-One

Three days later, Laura was running the laundry through the wringer of the washing machine out back in the shed. It was her last day of afternoons, and she was looking forward to a day off. But she didn't want to spend it catching up on chores, so she was trying to get as much done as possible. She wore an apron over her clothes and had her hair tied up in a kerchief.

Her fingers were like prunes, and she vowed that as soon as Edwin returned from the war and they bought a home, her first purchase was going to be an electric washing machine, just like the ones she'd seen advertised in the women's magazines.

She stopped halfway through running one of the girls' nightgowns through the wringer, as she thought she heard someone calling her. Wiping her hands on her apron, she opened the door and found Edna calling for her.

"What is it, Edna?"

"Phone call, Mommy." With the message delivered, Edna skipped off around the side of the house.

Looking at the two baskets, one of dirty laundry and the other filling up with wet laundry needing to be hung on the line, Laura rubbed the back of her hand against her forehead. She removed her apron and threw it over an old chair in the corner.

She ran to the house, going in through the kitchen door, and went for the phone in the front hall.

"Hello?"

"Is that you, Laura?"

Tentative, she replied, "Yes?"

"It's Mrs. Quinn."

"Hello, Mrs. Quinn, how are you?"

"We're not too well over here. It's Diana."

Laura frowned. "Is she sick?"

"No. She hasn't come out of her room in two days." Mrs. Quinn did not elaborate.

Putting two and two together, Laura said, "I'll be right there."

Her parents were out at some luncheon for friends who were celebrating their fiftieth wedding anniversary. She couldn't leave the girls home unattended. Joan had made it clear that she didn't mind cooking and cleaning, but she wasn't babysitting. Laura often thought it had nothing to do with children in general, only her two girls, who were a handful.

She'd have to take them with her. She didn't bother calling Joy, who lived all the way over in the next town.

Holding both girls by the hand, they walked over to Peony Lane which wasn't too far away, only a block or two.

As the three of them approached the front porch of the Quinn house, Laura said to her daughters, "Behave yourselves in here or you'll be in a whole heap of trouble when we get home." She leveled her meanest glare at them, the one that said she meant business.

Taking each girl by the hand, she walked quickly up onto the porch and rang the bell.

Mrs. Quinn opened the door, and her expression was one of pure anguish.

Laura herded the girls into the house. "I'm sorry, I had to bring them with me as I had no one to watch them. This is Edna, and the younger one is Edith."

Mrs. Quinn smiled but it didn't reach her eyes. "Two pretty names for two pretty girls."

"Is she in her room?" Laura asked.

Mrs. Quinn nodded, looking in the direction of Diana's bedroom. "No matter what I say, I can't get her to come out of that room."

"The visit with Preston didn't go well?" Laura asked, afraid of the answer but already knowing it.

Mrs. Quinn lowered her voice. "No. It turned out as she feared."

"Gee whiz, that's awful. I'll go back and talk to her."

"Thank you for coming over so quickly, Laura, I appreciate it." Then, turning to the girls, Mrs. Quinn asked, "Who likes oatmeal cookies?"

Both girls jumped up and down and yelled, "Me, me!"

Laura put a hand on each shoulder. "Hey, hey, tone it down."

They nodded and followed Diana's mother to the kitchen.

Laura walked down the narrow hallway to Diana's room, knocking gently before poking her head inside and saying, "Diana, it's me."

Diana was on her side in her bed, facing away from Laura, and barely lifted her head in acknowledgment. Laura closed the door behind her, went over to her friend, and sat on the edge of the bed. She placed a hand on Diana's shoulder.

"Your mother called."

Diana did not turn over. In a flat voice, she said, "There was no need for that."

"She said you haven't been out of this room in days. She's worried about you." Laura was too.

"There's no need for me to come out of this room anymore."

"Come on, Diana, you can't say that. Tell me what happened with Preston," Laura prompted.

"We broke it off, just as I predicted."

"Sit up and tell me."

"I don't want to go into it," Diana said.

"When's the last time you ate?"

"I don't know." Diana shrugged and added, "and I don't care."

Laura jumped up, glad for something to do. "Nothing can be done until you eat something." Before her friend could insist otherwise, she slipped out of the room.

She found the girls seated at the table with Mrs. Quinn. Each girl had two cookies on a small dessert plate and a glass of milk. They were talking about their adventures with Diana's mother, who seemed amused despite her worry over her daughter.

"She'll have something to eat," Laura said.

Mrs. Quinn jumped up from the table and fixed a chicken sandwich and a cup of tea for her daughter.

Laura balanced the serving tray in one hand as she opened the door to Diana's room. Diana was now sitting up in the bed.

Progress.

Laura set the tray onto Diana's lap. "Try and eat something."

"I'm not hungry."

"Try." Laura's tone was firm, indicating she would tolerate no resistance. She pulled the chair up closer to the bed and sat down and crossed her legs.

Diana looked pale, and there were purple circles beneath her eyes, which were glassy and bloodshot.

When she had eaten half of the sandwich, Laura said gently, "Tell me what happened."

Diana took a sip of tea and then a second one, setting the cup carefully down on the tray.

"At first, Preston seemed fine with it. Kept saying it couldn't be that bad." Diana rolled her eyes, and they filled up. She gathered her composure and in a shaky voice, she said, "He insisted on seeing it."

Laura didn't know how that could have been avoided. Diana had said they'd been talking about marriage before the accident. She'd been expecting to get engaged on his next leave.

Her voice became angry. "I kept putting him off and putting him off. His insistence made me feel like a freak in a traveling circus show." She sniffled. Ignoring the remaining half of the sandwich, she picked up the teacup and sipped from it.

With defiance in her voice, she said, "So I showed him on the third night of his leave."

Laura remained silent, giving her friend all the time she needed.

Diana bowed her head, and a teardrop fell on the tray. "It was his reaction. It just gutted me."

Oh no.

"I took off my scarf, and he looked stunned." Diana grabbed a hankie from the sleeve of her housecoat. "Then he looked horrified." A round of crying followed.

Laura didn't know what to say or how to comfort her friend. She reached out and rubbed Diana's arm.

"I'm so sorry," she whispered. "So sorry that you've been hurt."

In between sobs, Diana said, "You should have seen the look on his face. He made me feel like I was some horror creature. From your worst nightmares."

Laura wanted to get a hold of him and throttle him. He must have seen a lot worse in the war. He was supposed to love this girl. She wanted to reassure Diana that this fella wasn't worth it, that there was someone better out there for her. That he'd done her a favor by leaving her because she deserved better.

"And then he broke it off with you?"

Diana shook her head. "No, I broke it off with him. Told him I didn't feel like waiting for the war to be over to get married."

She'd given him an escape route.

"What did he say?" If he was the decent sort, he would have refused.

"He didn't say anything. But you should have seen the look on his face. It was one of pure relief."

Then Diana broke down, and her shoulders shook as she sobbed. Laura removed the tray so it wouldn't end up on the floor, and set it on the bureau. She nudged her friend over and sat beside her in the narrow bed, putting an arm around her. Diana sagged against her, her head on Laura's shoulder.

"That's it, let it all out," Laura said.

By the time she had to go, Diana had stopped crying. Laura didn't think she had any more tears. With a heavy heart, she departed with the promise to see her soon.

She found the girls in the kitchen, eating more cookies, not worried that they'd most likely spoiled their dinner. When she told them it was time to go, both girls protested loudly. But she leveled a glare at them that withered their protests on the vine.

Mrs. Quinn walked the three of them to the door.

"Thank you for bringing your daughters. They were a pleasant distraction."

"I'm glad to hear that." As the girls rushed out of the house and ran toward the car, Laura said, "I'll be back soon for a visit, but call me anytime."

As she drove home, she thought she and Joy would have to put their heads together to figure something out to help their friend.

1945

They visited Diana weekly when their schedules allowed. Sometimes, they brought their children with them. Diana was less self-conscious with the kids, and Laura thought she was a natural. She sent up a silent prayer that one day, Diana might become a mother herself. In the meantime, as spring approached, they tried coaxing her outside to sit on the front porch, but she refused.

On one visit, Laura brought two of Edna's dresses with her because of an offhand comment Mrs. Quinn had made about how Diana used to enjoy sewing and making clothes and bed linens but hadn't picked up her sewing box since the accident.

Although Laura did sew, she wasn't especially skilled at it, and there were always other things that needed doing. In other words, she just didn't have the time, not working six days a week. Maybe it was selfish of her, but she figured since Diana was home all day, maybe she could mend a couple of dresses for her.

At first, Diana simply stared at the dresses in Laura's hand.

"These are Edna's," Laura said. "She's a climber. Trees. Fences. The garage roof."

Mrs. Quinn looked concerned. "I'd be afraid she'd fall and break something."

"I am. But right now, I'm more concerned with all the tears in her clothes." Laura held up the first dress, which had a rip down the side of it.

Diana reached forward and fingered it. "May I?" she asked.

"Of course." Laura handed both dresses to her.

Diana set the dresses in her lap and lowered her head to examine the rents in the fabric. Finally, she looked up at Laura. "If you leave them with me, I'll see what I can do."

"I really appreciate it, Diana, you'd be doing me a favor," Laura said.

When she returned a week later, Diana was waiting for her with Edna's dresses folded neatly in her lap. She handed them to Laura.

Laura turned the dresses over in her hands. You couldn't even tell where the rips had been. "This is fantastic."

Diana pulled something out of a large bag lying on the floor next to her chair. "I had some extra fabric, so I made two more dresses for Edna. If you give me Edith's size, I'll do the same for her."

Laura was impressed. "Jeez, you didn't have to do that."

Diana shrugged, looking sheepish. "I had the time."

"How much do I owe you for these?"

Her friend looked appalled. "No, Laura. That isn't necessary. I wasn't expecting any payment."

"Are you sure?"

"Definitely. You've been a good friend to me. It's the least I could do. By all means, bring me your mending."

"You don't mind?"

Diana shook her head. "No, not at all." She opened her hands, palms up. "What else do I have to do?"

"All right then, that really helps me." But Laura was determined to help her friend. And if she insisted on mending Laura's clothes, she would be paid for it.

On the way out, Mrs. Quinn followed Laura to her car. "Please do bring your mending. Working on those dresses has been good for her. She's had something to do other than think about her problems."

An idea began to swirl around in Laura's head. "You can count on it. It was good to see you again, Mrs. Quinn. I'll see you next week. Joy couldn't come today because she switched shifts with someone at work, but she'll be here next time."

"Good. We look forward to your visits. They certainly brighten Diana's days."

"I'm happy to hear that."

CHAPTER THIRTY-TWO

May 1945

Laura had just shut her drill off when the alarms sounded. Toni jumped out of the hull of the plane and said, "Now what?" Laura hoped no one was hurt.

But Buster soon appeared, walking as fast as his mismatched legs would allow, and assured them that all was well. Mr. Treadwell had called an impromptu general meeting, he said, in the main hangar. As he hurried along, he said over his shoulder, "Pass it along."

Laura and Toni made their way to the meeting point along with a crowd of women, and Toni voiced what Laura was thinking. "I wonder what this is about."

"We'll soon find out."

It was a sea of coveralls and bright headscarves in the main hangar. Benches had been set up hastily in front of a podium. Beyond the podium, the doors to the hangar stood open, letting in the warm breeze.

Laura and Toni slid in along one of the benches toward the front. Laura leaned over and whispered to Toni, "It must be good news, because Mr. Treadwell is all smiles." Toni's gaze traveled to the front of the hangar, where their boss was clapping the back of the plant manager with a grin on his face.

Mr. Treadwell stepped up to the podium. "Take your seats, please. This will only be a moment." And then he laughed.

"Strange," Toni said.

Once everyone was seated and the room hushed, Mr. Treadwell, still smiling, said to the crowd, "I have great news." He paused before announcing, "Germany surrendered this morning!"

He barely had the last word out of his mouth when whoops and shouts erupted and everyone jumped to their feet. Headscarves were thrown into the air in jubilation.

The deafening roar that went up echoed through the cavernous space.

Crying, Laura and Toni hugged each other and danced around. When they pulled apart, Laura wiped her eyes with a handkerchief. She was stunned into happy disbelief.

It was over. *Finally.*

Soon, Edwin could come home.

By the end of the month, all the trees sported young green leaves and the air began to turn warmer. The sun, although weak and watery, added a brightness to everything.

Laura and Joy finally managed to coax Diana outside to sit on the front porch. It had taken months for them to convince her to leave her bedroom to sit in the living room or the kitchen, until she gradually became comfortable with moving around inside the house.

At first, she had balked at stepping outside, shaking her head back and forth, saying everything she needed was within the walls of her home. But Laura and

Joy would not take no for an answer. Somehow, Diana needed to get past this and move on with her life.

They sat on the front porch in chairs brought out from inside. Diana situated herself between her friends, with one of them sitting protectively on either side. Diana had put on a colorful turban, complaining that it made her feel like Carmen Miranda and all she needed was to add a bowl of fruit to the top of her head. But Laura had reassured her, telling her the turban accentuated her fabulous cheekbones. This seemed to mollify her.

There was a gentle breeze, and the air smelled of spring: like damp earth with some hope thrown in.

Laura was in a good mood. The war was over in Europe and hopefully winding down in the Pacific. She and Joy were counting down the days until their husbands returned home. The domestic landscape had changed, but she wasn't worried. They had weathered a depression and a war; certainly there were happier times ahead. And she and Edwin could face anything together.

Joy was in the middle of telling a funny story about something that went on at work. Laura had already heard it during the car ride, but she was content to relax, her legs stretched out, and enjoy the new pink and white blossoms on the cherry trees. She'd always wanted cherry trees, but her mother was against it, saying the petals got all over the place when they blew off and made too much of a mess. Laura felt differently. She thought it was a small price to pay to look at something so beautiful. She decided right then that when she and Edwin bought their own house, she'd plant a couple, right after she bought an electric washing machine.

"Diana, would you consider coming to my house for dinner on Sunday?" Joy asked.

Joy made sauce on Sundays, and Laura had gone over several times with the girls for Sunday dinner. She'd been introduced to the world of spaghetti, baked ziti, manicotti, stuffed shells, and lasagna, and she'd loved all of it. Now it was easy for her to see why Joy's husband spoke profusely about her cooking. Edna and Edith especially loved spaghetti. She didn't have to fight with them to clean their plates.

Diana looked panic-stricken.

"I couldn't." She shook her head.

"It'll only be us and the kids," Joy said. She cast a beseeching glance in Laura's direction, but Laura said nothing. Her opinion was that Diana shouldn't be forced. That she should get to the destination—the destination being moving on with her life—in her own way. And in her own time. Besides, they'd only just convinced her that day to step outside the house. Baby steps.

"Thank you, Joy." There was a tremor in Diana's voice. "I appreciate everything the two of you have done for me. I couldn't have asked for better friends. I don't think I would have made it without you. Everything seemed so bleak and desperate."

Laura didn't know what to say to that. Apparently, neither did Joy.

Diana continued. "After the accident and even after Preston and I broke up, I didn't want to live. I didn't."

"You shouldn't say that," Joy said. "Life is a gift."

But Laura added no comment to that. For she, too, had once felt that way. Funny how at the time, you thought it would never get better. That you would never know joy again. But you did. You laughed again. You felt happy again. Diana would have to find that out for herself.

"But it's the truth, Joy, and I can't lie about it," Diana said.

"No, of course you can't," Laura said. "Do you still feel like that?"

"Sometimes," Diana admitted. "But not all the time. Not like before."

Laura nodded. "Then that's progress." She wished her friend could see what she saw: a stunning young woman with beautiful eyes and fine bone structure.

"I wonder if I'll ever have peace," Diana said.

"It will come with time. But you have to make the effort."

On the other side of Diana, Joy slipped a necklace from around her neck, pulling it up and over her dark hair. She reached out and put it in Diana's hand.

"I want you to have this."

"I can't take this," Diana said, handing it back to her, but Joy pushed her hand away. "Joy—"

Joy put her hand up. "No, Diana, I insist. It's a St. Anthony medal. It was my grandfather's."

"Even more reason not to give it away," Diana said, attempting again to hand it back to Joy, but she refused to take it.

"No, listen, we pray to him for lost things."

"Can he find me a new scalp?" Diana quipped.

They all laughed.

"Seriously, he can help you find those things you're looking for: peace and happiness. You must trust him and pray to him." Joy was fierce in her devotion.

Diana struggled to put the chain around her neck. Joy took the medal and stood behind her, adjusting the clasp. Once done, she sat down. Diana touched the medal against her chest.

Joy looked out to the street as she spoke. "My grandfather was from Italy. They were dirt poor. He prayed and prayed, asking St. Anthony for help to get to America. Eventually, he won prize money in a fight, if you can believe that."

Laura raised her eyebrows.

"Anyway, he made it to America and he never looked back."

In time and with some gentle coaxing, after Diana had done all of Laura's and Joy's mending, they encouraged her to take in sewing projects from other people. At first,

Diana was mortified. The thought of people coming to her house to drop off mending caused her to blanche.

"I think it's a wonderful idea," Mrs. Quinn chimed in.

"They'll only come because they're curious, and I'll be like some sideshow attraction." There was bitterness in her voice.

Laura decided to go for honesty. "There will be some people who will do just that. But pay no attention to them. Once they see what fabulous work you do, they'll be back, and if not, then they will have had their curiosity satisfied."

Diana considered this. Laura's honesty had not turned her off.

Laura added, "It'll be a good way to make some money. There's only one seamstress in town right now, and she's getting on in years and won't be around forever."

Joy piped in. "It could be an opportunity."

Diana appeared contemplative. "How would I get customers?"

Laura was buoyed by the fact she hadn't totally nixed the idea. "That's easy. Word of mouth. And we can put up an advertisement in the post office."

"The canteen at work," Joy said excitedly. "You know, a lot of the girls ask about you."

"Do they?" Diana seemed genuinely surprised by this.

"Of course."

Diana bit her lip, and the expression on her face suggested she was struggling with some internal debate. "I wish someone else could handle the people."

Gently, Laura said, "Diana, it's a step toward rejoining the land of the living."

"Honey, you don't want to spend the rest of your life locked up in your bedroom," Joy said.

"I'll be here to help you as much as I can," Mrs. Quinn said with encouragement.

Diana threw her hands up in surrender. "All right, all right. I'll do it."

Laura was so overcome with excitement that she clapped her hands, which led everyone—including Diana—to burst out laughing.

Later, they tacked up notices in the post office and in the canteen at the factory in Cheever, and business began to trickle in. There were some who stopped by with the excuse of needing alterations or something mended when all they wanted was to see Diana's disfigurement, but Diana developed a toughened exterior, choosing to ignore those who stopped by simply to gawk. But throughout it all, she kept a headscarf on at all times. Once people saw the measure of her work, the trickle turned into a gush. Diana helped Mrs. Quinn convert a spare bedroom into a room where she could work and where customers had privacy to try things on.

She came to be in such demand that it was rare to see her without a tape measure around her neck alongside the St. Anthony medal Joy had given her. It kept her mind so busy she didn't have time to think about her problems. She still wouldn't leave the house to go out in public except to go to Joy's, but Laura figured with time, that would come about.

Chapter Thirty-Three

1946

Laura wanted to pinch herself. She couldn't quite believe it was true. The day she'd waited for for years was finally here.

She reread the small article in the town's weekly newspaper, *The Lavender Bay Chronicles*, for the umpteenth time.

Knickerbocker to Return Home
In the US Army since May 1943, during which time he served in France, Central Europe and Germany, Cpl. Edwin Knickerbocker, husband of Mrs. Laura Knicker-

bocker of 4312 Bluebell Lane, will soon return to Lavender Bay after his honorable discharge from Fort Dix, NJ.

Edwin was coming home.

She scurried around the house, doing some last-minute things before leaving for the train station. The girls wanted to go with her, but she wanted to be alone with him before he came home and demands were made on his time and attention. For just a few minutes, she wanted him all to herself.

It was drizzling outside.

"Go on, you'll be late," her mother said from the parlor. Her father had his foot up on a stool, his big toe suffering another gout attack. "Don't keep him waiting."

"We'll mind the girls, Laura," her father said. "Edna, come here and read the newspaper to me while we wait for your father to come home."

Edna skipped from the hallway into the front parlor. "Sure thing, Grandpa." She picked up the newspaper and sat cross-legged on the parlor floor.

"Edna, would you like to sit on a chair?" Eleanor asked.

"I'm okay, Grandma. I don't mind sitting on the floor."

"Well, all right, but it's not very ladylike."

"But I'm not a lady. I'm a kid."

Eleanor looked blankly at her granddaughter.

"What page should I start on, Grandpa?"

"I think I left off on page five."

Edna snapped open the paper, as she'd seen her grandfather do a hundred times, and started reading.

Laura glanced at the clock. "I'm going."

"We'll see you in a little bit," her mother called after her, but Laura was already out the door.

Seconds later, she backtracked into the front hall. When they all looked up at her, she said, "Forgot an umbrella." And she dashed out the door again, closing it behind her.

Standing on the edge of the porch, she opened the umbrella. It was more of a mist falling than a rain, but she didn't want to get her hair wet. She'd splurged and had it done at the salon, wanting to look nice for Edwin, and she was wearing her best dress.

As she walked to the car parked out front, some movement in the distance caught her attention. She narrowed her eyes to see better—*I really need to get a pair of glasses*—and noticed a man in uniform, Army cap tilted jauntily to the side of his head as he walked down the street. She opened the car door but took another look at the soldier. His walk was familiar. Her mouth fell open.

Edwin.

She dropped the umbrella and broke into a run, leaving the car door wide open.

Lifting her arm, she called out, "Edwin! Edwin! I'm here!"

After all those years of missing him, longing for him, aching for him, she ran toward him, laughing and crying at the same time.

"Laura!" he called out, a big grin on his face, and broke into a run.

They met in front of a neighbor's house, practically slamming into each other. The neighbor, who was out front watering her flowers, clasped her hand to her mouth, gasping in delight.

Edwin threw his arms around Laura and pulled her close, kissing her on the mouth. She didn't care who saw or what was said or whispered. She didn't care if neighbors thought she was brazen or indecent. She'd waited so long for this day. The man she loved had survived the war and returned to her. It was one of the happiest days of her life.

He scooped her up and swung her around, and she held out her free arm, laughing.

He stopped, put her down, and kissed her again.

"Mrs. Knickerbocker, you are a sight for sore eyes!" he said.

"You too! I was just leaving to drive over to the train station."

"My train came in early," he explained, picking up the duffel bag he'd dropped. "And I figured I'd walk home."

"I'm sorry I wasn't there."

He wrapped an arm around her shoulder and pulled her to him, kissing her on the forehead. "It's fine, my love. I'm so happy to be home."

They walked arm in arm down the street.

As they neared the house, Laura closed the car door and picked up the umbrella still lying on the grass. She looped her arm through Edwin's, and they walked up the porch steps and into the house.

Grinning widely, she said, "Look who I found outside wandering the streets!"

"Daddy!" Edna jumped up, dropping the newspaper, and ran to them, followed by Edith, both of them yelling, "Daddy! Daddy!"

Mrs. Wainwright clapped her hands and stood, if shakily. She grabbed her cane and made her way out to the front hall.

Leo struggled to get up, but Laura went to him and said, "Dad, don't get up. Edwin wouldn't expect that."

He cursed his foot. "This darn toe. I'd like to stand and welcome our war hero home."

Chapter Thirty-Four

Edwin had been home for a few weeks. Nothing had been decided about their future or where they were going to live. Laura still worked at the plant, but her days were numbered, and she knew it. The ratio of male to female plant workers was shifting as the troops returned home from the war and took back their old jobs.

Edwin needed time to decompress and do nothing, she'd decided. It was time for him to get reacquainted with his daughters. But at the end of the first week, Uncle Bert called, asking when he'd be coming back to the garage. Laura stood behind her husband, whispering, "Stall him as long as you can." With a laugh, he waved her away.

When he hung up the phone, she put her hands on her hips and stared at him. "Well?"

He gave her his winning smile.

"Oh, Edwin, I want you to relax and take it easy for a while."

"Honey, I can't do that. You know that. I can't sit still." He pulled her to him.

"But aren't you tired?" she asked. She figured fighting a war for a couple of years must be exhausting.

"Not really," he replied.

"When are you going back to the garage?" she asked, resigned.

"The day after tomorrow."

"That soon?" She was unable to hide her disappointment.

"It's time. We need to get back to normal as soon as possible."

"All right, but let's take the girls to the beach tomorrow. It's supposed to be nice."

"Sounds like a plan."

Later that evening after everyone had gone to bed, Laura and Edwin were in the kitchen, the stove still warm. The metal lamp hanging above the table illuminated them in a triangle of golden light. Edwin sat there with a scratch pad and a stubby pencil, working on sums.

"I'm trying to figure out how much we're going to need to buy a house," he said.

With excitement, Laura said, "I'd love our very own home."

He smiled at her. "Me too."

"It would have to be near my parents' house, though, so I could keep an eye on them and help out."

"Of course." Edwin leaned forward, elbows on the table, his voice excited. "You know, with that GI Bill President Roosevelt signed, we can get a low-cost mortgage. We just need to figure out how much we need for a down payment. Uncle Bert said he was giving me a raise. Said he couldn't expect me to work at 1941 wages." He laughed.

Laura stood and retrieved her bank book and slid it toward Edwin. "Hopefully, this will help."

"What's this?" He took the book and opened it, thumbing through the pages until he landed on the one showing Laura's most recent deposit. His eyes practically bulged out of his head.

She sat up straighter, her chest puffed up. Her cheeks hurt from smiling so hard.

"Laura..." Edwin's voice trailed off.

Unable to contain her excitement, she jumped up from her chair, and Edwin leaned back so she could sit in his lap. He slid an arm around her waist.

"Seventy cents an hour," she said. "I saved most of it."

Still stunned, Edwin said with a generous smile, "Well, I'll be damned!"

She blushed. It was hard to catch her husband off guard. "But once in a while, I did treat myself to a new dress."

"And rightly so!" He pulled her closer. "I'm so proud of you, honey."

Emotion overtook her, but she was determined not to cry. Instead, she kept right on smiling. She leaned in and kissed him on the forehead.

But now it was time to get serious. "But the thing is, Edwin, I like working. It makes me feel useful."

He nodded as he listened.

"I want to keep working," she said.

"But you don't have to work, Laura. I'll make enough at the garage to pay all our bills."

"I know, honey, but I want to. Part time, preferably."

His forehead creased. "At the plant?"

"No, no. We're all being let go," she said. As much as it wasn't fair, it was the way it was. Besides, she didn't think she could do that kind of work long term. If her hands and arms ached now after only a few years, how would it be after ten years? Twenty? "But I'd like to find something."

"What about the girls?"

"They're getting older, and although Mother and Dad aren't in any shape to watch them, we could find a sitter."

"You really want to do this?"

He hadn't said no, like Joy's husband had said upon his return. *No more working*, was what he had said to Joy, but Joy didn't seem to mind.

"Yes, I do. Like I said, even if it's only part time." The thought of that electric washing machine was always at the forefront of her mind. It had kept her going, especially on night shift when she was tired and weary and felt like her eyes were crossed.

"What would you do?" he asked.

She knew she was limited, as men were pouring back into the country and being given preference for jobs. That was only right, but she was confident she'd find something. The way she looked at it was if she could drill rivets into a cargo plane, she could do anything.

"The extra money would help," Edwin said.

"You've done your bit, Edwin, and now I want you to have a comfortable life," she said, her arms around his neck.

"That sounds good."

"It's perfect!" Laura declared.

Once Edwin went back to work, he and Laura began to look for a home of their own. Although her parents never complained and they were truly fond of Edwin, it was crowded with all of them under one roof. But still she worried about them. She and Lenore had devised a schedule where one or both would check in on them every day. And of course, Joan was there for anything emergent during the day.

They stood in the front hall of a smallish, modest Victorian. It wasn't as grand as Lenore's, but for the four of them, it was just right. It had a small porch and the gingerbread trim Laura loved. It had a lilac bush out front, which she found welcoming. She could imagine the two of them sitting out on the porch on a summer evening, watching the girls playing or riding their bikes on the sidewalk. And she could already picture where she would plant two cherry trees.

The house had three bedrooms upstairs, the beauty of that being that Edna and Edith would each get their own room, so no more fighting and arguing at bedtime. Laura could almost hear the golden silence. Also upstairs were a bathroom and an extra room that was too small to be a bedroom.

Downstairs, there was a front parlor, a kitchen, and a dining room.

There was even a garage out back at the end of the driveway.

"What do you think?" Edwin asked again. He was as excited as she.

"I love it!"

"Me too."

He hugged her.

The only nagging thought in Laura's mind was that she still hadn't secured a job. She'd tried the bank, the drugstore, and the grocery store. She'd even gone up to the hospital, and the nun she'd spoken to was kind but said there was nothing available. She was almost relieved, as she hadn't treasured the thought of working with the sick and the infirm. But she was beginning to feel she'd never get a job. Edwin had been encouraging, telling her again and again not to give up hope, that something would come up.

The day before they were set to move into the house on Orchard, Laura invited Edwin to go for a drive.

"Is this a mystery tour?" he asked.

"You can call it what you like. But we have an important task to do today."

"We do?" He frowned.

"Don't worry, you haven't forgotten anything."

"All right. Where to, Mrs. Knickerbocker?" he asked.

"Go to Main Street," she directed.

"As you wish."

They drove into the main thoroughfare of town, and Laura instructed her husband to find a spot near the appliance store.

He laughed. "Is today the big day?"

"It is. And about time. I've waited a long time for this." She was as excited as a kid walking into a candy store with a handful of pennies in his pocket.

After they purchased a Bendix washing machine, Laura walked proudly out of the store, arm in arm with Edwin. "Did you see that automatic dryer?" she said. "That's next."

Edwin laughed and they left, Laura eagerly anticipating the delivery of her brand-new appliance.

Chapter Thirty-Five

In the meantime, Diana's business was taking off. The women who used to work at the plant with them still sought her out for mending and dressmaking.

They'd been working on getting Diana out in public for the last six months. Initially, she'd only go to Joy's house for Sunday dinner. Although there was a small crowd, it was people Diana knew: Laura and the girls and Joy and her three kids, Frankie, Rose, and Sammy. The kids took no notice of Diana's headscarf, had become used to it. When Edwin and Sam, Joy's husband, had returned from the war, Diana had been shy. But Edwin was kind and solicitous and did his best to involve her in conversations. Joy's husband, on the other hand, was a hoot. He was always joking and teasing.

"Diana, I see you eyeing up that last piece of eggplant parmigiana," he started one Sunday afternoon.

Diana looked mortified, her face reddening. She put her hand to her chest and said in a voice barely above a whisper, "No, honestly, I wasn't."

Sam winked at her, and her posture relaxed. He reached over and helped himself to the last square. "Because the last piece is always for me."

Laura didn't know where Sam put it. He wasn't that tall, maybe five-five, five-six, but he packed it away like he was six-four and weighed two hundred pounds. He enjoyed his food, or more specifically, he loved his wife's cooking.

Diana realized that he was joking, and she smiled. It wasn't long before she caught on to his humor.

It was a start.

From regular Sunday dinners at Joy's house, they progressed to taking Diana out for tea and cake at one of the diners in Lavender Bay. The first time, Diana was extremely self-conscious, always looking around and touching her headscarf as if to make sure it was still there. But gradually, slowly, she calmed down a bit.

Finally, they convinced her to go to the beach. As Joy had said, it was the one place you could wear a hat or a bathing cap and no one would bat an eye.

It was a beautiful sunny day, and by late morning the heat was already bordering on unbearable. Beachgoers were spread out on blankets and towels, their bodies glistening with sweat. The sun was a large white-hot ball in the cloudless sky. Beneath it, the lake shimmered and sparkled, looking like a beautiful woman dripping in diamonds.

The three of them walked side by side onto the beach. Edwin and Sam followed, Edwin carrying the beach blankets and a bag of food, and Sam similarly burdened. Laura had made peanut-butter-and-grape-jelly sandwiches for all the kids and wrapped them in wax paper. As they trod through the hot, heavy sand, the conversation revolved around the Brooklyn Dodgers and President Truman. Every once in a while, Sam cracked a joke, and the air was punctuated with his machine-gun type of laughter. With a grin, Laura looked over to Joy, who smiled and rolled her eyes. The children ran on ahead, their skin already a light brown from summer days spent at the beach. Edna rushed toward the water.

"Frankie, keep an eye on everyone," Joy called out after her oldest boy, who was almost fourteen. He threw his hand up in a wave of acknowledgement, not bothering to turn around.

The three women shook out the blankets and spread them out over the sand, using a shoe on each corner to keep the blanket in place. They sat on one of the blankets together, with Diana at the edge and Laura in the middle. They rolled up towels and used them as headrests. Laura lay on her back and closed her eyes, not bothering to take off her sunglasses.

"I'll go in the water and keep an eye on the kids," Edwin said.

Without opening her eyes, Laura replied, "Okay."

"Any luck on the job front?" Joy asked.

"Not yet." She was trying not to get discouraged, but it was hard. She wanted to work. She liked making her own money. And if working at the plant in Cheever had taught her anything, it was that despite her lack of skills and education, she still had a contribution to make.

"Something will come up. Pray to St. Anthony. He'll help you find a job," Joy advised.

Next to her, Diana held up the St. Anthony medal she wore around her neck. "I second that." She was never seen without it. And every once in a while, when she was lost in thought, Diana fingered that gold medal that hung around her neck with a faraway look in her eyes.

"Maybe I'll try just that," Laura said, half joking.

"As for me, I'm done working. Those two years were enough," Joy said with a shudder. "I still dream about being at the plant, mostly frantic about being late for my shift."

"I have dreams about the plant as well," Laura said.

"I have nightmares about it," Diana said quietly.

The three of them went silent for a moment and before a pall could descend around them, Laura asked Joy, "You don't mind not working?"

"Not on your life. I like being a housewife. I was born for it. I like cooking and cleaning."

Laura looked at her, incredulous. "You do?" She did it because it was expected of her, but she found no enjoyment in it.

"I sure do," Joy said whole-heartedly. "Sam, would you hand me a Coke?"

Sam sat on the blanket next to them, his legs stretched out. He leaned over and rummaged around in the cardboard box that contained food and beverages and pulled out a bottle. "Joy, I forgot the bottle opener."

Joy sighed. "After I reminded you?"

"Yep." Sam jumped up, the Coke bottle still in his hand. "I'll see if someone around here has one."

"Okay."

Sam set off, and once he was out of earshot, Joy shook her head and muttered, "I remind him of things all the time and he still forgets."

The three of them were still lying on their backs, half listening to the shouts and laughter of their children in the water with Edwin, and the conversations on the neighboring blankets around them. Knowing that her husband was minding the girls allowed Laura to relax, and she hoped she'd doze for a bit.

That idea was short-lived. A female voice called out to them, "Hello!"

The three of them opened their eyes and propped themselves up on their elbows as Grace Gibson approached them. The young woman wore a brand-new bathing suit in red, and her dark hair, parted down the middle, hung in curls to her shoulders. But her face was thin since coming back from serving as a Red Cross worker in the Pacific, her clavicle bony. Despite her young age—she was only in her early twenties—she had an air of maturity about her. But then war would make anyone grow up quickly.

They all said hello and made small talk for a few moments. Grace informed them that she was going to work in her father's grape jelly factory.

"After being so busy for the last couple of years, it's hard to be idle now," she said in a faraway voice, looking out at the lake. She sighed and smiled quickly as if sweeping away a sense of gloom. "Anyway, I told Father I wanted to learn the business from the ground up."

"How did he take that?" Joy asked.

With a sly grin, Grace said, "He didn't need too much coaxing. I simply reminded him he had no sons, that I was it and no one would take more interest in the business than me, as grapes are in my blood. My mother was horrified, though. She wanted me to go back to college and finishing school and all that nonsense." Her laughter filled the air around them. "Anyway, I stopped by because I wanted to speak to Diana."

Diana used her hand to shield her eyes from the blinding sun, closing one eye as she looked up at Grace.

"Since I've returned," Grace said, "none of my clothes fit. Everything is hanging off of me. Father said I should buy a new wardrobe, but most of the clothes I have are perfectly good. I was wondering if you could take them in for me."

Diana nodded. "Of course."

"Can I come by on Tuesday?"

Diana thought for a moment. "I'm booked out that day. What about Wednesday morning?"

"Perfect."

"Did you want to join us?" Joy asked.

Grace shook her head. "No thanks." She looked over her shoulder. "I'm with some friends over there."

The three of them glanced in the direction she was looking and saw a group of similar-aged girls spread out on a blanket.

They said their goodbyes, and Grace turned and left with a wave.

"Gee, honey, that's great to get her business," Joy said to Diana.

"Yes, she's a lovely girl. You'd think with all that money, she'd be snobbish, but she isn't."

"Not at all," Laura murmured in agreement, settling back down and closing her eyes.

Chapter Thirty-Six

A month after they moved into the house on Orchard, Laura was upstairs in Edna's bedroom, taking down the curtains that had come with the house and replacing them with a set Diana had made. Edwin was at the garage, and the girls were at school. Summer was over, and they'd turned the calendar page to October. The girls were already chattering about Halloween and costumes and pumpkin carving.

She stood on a kitchen chair and hung the first panel. She'd already replaced the curtains in Edith's room. The girls had been excited about getting their own rooms, and she'd promised them that if they behaved, they could decorate them any way they liked. That seemed to be holding for now. She didn't remember her and Lenore fighting like that when they were growing up, but then Lenore was six years older than she. What she did remember was Lenore helping Hilda do all the work while she sat around and watched, more interested in looking in the mirror. She shuddered; she'd been an absolutely horrid sister. It amazed her that Lenore talked to her at all these days.

From the window, she had a bird's-eye view of the front lawn, and she admired the two cherry trees that Edwin had planted the weekend before. She was about to hang the second panel when she heard the phone ringing downstairs. Holding on to the back of the chair, she carefully stepped down and ran down the staircase to answer it.

Breathless, she picked up the handset from its cradle. "Hello?"

"Hello, Mrs. Knickerbocker?" said a male voice.

"Yes?"

"It's Alfred Block from Block Answering Service."

"Oh, yes, how are you?"

"I'm fine. I'm calling to see if you'd still like to come work for me," he said.

For a moment, Laura was speechless. It had been more than a month since she'd gone in there to apply for a job. She'd given up. It was swing shift: afternoons and overnights, and she thought it would be perfect for when the girls were home. Edwin hadn't been keen on her working any more overnights, but she'd reminded him that it was only part time.

"Mrs. Knickerbocker, are you still there?"

"I am, yes, yes, I'll take the job."

"Very good. Be here next Monday at four in the afternoon and you'll be trained on the switchboard."

"That's wonderful news, thank you so much, Mr. Block."

"You're welcome. See you Monday."

1948

With a heavy heart, Laura stood in the parlor of Bluebell Lane. Now that both her parents were gone, the house was going to be sold. There was an upcoming estate auction for the furniture and the dishes. She and Lenore had taken what they wanted. If she'd had the space, she would have taken everything. There was a memory attached to every piece of furniture, every plate, every knickknack, everything. She swallowed hard, trying not to cry. The red sofa in the parlor sat empty, and all she could think about was her parents sitting there together, her father with a newspaper, his foot usually up on the small, embroidered stool, and her mother next to him with her wooden embroidery hoop on her lap or reading a magazine.

Edwin came up behind her and placed his hands on her shoulders. "Are you all right?"

She nodded, unable to speak.

"The car is packed up."

"Okay. I'll be out in a minute."

"Take your time." He gave her shoulders a gentle squeeze, and Laura placed her hand over one of his for a moment. With a soft kiss on her cheek, he left her alone, going outside and shutting the front door behind him.

Lenore appeared from the kitchen. "That's everything, I think."

The two of them looked around.

"It's hard to believe, isn't it?" Lenore said. "That they're both gone, and we'll never come to this house anymore."

For Laura, who had lived most of her life in this house, the thought was downright depressing.

"I miss them," she said.

Lenore stood at her side and put a hand on her back. "Me too. Life won't be the same anymore."

"No, it won't." Laura heaved a large sigh. "For so long, they were my moral compass."

"They set a good example. But you've got your own compass now."

"What are you going to do with your inheritance?" Laura asked. After the furniture and the house was sold, the proceeds would be divided evenly between them.

Lenore sighed. "My house needs a new roof. I've got buckets and pails all over the attic. So that's where most of it will go: into the house. That, and I'll put a little away for Johnny's college education. You?"

"Edwin wants to invest it."

"That's wise."

"I've got my eye on one of those newfangled refrigerators."

Lenore laughed.

Laura looked around again, wistful and sad. Why couldn't some things remain the same? "Lots of memories here."

"Yes. Let's take one last walk around the house before we leave. For old times' sake."

Laura smiled. "You never struck me as the sentimental type, Lenore."

Her sister held up her thumb and forefinger as if she was going to pinch something. "Just a little bit. But don't tell anyone."

Laura laughed. "Your secret is safe with me."

Together, they walked through each room of the house they grew up in, their hearts heavy but reinforced by happy memories.

PART THREE

Maureen

Chapter Thirty-Seven

Although only June, it was the first uncomfortably hot day of the summer, and the air conditioning unit was on the fritz, the repairman unable to make it until the following day. Maureen didn't feel like cooking—she certainly couldn't see turning the oven on—and Allan suggested they go out for dinner, the four of them.

As soon as his final exams were over, Lance had packed up his belongings, vacated his dorm room, and headed home, immediately landing a job with a local landscaper and working six days a week from dawn to dusk.

Ashley had her final exams for senior year in another week, and her graduation ceremony was scheduled for the last Thursday of the month.

Things had been rough since Everett left. Some days, Maureen found herself driving around Lavender Bay, trying to get a glimpse of him. In a strange way, it reminded her of when she was back in high school and always on the lookout for a chance meeting with her crush of the moment, driving and walking around aimlessly, hoping to run into him.

But it seemed as if Everett had disappeared into thin air. Nights were always the worst, when worry kept her awake. She'd lie there on her back, wondering if he was hurt or lonely or hungry, or worse, unconscious with no one to look after him. Beside her, Allan was also awake, but they didn't speak, neither one of them wanting to voice their darkest fears. Every night, they lay there on their backs, staring up at the ceiling in the dark.

Maureen was relieved when Allan suggested eating out. Even though the Annacotty Room was their favorite restaurant, they all agreed they'd like to get out of Lavender Bay for a bit, and Allan drove them to Cheever, where one of his hygienists had recommended a place.

The restaurant was a former home, three stories, painted a pale yellow with white trim. Several white wooden rockers sat on an expansive front porch with thick white columns. The building was on an elevated site, and the back terrace overlooked a gentle downward slope of trees and a man-made lake. The trees were in full foliage, lush and green. A flock of ducks paddled quietly across the lake. It was such a pleasant evening that they sat outside at one of the heavy wrought-iron scrollwork tables on the terrace, enjoying the scenery.

"I bet it's beautiful here in the autumn with all the colors," Maureen said, settling into her chair with its thick, comfortable seat cushion.

Allan nodded, pulling out his readers and scanning the menu. "Aha. They have rack of lamb. That's for me." And he snapped his menu shut, smiling, satisfied with his choice.

Maureen couldn't make up her mind. She was more tired than hungry. Too many sleepless nights. She'd dozed with her head against the window in the car on the way over. Yawning, she looked again at the menu. The offerings looked good, but nothing appealed to her.

When the server arrived to take their order, she simply picked the first thing on the menu, ordering something called Chicken Supreme. Lance went with the filet mignon, and Ashley chose the chicken as well.

A silence had descended over the table. Maureen missed their lively dinner conversations, the in-jokes, everything. But since Everett left, it felt like someone had died.

Forcing a brightness she didn't feel, she leaned back in her chair, clasping her hands over her belly. "What's new with everyone?"

"One week until graduation," Ashley said enthusiastically.

"That's right." Was that already upon them? Everett and Lance had each had a graduation party when it was their turn, but she wasn't feeling it this year, though that wouldn't be fair to Ashley. If you did for one, you did for them all.

"Mom, when can we go shopping for things for my dorm?" Ashley asked.

Allan laughed. "Gee, honey, you're not leaving until August, do you need to do it now?"

"Dad," Ashley said.

Maureen understood her daughter's excitement. "Right after graduation, Ash." She looked over at Lance, who hadn't said two words.

"Everything all right, Lance? You're awfully quiet."

Lance played with his knife, flipping it around in his hand.

"I saw Everett," he said.

Maureen blinked. "What?"

"You saw Everett? When?" Allan demanded.

Ashley shrank back in her seat, sipping from her glass of water.

"I saw him last night. And I didn't tell you because I left early this morning and neither of you were awake yet. And I didn't think it was the type of news to send by text."

"Never mind all that," Maureen said. "How is he? Is he all right?"

"Where is he?" Allan asked.

Lance's gaze swung between his parents. "He seemed all right. I saw him at a party."

Maureen and Allan peppered him with questions.

"Did you talk to him?"

"Do you think he's still doing drugs?"

"Yes, and yes." Lance sighed and looked at the knife he was playing with. "He seemed a little bit out of it. I asked him if he was okay, and he said he was never better."

Maureen flinched.

"Do you know where he's living?" Allan asked.

"Any mention that he might come home?"

"He wouldn't give me the address. Said it was better that way," Lance explained. "But I have an idea of where he's staying."

"Where?"

"And with who?"

Lance shook his head and set the knife down. "No. Look, it won't help for the two of you to show up there and interrogate him. It'll only chase him further away. I'll keep an eye on him as best as I can."

"But he's not on the street, living in some cardboard box, is he?" Maureen's voice betrayed her anxiety. That was one of her many worries.

"No, he has shelter and a bed."

"But you won't tell us where?" The tone of Allan's voice indicated he wasn't happy about that. Maureen didn't like it either, but she thought Lance had a point. Everett wasn't ready to do what needed to be done. And them coming after him would only make things worse. As much as it killed her, she knew she had to back off. This was one thing she couldn't control.

"No, Dad," Lance said.

The server appeared with a round of salads, and they all went silent as she passed them out. As soon as she left, Lance spoke, picking up his fork and spearing a cherry tomato. "The way I see it is Everett has always been smart. Really smart."

"Maybe too smart for his own good," Allan said.

"Someday, he'll come to his senses," Lance said.

"What if it's too late?" Ashley asked, voicing the deep-seated fear they all felt. Her salad sat in front of her, untouched. Maureen knew how deeply this was affecting her daughter. Being the youngest, she'd always looked up to her brothers, and they'd looked out for her.

Maureen decided it was time to address the issue. "Look, we are a family of five, and when one of us is going through a tough time, we're all going through it. And although Everett won't let us help him, it's important to keep the lines of communication open. And also, to support each other."

Allan waved his fork in the air. "Everything your mother says and then some."

She looked from Ashley to Lance. "This must be very difficult for you. We've never had to deal with something like this before."

Lance shrugged. "Everett and I have always been kind of close. But this last year, I feel like I don't even recognize him."

Allan looked over at his daughter. "Ash, how do you feel?"

Ashley had picked up her fork but was pushing the contents of her salad plate around in a circular motion. She looked at her dad and squinted. "Can I be honest?"

Allan nodded. "Of course, honey."

Her face went red, and tears filled her eyes. "I'm really, *really* angry at him. That he'd do this to himself. That he'd do it to you guys and to all of us. Because no matter what we're doing in our lives, in the back of our minds is Everett." She picked up the napkin and wiped her eyes.

Maureen was seated across from her and wished she was next to her so she could reach over. As much as she wanted to, she resisted getting up and going over to hug her, because Ash would be horrified at having attention drawn to her. Allan reached for her hand and gave it a squeeze. "I think we all feel some of that."

Lance spoke. "You always have me, Ash." He made a goofy face by screwing up his eyes and sticking his tongue out of the side of his mouth.

Despite everything, this made Ashley laugh.

"One last note on this, and we'll change the subject," Maureen said, pushing her salad plate away. She'd eaten most of it. "Dad and I will continue to look at different rehab places—inpatient and outpatient—for Everett. We'll continue to talk to our doctor, and we'll continue going to the support group for parents of kids addicted to drugs. If you think you might be interested, I'll find something like that for you as well."

Allan finished his last forkful of salad. He shook his head and smiled. "Listen to me when I tell you that your mother is amazing. The way she takes care of everyone and everything. If it wasn't for her, we wouldn't have the life we have today. If it had been left up to me, we'd still be living in that two-bedroom apartment in the city." He sat back in his chair and smiled at her.

He said things like this from time to time, always talking her up. At that moment, as terrible as she felt, he made her feel appreciated. Sometimes, she couldn't quite believe how lucky she'd gotten with a partner. During really dark times, it was like the small flicker of a candle.

Chapter Thirty-Eight

It became part of Maureen's morning routine to take a walk on the beach. And now that summer was in full throttle, the morning light was dawning earlier, so that some days, like today, she found herself arriving before six. Even this early, the air was warm and heavy, promising another glorious summer day.

She had the shoreline to herself, almost. There was one other woman, slightly older than she, who walked in the distance, a small dog running along and yipping at her side. Maureen had never walked on the beach as a matter of routine; she'd been too busy working and raising kids. But she understood now why it was so popular; it was peaceful and relaxing. The sight of the water rolling in, the sound of the surf, and the briny smell that every beach seemed to have. What a comfort.

She fingered the St. Anthony medal in her pocket. She carried it everywhere with her, like a talisman.

As she walked north, her gaze naturally swung toward Nadine's house on Pearl Street. She spotted her sister sitting out on her back porch with a coffee cup in hand. She threw her hand up in a wave.

Maureen was surprised to see her sister up this early, but then maybe she shouldn't have been, because she knew Nadine served breakfast between seven and nine every morning for her guests.

She changed her course, walking away from the shore and across the thick, heavy sand until she reached her sister's property.

Herman jumped up and wagged his tail and whined until Maureen petted him. She laughed. "You're nothing but a big baby, Herman."

"You're up early," Nadine said.

"Can't sleep. I've been coming out in the mornings to walk and to think."

"It's a good place for it."

Maureen sat down in one of Nadine's new chairs. "I see you've gone with the turquoise. It looks great."

"I wasn't going to argue with an interior designer." Nadine stood up. "Coffee?"

"I'd love some if it isn't too much trouble."

"Not at all." She walked over to a small table against the back wall of the house, where she had a coffee station set up. She picked up a carafe and poured coffee into a mug. "How do you like it?"

"A little cream." Maureen admired the setup. "You're very organized."

"I like to sit out here before the breakfast rush. Sometimes, some of the guests are up early and like to sit out here and enjoy the view. I figured they might like to have a cup of coffee while they do."

"Smart thinking. Thanks," Maureen said as her sister handed her the mug.

Nadine sat down, and Herman moved to sit next to her, looking up at her expectantly.

"You've already had your breakfast, mister."

He put his paw on her thigh.

"No, you can't sweet-talk me."

Maureen laughed.

"I had him at the vet last week. He's put on three pounds!" Nadine pressed her lips together and looked at the dog. With a hand at the side of her mouth, she whispered, "He's on a diet."

"Welcome to our world, Herman," Maureen said.

"The guests like to feed him. I know they mean well, but carrying any extra weight will wreak havoc on his joints."

Maureen nodded, amused. She was grateful for the distraction.

"I had to post a sign in the dining room, asking the guests not to feed the dog."

"Is it working?" Maureen cradled her mug, enjoying the aroma of the coffee.

"Ninety percent. There's one guest, Mrs. Habermehl, who's eighty and has brought a box of Milk-Bones with her."

Maureen winced sympathetically.

"Luckily, she leaves the day after tomorrow."

"Poor Herman."

"Anyway, enough about that. How are you doing?" Nadine asked.

Sensing that the conversation was no longer about him, Herman lowered himself to the porch floor, groaned, and closed his eyes.

"I'm all right," Maureen said.

"Any word on Everett?"

"No, but Lance knows where he is. At least he's indoors and not sleeping rough." She never thought she'd use those words in reference to a child of her own. It was beyond the scope of her imagination.

Nadine grimaced. "I don't know how you do it. How do you hold it all together?"

Maureen sighed. "I won't lie. It's not easy. I keep busy, and I remind myself I have two other children I'm determined won't get lost in this shuffle."

"How's Allan?"

Maureen shrugged. "The same. Worried. Doesn't sleep well. Waiting for Everett to come to his senses and go into rehab."

"I don't know what I would do if that ever happened to Emma."

"I don't think you have to worry about that with Emma. Besides, I'll give you the handbook if you ever do."

"I give you a lot of credit, Maureen."

Maureen lowered her head, staring at the inside of her mug, coffee half drunk and growing cold. "Don't give me too much credit. We haven't convinced him yet to give up the drugs and go into rehab."

"That's a decision only he can make. It must be so painful to stand by and watch." Nadine's voice had a sympathetic tone.

"You feel so helpless. Like you're powerless. Like you've been swept up in an awful current and you can't get out of it."

Nadine listened.

Maureen stared out at the lake, squinting. She'd seen a flash of something on the horizon, but it was gone. "You know, I always thought my life was just about perfect. And I'll admit that at times, I was smug about it. *Oh, look at me and my perfect husband and kids, I'm so lucky*," she said in a singsong voice.

Gently, Nadine said, "No one's life is perfect."

Maureen smiled sadly. "I know that now."

"But everyone has perfect moments in their life."

Maureen thought about that. "I like that." She tucked it away for future reference.

Nadine continued to talk. "I wish there was something I could do. You know, Angie and DeeDee and I have talked about this. We wish we could help you, but we don't know how."

Maureen smiled, touched by their concern. Sometimes, sisters were great. She lifted her coffee mug. "This helps."

"Good."

"How's DeeDee?" She hadn't heard from their youngest sister in a while. It was news to her that she knew what was going on with Everett. But she supposed her mother or one of her sisters must have told her.

"She's good. I spoke to her the other day. Working. Dating some guy, but she was kind of vague on the details."

"Is he an actor too?" DeeDee had caught the acting bug early, always doing plays at home and forcing her older sisters to perform the parts. Their grandmother, who'd lived with them, encouraged her, even going so far as to sew costumes for the various roles.

"She didn't say." Nadine stared out at the water for a moment. "Now that I think about it, she doesn't say much. It's all general. You know, 'Everything's fine. I'm good.'"

"Do you think she's not telling you something?"

Nadine shrugged. "I don't know. It's just a feeling I get."

Maureen was about to say something when Nadine added, "I forgot to tell you. Richard got married."

Maureen arched an eyebrow. "As in, your ex? Did he marry that woman he was cheating with?"

Nadine nodded. "Julie. Yes. They got married two weeks ago."

"How do you feel about that?"

"To be honest, kind of philosophical. Our relationship went as far as it could. We came to the end of the line."

"That sounds healthy."

"The thing is, I'm happy here. Really happy. I mean, I've been content all my life, but here, I'm happy."

Maureen couldn't help but smile. Her sister had gone through a rough period at the end of her marriage. "That makes *me* happy to hear that. What about Emma?"

"She still bears a lot of anger and resentment toward him, but I'm encouraging her to keep the relationship going. She's loyal to me. He was a jerk for a husband, but he was always a good father."

"She'll come around. She's a good kid." Maureen glanced at her phone and stood up from her chair. "I better get going. I know you have to get breakfast ready for your guests."

Nadine also stood, and so did Herman.

"Full house?" Maureen asked.

"No, one empty bed, but I'm expecting guests for that room tomorrow."

"Good." As Nadine headed toward the sliding glass door to go inside, Maureen said, "I'll wait. I want to see this Herman thing again."

Nadine laughed, rolled the door open, and stepped in. "Come on, Herman."

The dog faced away from the door, looked over his shoulder, and walked backward into the house.

Maureen chuckled. "That never gets old."

CHAPTER THIRTY-NINE

Maureen had tried to find the owner of the lost medal, which she continued to carry around on her. Never one to be considered superstitious, she thought of this medal as sort of a good luck charm, though she hated the term. It meant something to her that she was the one who found it. As if it was meant to be. She scoured the lost-and-found section in *The Lavender Bay Chronicles* for months, to no avail. She'd even placed an ad of her own and received no replies. She posted a photo on her rarely used Facebook page, and although it received a lot of likes and comments, no one came forward to claim it. At the post office, she tacked up a notice on the corkboard, but again, nothing. Crickets. She showed it to everyone she knew but was met with blank stares.

If everything else had been all right in her life, this lost medal wouldn't even have been a blip on her radar, but it bothered her that someone was out there missing their medal. It might have held significance for them. As for herself, the medal depicting St. Anthony, the finder of lost things, gave her an inexplicable sense of comfort.

In her quest to locate the owner, she showed it to her mother, lamenting the fact that she was no further ahead in her search. As usual, Louise took a practical stance. "It's obviously very old as evidenced by how worn it is. Of course, the lake will do that. But whoever lost it is probably long gone. I would consider this a case of finders keepers. But why don't you take it down to Aunt Gail and see if she can help you?"

"Would she know anything about a religious medal?"

Louise shrugged. "You won't know until you ask. The things that Gail knows would surprise you."

Maureen nodded. "I'll take a walk over there."

"Go now, her afternoons can be quiet."

Maureen would have preferred to walk, but it was raining, so she took the car. Her aunt's antique shop was located on the corner of Main Street and Pine, but there was no parking on either, so she ended up a block away on Cedar. She got out of the car, opened her umbrella with a click of the button, and covered her head as she made a run for Prime Vintage.

The shop was lit up by the various chandeliers and light fixtures hanging from the ceiling at different heights. They cast a bright golden hue over all the paintings and gave the antique furniture a glossy shine. The place smelled fusty, of old things and furniture that had long outlasted its owners.

Rufus the retired bloodhound was ahead of her, waddling toward the back of the shop, his tawny ears dragging on the ground. He paid no notice to Maureen. Gail was at the back counter, putting a new consignment of jewelry into the glass case. She wore a colorful dress of purple, turquoise, and green, and a pair of Skechers on her feet.

"Maureen!"

"Hi, Aunt Gail."

Rufus shuffled off to the back room behind the counter.

"Your dinner's there, Rufus." Gail looked at Maureen and asked, "How's Everett doing?"

Maureen shrugged and sighed. "Your guess is as good as mine. Apparently he's somewhere in Lavender Bay, but I don't know where."

Aunt Gail nodded. "Your mother said Lance knows where he is. That's good. That way he can keep an eye on him."

"I wish he would come to his senses and come home."

"He will. He's an intelligent kid and someday, he'll wake up. Unfortunately, with addiction, sometimes you have to hit rock bottom before you can change."

Maureen tilted her head. "You sound like you have experience with this."

Aunt Gail shrugged nonchalantly. "I've seen a lot of things in my life."

She didn't elaborate, and Maureen didn't push.

"I wanted to ask you," Gail said, "has my daughter roped you into joining her bowling team?"

"She has," Maureen replied. "You too?"

Her aunt had a concerned look on her face. She stepped back from the counter and held out her hands. "Do I look like a bowler to you?"

Maureen couldn't help but laugh. "That makes two of us. But I've agreed."

Gail shook her head. "Sometimes, I worry about her."

"Aw, don't, Aunt Gail. Esther is her own person. And if she likes bowling, she likes bowling."

"She didn't get that from my side of the family," Gail said.

"None of us did."

Her aunt changed the subject. "Take a look at this fabulous jewelry that was part of an estate." She pulled a ring out from the tray. "Would you look at this beauty."

The ring, a large rectangular topaz in a gold setting, was still in its original box with the jeweler's stamp on the lining.

"Wow, that's gorgeous."

"It's about one hundred years old. Art deco." Aunt Gail turned it around in her hand, admiring it.

"It's lovely."

Gail slid the ring onto her finger but couldn't move it past her knuckle. "I keep trying it on, hoping my fingers have thinned out since the last time I tried, but no luck."

Maureen laughed.

"Did you want to try it on?" Gail asked.

"No thanks. I've got something I was hoping you'd look at."

Gail set the ring aside. "Let's see it."

Maureen pulled out the medal from her pocket and set it on the counter.

Gail frowned and picked it up, turning it over, studying both sides. She looked up at Maureen. "Where did you get this?"

"If you can believe it, I found it on the beach."

Gail sighed. "These days, I'd believe anything." She pulled open a drawer behind her and dug through it, pulling out a jeweler's loupe. She turned on the desk light she kept on the counter, unfolded the loupe, and brought it up close to her eye, picking up the medal with her other hand.

After studying both sides, Gail announced, "It's a St. Anthony medal. Looks vintage. Made in Italy. The writing is in Italian, but it's too worn to read it properly."

"St. Anthony was an Italian saint?"

Gail shook her head. "Portuguese." She put the loupe and the medal down and stood there and stared. Maureen frowned. Her aunt looked as if she'd seen a ghost.

Alarmed, she asked, "Aunt Gail, are you all right?"

"I am. Tell me, how many of this exact type of medal do you think are lost in that lake out there?"

"Honestly, I'd be surprised if there were two."

"That's what I thought."

"What's the matter? What does it mean?"

Aunt Gail swallowed hard. Maureen was nervous; she'd never seen her aunt at a loss for words before.

"I think this medal belonged to my mother."

Chapter Forty

"Wait. What?" Maureen stared at Gail, who blinked several times, taking a moment to recover.

"I'm pretty sure this belonged to my mother." Gail turned it over again in her hand, studying it.

"Grammie?" Maureen placed a hand over her chest for emphasis. "My grandmother. Your mother?"

"Yes."

"Are you sure? I showed Mom the medal, and she didn't say anything about it being Grammie's."

"Because she might not know the story. Might never have heard of it."

"Can you tell me?"

Gail smiled. "Of course." She leaned on the counter, the medal still in the palm of her hand. "You know

Grammie had an accident at the plant during the war, right?"

Maureen nodded. Sure, she knew the story. They all did. During the Second World War, Grammie had taken a job at an aviation plant over in Cheever that had been repurposed to make cargo planes for the military. She wasn't there long when her beautiful hair got caught in a buffer, leaving her disfigured. She spent most of the rest of her life wearing scarves and wigs but as she got older, especially when she wasn't going out as much, she didn't bother. As Grammie and Granddad had lived with them, Maureen was used to it and took no notice of it. Her sisters were the same, she was sure. Thinking about it now, it must have been a horrific ordeal for her grandmother to go through.

Gail picked up her story. "Anyway, she took the accident pretty hard at the time."

"That's understandable."

"She was going out with a guy, a soldier, and when he came home on leave, they broke up."

"Poor Grammie!" Maureen had not known this story. Or that her grandmother had had a boyfriend before Granddad. But that wasn't surprising. She'd seen old black-and-white photos of her grandmother before the accident, and she'd been stunning. Statuesque with long golden, honey-colored hair, she'd certainly been a looker. It came as no surprise that she would have had a boyfriend, or maybe even more than one.

Her aunt appeared thoughtful. "Though I suppose if they hadn't broken up, she would never have met Dad, and we wouldn't be here having this conversation."

Maureen lifted an eyebrow. "I didn't know you were such a deep thinker, Aunt Gail."

"I surprise even myself." Gail laughed, but it turned into a fit of coughing.

"Are you all right?"

Gail waved her off and soon stopped coughing, though her eyes were watering and her face was red. "Anyway." She pulled a tissue from the pocket of her dress and wiped beneath her eyes where her mascara had smudged. "She said a religious medal had been given to her by a very dear friend, and when she lost it swimming in the lake, she was heartbroken. Looked everywhere for it and even though we aren't Catholic, she prayed to St. Anthony."

"Funny that I would be the one to find it," Maureen said. "If you think about it, I mean. All those years that have gone by. *Decades*. All the people on the beach since then, and it's her granddaughter that finds it."

Aunt Gail shivered even though it wasn't cold. "I know. My hair is standing up on the back of my neck." She shuddered again.

Maureen wondered if this was one of those cosmic, there's-no-such-thing-as-coincidence moments, as if there were greater forces at play here.

"It's almost as if it was you that was meant to find it," Gail said.

A shiver ran up Maureen's back. When she and her sisters were kids, they'd say someone was walking over their grave.

Gail picked up the medal and handed it back to her. "For whatever reason, it was supposed to find you."

"Do you really believe that?"

"I most certainly do!"

Maureen pocketed the medal.

"St. Anthony is the saint you pray to when you lose something," Gail said.

"So, if I lose my car keys, I should pray to him?"

Gail put the loupe away, back in its drawer. "Not only items. If you lose anything, pray to him." Then with a shrug of her shoulders, she added, "That's what they say, at least."

Coffee Girl was packed when Maureen stopped there shortly after lunchtime on Friday afternoon. Immediately, she spotted Angie running from the kitchen to behind the counter and back through the stainless-steel butler doors. The place smelled of coffee and sugar and vanilla, a heady combination.

Maureen approached the counter and surveyed the long glass case full of every pastry imaginable. There were scones, cakes, pies, muffins, and cheesecakes. Her mouth watered.

"Who's next?" Angie asked in a tone that said she better have her order ready.

Maureen stepped forward and Angie's features softened. "Hey there. Good to see you."

"You too."

"I'll have the usual," Maureen said.

"Café au lait and the white chocolate raspberry muffin?"

Maureen nodded and pulled her wallet out of her purse.

"This is on me," Angie said.

"No, Angie. We've had this discussion. You're running a business. No freebies for the family."

Angie chuckled. "Okay, boss. You're owning your big sister shoes today."

Maureen had to laugh.

Angie punched in her sister's order, and Maureen tapped her bank card against the card reader to pay for it.

"Go on, grab a table and I'll bring it over to you."

Maureen turned around and scanned the shop, spying a small open table for two toward the back. She wound her way through the packed seating area and set her purse on the floor by her chair and waited.

Angie appeared and set her beverage and muffin down in front of her. She pulled out the other chair and sat down. "It feels good to get off my feet for a minute."

"I bet. Aren't you having anything?"

Angie shook her head. "No. I just had my lunch." She paused and asked, "How are you doing? How is everything?"

Woven throughout her questions was the more specific one: *How's Everett?*

With a slow nod, Maureen said, "Okay. I'm taking it one day at a time."

"That's smart. Any word?"

"No, nothing." Maureen took a tentative sip of her café au lait and decided it needed another minute to cool down.

Angie heaved a sigh. "Hopefully, Everett will come home soon."

"Hopefully." She broke off a piece of her muffin and put it into her mouth, chewing thoughtfully. "I still don't know what I did wrong."

Angie scowled. "Who said you did anything wrong?"

Maureen shrugged. "I keep going back down through the years, wondering what we could have done differently."

"This has nothing to do with you or Allan. At the end of the day, it was Everett's choice."

Maureen wasn't totally convinced. "Everything was so perfect. Or at least I thought so, with the boys in college and Ash getting ready to go off in the fall."

Angie leaned back, draping one arm over the back of the chair. "Can I be blunt?"

Maureen laughed. "When are you not?"

Her sister tilted her head slightly. "True, but my directness usually serves a purpose."

"Go on."

"Maureen, you're a little bit of a perfectionist. Always have been. I think you need to let go of that concept, or at least change your definition of it. You're hung up on how things appear to the outside world."

Maureen reserved comment. There was some truth in what her sister said. And it stung a bit.

Angie's assistant manager approached the table and relayed some problem to Angie about something going on in the kitchen.

"Okay, thanks, Melissa. I'll be right there." She shifted in her chair, ready to stand up.

"Speaking of perfectionism," Maureen said with a lift of the eyebrow. "When are you going to let Melissa take on more duties? You're going to run yourself ragged."

"It's just habit."

"Not a good one," Maureen continued. "I'm not the only perfectionist in the family. And in the spirit of honesty, you're also a control freak." She said this in the most loving way possible, because her younger sister could sometimes be prickly.

"Guilty as charged on both counts." Angie stood up from the table. "I've got to go."

"All right, take care of yourself."

"You too. Keep me posted about Everett." And she was gone.

After she left the coffee shop, noting the line outside Java Joe's across the street, which would surely send Angie into orbit, Maureen wandered down Main Street, in no hurry to go to work. She had some details to go over, but she couldn't concentrate.

She walked to the end of the block and looked across the street at Prime Vintage. Brutus was not in his usual spot by the front door. She did a double-take and spotted him in the front window, ensconced between an antique globe and a small table. He seemed vigilant.

On a whim, she stopped into Gloria's Gifts on the next block to browse. The gift shop was a hodgepodge of things. There was soft, pleasant music playing in the background, no doubt from a CD the store sold. The air was fragrant with a scented candle. She lifted a few from the display, sniffing them, deciding she liked the lavender and thyme one best.

She strolled through the aisles, looking at all the wares and falling in love with a ceramic butter dish that would match her kitchen perfectly, but then deciding against it, thinking she had enough butter dishes at home. In the aisle of wind chimes, she had to duck a few times to avoid getting hit in the head with one of them. She had enough of those at home as well.

At the back of the shop was the novelty section. Some retro stuff and gag gifts. There were things like rain bonnets, plastic change purses, mood rings—she'd had one as a teenager that turned her finger green, and all it had confirmed was that she was moody—and whoopee cushions.

Edna Knickerbocker was in the middle of the retro section, holding a squirt gun. Why an eighty-five-year-old woman would be looking at a fluorescent orange squirt gun aroused an unusual amount of curiosity in Maureen.

Maureen approached her, and Edna looked up. Her gnarly fingers kept squeezing the white plastic trigger.

"Hello, Maureen, how are you?"

"I'm fine, Mrs. Knickerbocker, how are you?"

"I'm good for my age. How's Everett? Has he come home yet?"

Maureen's mouth went dry. That was the problem with Lavender Bay. Like other small towns, not only did everyone know your business, they also felt it was okay to comment on it and ask questions. If you were looking for privacy, this wasn't the place.

"No, he hasn't."

Edna shook her head. "Addiction is tough. I'm praying for him."

"I appreciate that," Maureen said sincerely. They not only needed prayers, they could use a miracle or two. Wanting to change the subject, she nodded toward the squirt gun. "What's up with the water gun, Mrs. Knickerbocker?"

Edna looked at it and chuckled. "This? It's for my neighbor, Hal."

Maureen knew of Edna's neighbor. He was as old as Edna. "Hal wants a squirt gun?"

"No, of course not," Edna said in a tone that suggested it was ridiculous to assume an eighty-five-year-old man would want a squirt gun. But then there she was, holding one in her hand. "We like to play practical jokes on each other. This should take him by surprise." She broke into a fit of laughter, and Maureen found herself laughing too, buoyed by the idea of having that much fun when you were in your eighties. She tried to call up an image of her and Allan playing with squirt guns, but it seemed ludicrous. Maybe when they were in their eighties, it wouldn't seem as ridiculous.

"Hey, whatever happened to that raccoon?" Edna asked.

"I hired a company who offered a compassionate removal service," Maureen explained.

"Ha, they probably took him to the park like I did."

Maureen was about to say something, but Edna kept talking. "I better go. At my age, I could go any minute," she said. She waved the squirt gun around. "So it's best if Hal gets a belt of this today."

"I'm sure he'll be delighted," Maureen said.

"I think so too. Ta-ta!" The old woman disappeared, nimbly walking down the aisle to the front of the store.

As Maureen exited the store, having made no purchases, the narrow storefront of the jewelry store across the street caught her eye, and she had an idea. Looking both ways before crossing the street, she dashed across it to the jeweler tucked neatly between the Annacotty Room and the Quirk and Quill.

Chapter Forty-One

Maureen was in a deep sleep, the kind of sleep that felt like you were at the bottom of a deep well of darkness.

"Mom. Mom."

Someone shook her shoulder. From the depths of sleep, she swam up to the surface. She opened her eyes to see Lance standing over her.

"Lance? What is it? What time is it?" Immediately, she sat up, reaching for the bedside light and turning it on. Allan rolled over on his side, slowly opening his eyes.

"It's a little after three," Lance said. "You and Dad need to get up. Everett is on his way to the hospital."

Maureen and Allan jumped out of the bed, hair mussed, eyes heavy with sleep.

"What happened?"

"Is he all right?"

Lance sighed. "He's overdosed again."

"Oh no," Maureen cried.

"How did you find out?" Allan asked.

"I gave my number to someone he's living with. He just called me. They found Everett face down in a pool of his own vomit. They called an ambulance."

Maureen thought, *Thank God.* Thank God there had been one person clearheaded enough to notice Everett needed medical attention.

"Come on, let's get dressed," Allan said.

"Can I go to the hospital with you?" Lance asked.

"No, please stay here with your sister. I don't want Ash to be alone. If she wakes up and we're all gone, she'll think the worst." Allan opened the top drawer of his dresser and pulled out a clean pair of socks.

Lance closed the bedroom door behind him to let his parents get dressed.

Maureen stood there for a moment, numb. She'd always known this day was coming, and she had dreaded it, but now it was actually here. With the choices her son had made, this end result had been inevitable and deep down, they both knew it.

"Maureen, come on," Allan said, pulling on a pair of jeans.

"Okay, okay," she said, putting up a hand. She made her way to the bathroom to brush her teeth and use the toilet.

The streets were quiet, and Allan did not bother to obey the speed limit. Usually, Maureen would say something, but she was just as anxious as her husband to get to the hospital.

He pulled up in front of the emergency room entrance to drop her off at the door. "I'll go park the car."

"Okay." Maureen was alert and frantic as she rushed into the emergency room and went to the reception area. The desk was empty, but there was a crowd in the waiting area. In front of the vacant desk, she paced back and forth until a nurse in purple scrubs appeared. Maureen rushed her.

"I'm here about my son. Everett Peterson."

The nurse nodded. "He's here."

"How is he?" Maureen asked.

"The doctors are with him right now. That's all I know." And before Maureen could ask any more questions, the nurse disappeared through a door.

Maureen found two vacant seats directly across from the reception desk, where she could keep an eye out for any hospital employee. She'd even speak to the janitor if they had information about Everett.

The fluorescent lights in the waiting room were harsh and unforgiving at this time of night. Maureen, who rarely went out of the house without wearing a light covering of makeup, was devoid of it. At this point, she didn't care.

Allan joined her, slipping his keys into his pocket and sitting in the chair next to her. "Anything?"

"No. They're with him right now."

They sat quietly next to each other, watching the comings and goings of the waiting room. A young man in his late twenties sat across from them with a towel against his forehead to stem the flow of blood. The towel, whether a conscious choice or not, was scarlet in color, so it was hard to tell how bad the wound was. But overall, it looked as if it had been a rough night. Behind him sat two elderly people, the man, in his pajamas, wearing a nasal canula and having occasional violent coughing fits. The problems of other people kept Maureen slightly distracted. But she kept glancing at the desk until finally another person dressed in scrubs—Maureen was unsure whether she was a nurse or not—pulled out the chair at the reception desk.

Maureen bolted out of her seat and approached her.

"Hi, I'm Maureen Peterson. My son Everett was brought in."

The woman never looked away from her computer screen. "All right. I'll let them know."

Maureen waited for the woman to make eye contact and acknowledge her, but it never happened. Feeling discouraged, she returned to her seat.

"What did she say?"

"Nothing," Maureen said sourly. "She'll let them know we're here."

"It's taking a long time," Allan remarked. "Did it take this long when you brought him in the last time?"

Maureen had to think for a moment. She frowned. "No, it didn't." That couldn't be good. Fear gripped her.

Allan tried to reassure her. "I'm sure they're very busy back there. Emergency rooms are notoriously busy on a Saturday night."

She hoped that's what it was but was doubtful.

Within an hour, a man wearing a white lab coat over navy scrubs appeared, went to the desk, and asked the woman a question. She actually looked away from her computer screen this time and nodded toward Maureen and Allan.

Maureen laid a hand on Allan's thigh. He'd dozed off.

"Hmm."

"Here comes the doctor."

The doctor was tall, had to be about six-five. He was young. He looked exhausted and fed up.

"Everett's parents?" He stifled a yawn.

"Yes. I'm Maureen Peterson and this is my husband, Allan."

The doctor did not comment on that, instead looked through a folder. "Yeah. He was brought in for a drug overdose. Opioids. Specifically, oxycodone." Now he looked at them. "Were you aware of your son's drug problem? I understand this is his second visit to us in recent months."

Allan spoke. "Yes, we're aware. We've been trying to get him to go to rehab."

"Yeah, well, good luck with that."

Maureen didn't care for this man's abrupt manner. Must have been sick the day in med school when they were covering bedside manner one-o-one.

"He's in pretty rough shape. But he'll live." The doctor's tone indicated that he almost seemed disappointed.

"How bad is he?" Allan asked.

The doctor looked directly at them. "Your son went into cardiac arrest and was clinically dead for two minutes."

Maureen crumpled, putting her hand to her mouth and gasping.

The doctor was still speaking. "We've got him ventilated right now, which is helping him breathe."

On a ventilator? Oh, dear God.

"He's been transferred to the intensive care unit, and you can go see him. Going forward, check with the nurse regarding visiting hours."

"Where's the ICU?" Allan asked.

"Up on the third floor. Follow the signs." The doctor paused and said, "Look, I'm going to lay this on the line. Your son is on a trajectory that will not end well for him. I see it all the time. Unless he gets clean, he'll be in here again. And again. Until someday, he'll show up and we won't be able to save him. They're our frequent fliers." He paused. "He'll graduate to things other than pills. Syringes. Heroin. Because there will come a point where he will no longer get the high he needs from the drugs he's currently using."

Maureen felt like she might throw up.

"I'm sorry if that was brutal," the doctor said.

Maureen was speechless, but Allan said, "Thank you for your honesty."

She wondered how her husband was managing to keep his composure. She hoped his strength was contagious.

The doctor left them, and they headed toward the bank of elevators.

"I didn't care for his attitude," Maureen finally said.

Allan punched the "up" button several times, and they waited for an elevator to appear.

"He's fed up, and I don't blame him." There was a trace of anger in Allan's voice. "He sees these young kids hopped up on dope, and he has to save them. He sees them throwing their lives away, and he's pissed off. I'd feel the same way." He waved his arm around. "Look at all these sick people in here. People who need help."

"What's the difference between Everett and those people who are in here because of lifestyle choices?" she demanded. "They drink too much or they eat too much. Why should one addiction be singled out? Are you saying they shouldn't treat people who overdose on drugs?"

"Of course not!" Allan snapped.

The elevator doors opened, they stepped in, and he stabbed the button for the third floor with his finger.

He sighed. "Maybe we're going about this the wrong way."

"What do you mean?"

"Maybe we have to force him into rehab."

"I want him to go to rehab just as much as you, but I disagree. I don't think forcing him is a good idea. It would be unsuccessful."

Allan looked down at the floor. "I know. You're right. But I want him to see some sense. He's throwing his life away."

The doors pinged open, and they stepped out and followed the signs for the medical intensive care unit, walking down empty corridors and turning left and then right.

"Where *is* this place?" Allan asked, frustrated. "It's starting to feel like the Camino de Santiago trek."

Despite everything, Maureen chuckled.

Unlike other areas of the hospital, the ICU was whisper quiet. The first nurse they approached said she'd show them to their son's room.

Everett was in a room by himself, as were all the patients in the intensive care unit. The nurses' station was in the middle of ICU with patient rooms surrounding the desk. Each room had a full glass window, and some had a blue curtain pulled across the length of it. But there were glimpses of other patients. All in bed, in various states of illness, all on ventilators and all unconscious. It was so quiet it was eerie.

The curtains on Everett's room were drawn, and Maureen drew in a sharp breath to brace herself before she walked into the room.

But nothing would have prepared her for what she walked into.

Everett lay on his back in the middle of the bed, eyes closed. A ventilator tube snaked from his mouth, down his chest, to a machine at the side of the bed. The tube was anchored in place against the side of his mouth with medical tape.

Maureen gasped at the sight, feeling her knees give way. Allan was at her side, propping her up. In a voice that trembled, he said, "Come on, let's get you to a chair."

The nurse, who had her long brown hair clipped up and looked not much older than Everett, pulled over a chair for Maureen. She spoke to them in soft, hushed tones.

"My name's Adele. I'm Everett's nurse for the rest of the shift. Right now, he's stable, and the doctors are hoping they can wean him off the ventilator soon."

Maureen couldn't get past the sight in the bed in front of her. How could this be her little boy, who'd always stayed up way past his bedtime, reading books? How could this be him?

And how would she get through this? How would they cope? Allan stood next to her, rubbing her back.

"I'll get you another chair, Mr. Peterson," the nurse said.

"Thank you," Allan replied.

When they were alone, Maureen said, "I can't believe this. This is like some kind of nightmare we can't seem to wake up from." She covered her mouth with her hand.

Allan sighed. "I know."

Adele returned with another chair, and Allan rushed to the door to take it from her. She spoke with them for a few minutes.

"Even though he's unconscious, he can still hear you, so please speak to him and let him know you're here." The young nurse was so soft-spoken that Maureen thought she was perfect for the ICU. "If you need anything or have questions, I'll be out at the desk."

"Thank you, Adele, we appreciate it," Allan said. When she was gone, he arranged the two chairs, one on each side of the bed, so they could hold Everett's hands.

Before Maureen sat down, she reached over and brushed Everett's hair off his forehead, just like she used to do when he was a little boy. She leaned in and kissed him on the cheek.

"We're here for you, honey," she said. "Dad and I are here."

There was a fluttering behind his eyelids.

She sat down in the chair and grasped his hand. Allan, still standing, leaned over the bed and spoke to Everett.

"Everett, it's Dad. You're not alone. Mom and I will help you get through this."

More fluttering behind the eyelids.

Allan crossed his arms over his chest and looked over every line connected to his son's body, and then his gaze swung around the room, looking at the IV bags hanging from a pole above Everett's head and then over to the monitor that recorded his vital signs.

"His vitals are good," Allan said with a nod toward the monitor. Finally, he sat down and took Everett's other hand.

Maureen laid her head on the edge of the bed, still clasping her son's hand. She had no idea how to fix this. She had ideas and plans, but she had no idea how to make her son stop taking drugs. And she was beginning to doubt that they could get through to him.

As if reading her mind, Allan said to Everett, "Mom and I aren't giving up hope. We won't give up on you, Everett. Never."

Chapter Forty-Two

Once Everett was weaned off the ventilator, he was groggy but complained that his throat was sore. The nurse explained it was from the ventilator tube.

Maureen and Allan had discussed over breakfast how they were going to approach him. He had to go into rehab. But getting him to agree to go, to see that it was in his best interest, was going to be a challenge.

In the meantime, Maureen's phone had been bombarded with texts from her mother, her sisters, her aunt, her cousins, and friends. The news had apparently spread like wildfire. At this point, she didn't care. She wasn't going to hide it anymore. She wanted it out in the open. She needed all her energy to help her son; she couldn't waste it on maintaining a façade, pretending everything was fine within her family when it wasn't.

On the way to the hospital, she responded to as many texts as she could.

They'd agreed to handle Everett with care but be firm, as Allan had said.

Maureen agreed but did not want to be aggressive.

Allan looked over at her. "Aren't you angry?"

"Of course I am. What would make you think I wasn't?" She was angry that her son had decided that these were going to be his life choices. "But I don't think coming on like gangbusters is the answer either."

They found Everett out of bed and sitting in the chair, dressed in a hospital gown. He wore a second one as a bathrobe. She made a mental note to bring some of his clothes from home. His breakfast tray was on the table in front of him. A quick glance showed he'd eaten much of his meal, which Maureen took as a good sign. The good signs were slim on the ground, and she had to take them where she could get them.

As soon as they entered the room, Maureen went to him and kissed his forehead. When she stepped back, he hung his head.

"How are you, Everett?" Allan asked. He indicated to Maureen that she should take the other unoccupied chair.

In a voice barely above a whisper, Everett said, "I'm okay."

"You gave us quite a fright, you know," said Allan.

"I know."

"We almost lost you," Allan told him.

"I know. The doctors told me."

"Did they?"

Everett nodded. "They were in earlier this morning to talk to me. Told me I was dead for a few minutes."

In a wobbly voice, Maureen said, "That is a hell I never want to go through again."

He looked up at her. "Okay, Mom."

"Maybe you should apologize to your mother," Allan suggested.

Irritated, Maureen put up her hand. "That's not necessary."

Sighing, Allan said in a placatory tone, "All right."

Maureen chose her words carefully. "Everett, I know you've said you can stop taking drugs, but can I ask you a question?"

"Sure."

"Do you *want* to quit?"

It took him a moment, but finally he said, "Yes."

Allan let out the breath he was holding. "That's encouraging."

Maureen leaned forward in her chair. "Will you go into rehab?"

Everett bent his head. "Yes."

Maureen and Allan let out a collective sigh.

Chapter Forty-Three

Everett remained in the hospital for twenty-eight days to undergo medically supervised detoxification which included medication-assisted treatments. They were allowed to visit him in the visitor's lounge for scheduled visits. Maureen and Allan attended therapy sessions at the hospital and Nar-Anon meetings in the community.

At the end of his stay, he was transferred to a residential rehab facility on the other side of Cheever for further help.

In the middle of August, Maureen and Allan traveled with Ashley to the West Coast to see her off to college. Although she was excited to be starting this next adventure in her life, she did get a little misty-eyed as they left. The one thought swirling through Maureen's mind as she hugged her daughter goodbye was, *What if she starts taking drugs too*? A year ago, that thought wouldn't even have popped into her head. But the landscape was now different.

The only one left at home was Lance. After working all summer outside and usually shedding his T-shirt as soon as it got hot, their son was now a bronzed god, and his hair had lightened. It hadn't escaped Maureen, the number of girls walking by their house on a Sunday afternoon, which was Lance's only day off. But Lance was never home on a Sunday.

The first night after they returned from the West Coast, he actually joined them for dinner. As it was so hot out, Maureen decided on a simple meal of make-your-own bacon, lettuce, and tomato sandwiches.

She set down plates of sliced beefsteak tomatoes, lettuce, and cooked bacon in the middle of the table. There was butter for the toast and mayo for the sandwiches. She then manned the toaster. Allan and Lance sat and helped themselves to the first pieces of toast on the table and began putting their sandwiches together.

As Maureen carried another plate of toast over to the table, she asked Lance, "When are you heading back to UB?"

He didn't answer right away. He sat there, silent, staring at his half-eaten BLT.

"Lance, didn't you hear your mother?" Allan asked.

"I wanted to talk to you about that," Lance said. He looked up, first at his mother and then his father.

"Talk to us about what?" Maureen buttered a piece of toast and laid a few strips of bacon on it, followed by lettuce and tomato. She looked over at Lance.

He looked back down at his plate. "I'm not going back."

Maureen laughed. "What do you mean? Of course you are."

Lance shook his head. "I don't want to go back."

Allan frowned, finished chewing, and asked, "Don't you like it?"

"No."

"But you did well in your classes." Maureen didn't understand this. They'd seen his grades at the end of the last semester, and he had done quite well. They'd been pleased.

Silence descended. Maureen blinked several times, never taking her eyes off her second-born child.

What was going on? What kind of fresh hell was this?

"Why?" Allan demanded.

Lance shrugged, but he finally tore his gaze away from his sandwich and looked up at them. "I don't like school. I never have."

They knew this. Lance liked the social aspect of it and the sports, but cracking open the books was low on his list. This was the kid that had declared at the age of nine, "I don't know why I have to go to school. I know everything."

"You don't like the course," said Allan.

"Why didn't you tell us?" Maureen asked.

Lance turned to look at her. "I tried a few times to talk to you when I was home for spring break."

Immediately, she thought of the missed breakfast, and then missing him before he'd left to return to school.

"That was months ago. What about all summer?" Allan asked.

"I was working every day, and you guys were kind of busy with Everett."

Allan shook his head. "You had plenty of time to talk to us about this instead of waiting until the last minute."

Maureen understood why Allan was irate, but she tried to smooth things over.

"You've only been there a year," she said. "Why don't you see how the second year goes before you drop out?"

But Lance shook his head. "No. I'm not going back. I've already dropped out."

"What? You went ahead and dropped out without even talking to us?" Allan said.

"If you were having trouble, you should have told us," Maureen said.

"I wasn't having trouble, Mom. I've decided it isn't what I want to do anymore. College isn't for me."

She didn't know what to say. The landscape of her family was shifting so dramatically she no longer recognized it. It was like someone had dropped her on another planet. How could things change so drastically from one year to the next?

"Do you know what you want to do?" Allan asked. "Because if you're not in college, you'll have to get a full-time job."

"I know that, Dad, you said that enough times when Everett and I were in high school. That if we didn't go to college, we had to go to work."

Allan had nothing to say to that.

"It's no secret that I've never liked school," Lance continued. "Not like Everett and Ash." He picked up the other half of his sandwich, took a large bite, chewed for a moment, swallowed, and said, "I went to college because that's what everyone does."

Did they?

"What would you like to do?" Allan asked.

"I want to be an electrician."

"Electrician?" Maureen repeated. "I didn't even know you were interested in that." How had she missed this? He might as well have said he wanted to take a rocket to Mars.

Lance finally smiled for the first time since he sat down to dinner. His bright, cheery smile that always reminded her of when he was a little boy.

"Electricity lights up my life," he joked.

Neither Maureen nor Allan laughed. But Maureen could feel the tug of a smile.

"What about going to college for electrical engineering?" Allan suggested. "UB has a great engineering school."

Lance scrunched up his nose. "Nah. I thought about that for about thirty seconds. Not interested."

"I don't know what to say. Have you looked into this?" Allan said.

Lance nodded, helping himself to more fixings for another sandwich. Maureen stood from the table to make more toast.

"There's a year-long course at a trade school and then a five-year apprenticeship if I can get into the electricians' union."

"Do you have to do both?" Maureen asked. Although she frequently dealt with electricians with her work, she had no idea what the process entailed to become a qualified one.

"No. But I could handle the one year of trade school. And then try for an apprenticeship with the union. I've already spoken to Matt's dad; his brother is in the electricians' union. He'll see what he can do for me."

"Where's the nearest trade school?" Allan asked.

"Over in Cheever," Lance replied.

Four slices of toast popped up, and Maureen plated them and carried them over to the table. "At least you'd be able to live at home."

"Thanks, Mom."

"When do you need to apply?" Allan asked. Maureen passed him the plate of toast. "Thanks, hon." He took two slices and laid them on his plate.

"I already applied last spring. I've been accepted. It starts the first week in September."

Allan looked up from the second BLT he was making for himself and nodded. "Good for you. That shows initiative. When does the tuition need to be paid by?"

"It's not that expensive, and I've saved enough money working this summer to pay for it."

"You know the arrangement. I pay for college," Allan reminded him.

"I know, Dad, but I can afford this. I'd like to pay for this myself. It's only for a year."

"Great. But if you need anything, you'll come to me, right?"

"I will," Lance promised.

After dinner, Maureen and Allan sat out in their backyard around the new firepit that Allan had purchased the previous weekend. Their chairs were set back from the blazing fire. The brutal heat of summer was behind them, but the evenings were still warm. Maureen lit several citronella candles as the mosquitoes were out in full force.

Allan slapped his arm.

"Do you want me to go in the house and get the bug spray?" she asked.

"Nah, honey, don't bother." He looked over at her. "Do we have the ingredients to make s'mores?"

She laughed and shook her head. "The kids haven't had s'mores in years. Except when they go to my mother's house and she does them on the grill."

They sipped beer from ice cold bottles. It was refreshing. Maureen wasn't a big beer drinker, but she liked the odd one in the summer.

After a few moments of silence, he asked, "So what do you think of Lance's news?"

She sighed. "I don't know what to think. I had no idea he was that unhappy in college."

Allan crossed one leg over the other and leaned back in his chair. "I don't think he was unhappy, just that it wasn't for him."

"I'd prefer he went to college rather than the trade school."

"Why?"

She looked at her husband. Did he really not know? "Because I think he has a better chance of supporting himself with a four-year degree."

"Electricians make good money."

"I don't doubt that."

Allan probed gently, "Maybe it looks better if he's a college graduate."

Maureen reddened. "Gosh, that makes me sound shallow."

Her husband was quick to reassure her. "Which you're not."

"Everything is so different." Her voice was quiet.

"It's no lie that we've got some challenges with Everett. But as far as Lance is concerned, I'm impressed that he took it upon himself to drop out officially from college and enroll in trade school. That's a good sign of maturity."

Maureen had to agree.

Allan took a swig of his beer. "Look, honey, as long as they're happy, they'll be fine. They'll land on their feet."

Deep down, that was what Maureen wanted more than anything else: for her children to be happy. After all, a mother could only be as happy as her unhappiest child.

Chapter Forty-Four

The following day, Maureen stopped at her mother's house after work.

Louise was out back, sitting in one of the webbed lawn chairs that had been around since Maureen was a child. She peered through a pair of binoculars at a couple of birds at the back fence. Open on the table next to her was her bird book.

When Maureen came in sight and said, "Hi, Mom," Louise put down her binoculars.

"This is a pleasant surprise."

Maureen plopped down in the other chair. A faint scent of Louise's perfume, Amazing Grace, hovered in the air around them, a fragrance Maureen would always associate with her mother.

Louise handed her the binoculars. "Look at that bird near the blue birdhouse."

The wooden fence around the backyard was dotted with various and sundry birdhouses that had been put up long ago by Maureen's father. Every year, her mother removed the empty birdhouses, cleaned them out, and gave them a fresh coat of paint.

Maureen looked through the binoculars at the bird. Its body was a mixture of black, white, and light brown, and the top of his head was black with a splash of red.

"I think that's a yellow-bellied sapsucker," Louise said next to her.

"I wouldn't know a yellow-bellied sapsucker from a finch," Maureen admitted. She wondered if she would take up birdwatching like her mother when she retired.

Maureen set the binoculars down on the table as her mother handed her the bird book, thumping the page on the right-hand side. "See? It looks like that bird there."

Maureen studied it and had to agree with her mother.

Forgetting all about the bird, the binoculars, and the book, Louise gave Maureen her undivided attention.

"Do you want something to drink? Something to eat?" she asked.

Maureen shook her head. "I was finished with work early and thought I'd stop by."

"Mrs. Kovach loves what you did for her. All that black and gray was dreadful." Her mother grimaced.

"It was a little much. I'm glad she's happy with the results."

"She's been singing your praises up and down the street," Louise crowed.

Maureen laughed.

"Don't laugh, word of mouth is the best form of advertisement."

"I know."

"How's Everett?"

"He's going to be discharged next week."

"Already?"

"It went by fast, didn't it? It's been such a relief knowing he's safe, not using, and getting three meals a day." In the past two months while Everett was in the hospital and then rehab, she'd slept better than she had in a long time. And she knew the same to be true for Allan. Although Lance's situation weighed on her mind, as did

Ashley being three thousand miles away from home. When did you stop worrying about your children? Obviously never.

"Now," Louise said, "why don't you tell me what's troubling you."

"How do you know something's troubling me?"

"Please. I'm your mother."

Best to just spit it out. Maureen relayed in detail the conversation they'd had with Lance at the dinner table the previous evening.

"What?" Louise was as stunned as Maureen and Allan had been, but she quickly turned philosophical. "Well, he was never keen on school. Even from an early age."

"I know, but sometimes we have to do things we don't want to do."

Her mother narrowed her eyes. "I think I used to say that."

Maureen nodded, smiling. "You did. A lot."

"You know, I applaud Lance's decision," Louise said, nodding sagely.

"You do?" Maureen couldn't hide her surprise.

"Yes, of course. You've said yourself there's a shortage of tradespeople out there. We need carpenters, plumbers, and electricians. Do you know how long it took me to get a plumber? Weeks. And not everyone is college material. Not everyone is cut out for it, and kids shouldn't be made to feel guilty or less than if they aren't."

Maureen agreed in theory with what her mother was saying, but she wasn't there yet.

"It's just that it wasn't too long ago that I had two sons in college, and now both of them are out. I feel like such a failure."

Louise spoke sharply. "Maureen, you're not a failure. You're a great mother. You can only raise them. They have to make their own decisions."

Maureen didn't say anything.

Her mother continued to speak, but the sharpness was gone. "I know you're disappointed, and it has certainly been a rough year for your family, but you can't blame yourself. If you fall into the rut of self-blame, you'll be no good to anyone."

That was sensible advice.

"Easier said than done," Maureen said.

"I know. Sometimes motherhood is painful. There's no way around that." Louise paused and crossed one leg over the other, swinging it slightly. "And let's look at this. True, Everett's problems are very serious. But Lance?" She shook her head. "There's nothing to worry about there. He's made a different career choice, and there's nothing wrong with that."

"You're right, of course."

Louise winked at her. "Of course I am. I'm always right."

Chapter Forty-Five

Everett's thirty days were up at the residential rehab facility. Maureen and Allan were eager to bring him home. The treatment center was pretty strict with their rules: they did not allow cell phones or any kind of electronic devices, but they had been allowed to send online messages of support and encouragement to him through the facility. They also attended weekly family therapy sessions. Although Ash was unable to attend, Lance went to everyone. As the weeks progressed, they had seen a definite improvement in their son's appearance and demeanor, and they were cautiously optimistic.

The rehab facility was set back from the road so you couldn't hear any of the traffic from outside. The campus was surrounded by mature trees of various heights and different foliage, giving it a feeling of seclusion. Benches were placed throughout, and there was a bird bath and numerous bird feeders. It was a lovely, leafy spot.

On arrival, they'd been subjected to an inspection to make sure they weren't smuggling in any contraband. But the security guards had been pleasant enough while they searched through Maureen's purse and asked Allan to empty his pockets.

They met Everett in his room, which was clean and brightly decorated in pastel colors. It was quiet, and soft sunlight filtered in through the window. He looked well. Better than he had in months. He'd put on a little weight, his clothes were clean, and his hair had recently been washed.

"How's it going?" she asked him, settling into one of two armchairs and setting her purse on the small end table. Allan took the other chair, crossing one leg over the other and resting his arms on the armrest.

Everett sat in the middle of his made bed. A slim hardcover copy of *The Old Man and the Sea* by Ernest Hemingway lay on the bedside table. "Good," he said.

They'd been advised to keep the conversations light.

Always at the back of Maureen's mind was the thought that he might relapse. Opioid addiction was tough. But she supposed all addictions were tough whether it be cigarettes, alcohol, drugs, or food. She pushed these thoughts aside, deciding to focus on the present moment.

"What's new at home?" Everett asked.

"Lance will be starting trade school next week," Allan replied. "He seems excited about it."

"Hopefully he'll like it," Maureen said.

"Mom, jeez, don't be so negative."

Duly chastised and not wanting things to escalate, she said quickly, "You're right. This is what he wants to do, and he has our support. As do you."

"I know, Mom. Thanks. How's Ash?"

Maureen smiled. "She's settling in. Likes her roommate. Looking forward to the college experience."

Everett nodded. "Good for her." He appeared thoughtful for a moment. Maureen noticed his face had filled out a bit; he didn't appear as gaunt as before.

"I'd like to go back," he said. "Someday."

"You would?" Allan asked, unable to hide his surprise.

But to Maureen, this sounded promising. Having taken a leave of absence, he'd have to redo the semester, but no matter.

"Yeah, I would. I miss it. The classroom stuff."

This was the best news she'd heard in a long time.

"That's positive," said Allan.

Everett nodded. "If I can stay clean."

"Take it one day at a time, honey," Maureen added, trying to remain positive. It was important for him to remember this. He had a roof over his head and the support of his family. Employment would be the next step. But one thing at a time.

"Okay, Mom."

They spoke a few more minutes about Everett's desire to return to college, with Allan suggesting that maybe he could enroll in the local community college and take a few classes until he was ready to go back full time.

Maureen reached into her purse and pulled out the St. Anthony medal, now hanging from the chain she'd purchased for it at the jeweler in town. She stood up from her chair and handed it to her son.

"What's this?" he asked, turning it around in his hand.

"It's actually a funny story." She returned to her seat. "I found that one morning on the beach. It's a St. Anthony medal. Supposedly, you pray to him for lost things. Not only material but non-material things as well."

"What's so funny about that?" Everett asked.

"I was getting to that. As I said, I found it on the beach. Aunt Gail says it's over a hundred years old. But here's the funny part. Aunt Gail thinks it belonged to Grammie."

"Your grandmother?"

Maureen nodded. "Yes, if you can believe that. She remembers her mother telling her she'd lost one." Maureen paused. "Aunt Gail said she lost it in the lake which makes sense because I found it on the beach."

"Sounds about right," Allan said.

"Mom, we don't pray to saints."

"Maybe we could use a little heavenly help," she said.

"Maybe." Everett studied it, then slipped the chain over his head and straightened the medal against his chest.

Her instinct had been right; he did appreciate it. Her quiet child, who'd always been a deep thinker, valued things like this. It was as if he was meant to have it, and she couldn't help but wonder if Grammie had been working behind the scenes on the other side of the veil.

Lance would have said, "Cool," and tossed it into a drawer.

And Ash? She would have frowned, decided it wasn't fashionable enough, and tossed it into her drawer as well.

Allan joked, "Don't lose it or we'll have to pray to St. Anthony to find it again."

Seriously, Everett said, "No, I won't lose it." And he patted the medal now lying against his T-shirt.

She said a little prayer herself that her oldest son, her firstborn, the one who'd made her a mother, would find his way out of this mess. Would find his lost self.

Chapter Forty-Six

Everett had been home for a week, and things were going well. Maureen and Allan had laid down some ground rules, including unannounced searches of his room if they deemed it necessary, as well as a curfew of eleven p.m. He'd been agreeable to all.

September was shaping up to be a beautiful month. The early autumn sun cast a golden hue over everything. There was still the warmth of the summer without the blast-furnace heat. The trees were still a lush green, and the nights were comfortable.

Maureen stopped at Coffee Girl to say hello to Angie as she hadn't seen her in a while. As she approached the front door, she spotted her sister exiting Java Joe's across the street, followed by Java Joe himself.

Angie's mouth was set in a grim line. From behind her, Java Joe said something to her, but she did not turn around, only held up her hand to indicate that he should stop. But he wasn't easily dissuaded and followed her across the street toward her café. As they neared, Angie spotted Maureen and rolled her eyes.

Maureen wanted to laugh but refrained. These two were something else.

Angie and Java Joe stepped up onto the curb together.

"Hey," Angie said. "How's everything?"

"Today, everything is good," Maureen said honestly. She was trying not to look too far into the future. Taking things one day at a time was proving to be challenging.

Java Joe stood next to Angie and folded his large, muscled arms across his chest. "I heard your son—Everett, right?—is home from rehab. How's he doing?"

Angie rounded on him. "What business is that of yours?"

He immediately threw up his hands. "Only asking out of concern."

Before the two of them went off, Maureen said, "He is home. So far, he's fine. Thanks for asking."

"He need a job?" Java Joe asked. Angie scowled at him.

"Actually, he does," Maureen said. It had been almost impossible for Everett to find a job; the whole town was aware of his problem with drugs. And as much as everyone sympathized and asked after him, no one wanted to take on the risk of employing him. She supposed she couldn't blame them.

"Great. Tell him to meet me tomorrow morning at eleven after the breakfast rush. Everyone starts at the bottom."

Maureen was overwhelmed. "I appreciate this. Thanks for giving him a chance."

He shrugged it off. "I've been there. Not drugs but alcohol. I know firsthand what rock bottom is all about. Couldn't get a job or if I did, I couldn't hold one down. Once I got sober, one man gave me a second chance and I never forgot it."

"How long have you been sober?" she asked. She slid her gaze over to her sister, who stared at Java Joe, her expression softening. Slightly.

"Fifteen years, three months, and twelve days," he said proudly.

"That's wonderful." Maureen sighed. "It gives me hope."

"I'll keep him busy, and I'll keep an eye on him," he promised.

"Thanks, Joe."

A grin spread across his face. "Actually, my name isn't Joe. It's Tom."

Angie looked at him, her mouth hanging open. "I always thought your name was Joe." She rolled her head back and forth for emphasis. "You know, *Java Joe*?"

Still grinning, he said, "You know what happens when you assume, Evangeline."

Angie opened her mouth to say something smart, Maureen was sure, but Joe—er, Tom—cut her off. "Besides, Java Tom doesn't work at all!"

Maureen scrunched up her nose. "I agree. But you know, you'll probably always be known as Java Joe."

If her sister ever smiled, it would be a miracle, Maureen thought. She gently nudged her with her elbow and gave her a look that read, *lighten up*. The man had offered her son employment; going forward, Angie would need to cut him some slack.

"I've got to get back to my crib," he said. "Maureen, tell Everett to come by in the morning." And then with a grin, he said to Angie. "Evangeline, I'll see you around."

"Thanks, Tom," she replied softly.

He lifted an eyebrow, grinned, stepped off the curb, and ran across the street to his restaurant.

Angie stared after him. "I did not know that his real name was Tom."

"See? You learn something new every day," Maureen said.

"It was nice of him to offer Everett a job," Angie admitted, but then she looked at Maureen, narrowing her eyes. "I would have given him a job."

Maureen shook her head. "No, I don't want any trouble between us."

"It wouldn't have caused trouble between you and me," Angie said.

"Anyway, never mind that now," Maureen told her. "It's all taken care of."

They continued to stand there, looking across the street.

"You know, I think he's quite smitten with you," Maureen ventured.

Angie pursed her lips before asking, "What's wrong with you?" She turned on her heel. "Come on, let's go inside and get coffee and a pastry."

"Sounds good." Maureen followed her sister inside Coffee Girl, noticing that Angie had not disagreed or even protested about her comment regarding Java Joe.

Chapter Forty-Seven

Cousin Esther had gathered everyone she could for a night of bowling. The league didn't start until the end of October but as she explained, she wanted to see "where everyone was at." With a laugh and a raised eyebrow, Allan had begged off, despite the coaxing and cajoling from his wife.

"What about you, Everett?"

Everett was settling in. He was working thirty hours a week at Java Joe's, and it was decided that for the time being, he would not return to college out of state. It was too much of a temptation. His sobriety had been too hard-fought. Currently, he was looking at courses at the local college. His appetite had returned, and Maureen delighted in cooking again. On the weekends when she was home, she baked pies and cupcakes.

But Maureen and Allan kept an eagle eye on him. They did not view this newfound equilibrium through rose-colored glasses. Although his recovery had been encouraging, they were not euphoric. They knew the statistics for relapse were high; the actual percentage had been both eye opening and sobering, not to mention worrying.

One day at a time.

They'd encouraged Everett to find new hobbies, especially things that relaxed him. Under their advice, he'd started to see a therapist weekly to find better ways to deal with stress and to find better coping mechanisms.

In answer to Maureen's question about joining her for bowling, he held up a book. "Nah, I want to finish this." He flipped through the pages and announced, "It's not that long, and I may be able to finish it tonight."

"Okay, I'll see you later." She picked up her phone from the end of the counter, tossed it into her purse, and dug around for her car keys. Once she had the keys in hand, she waved goodbye and was out the door, heading to her car. The night was frosty for early October, and there was the rustle of falling leaves along the driveway and sidewalk. Maureen inhaled deeply because there was a strong smell of woodsmoke in the air.

The Lakeside Bowling Lanes was on Thistle, directly across from Dog Days Bar. It was a well-known fact that many a bowler over the last sixty years had stumbled out of the bowling alley after a disappointing game and staggered right across the street and into the bar. And there'd been the odd character who stumbled out of the bar after a night of drinking and got it into his head that he might like to go bowling, and from there, went home half in the bag wearing bowling shoes, leaving his good shoes behind in a little wooden cubby.

Maureen was one of the last ones to arrive. She wore jeans and a long-sleeved lilac-colored T-shirt and carried a hoodie with her in case the lanes were cool. She had no idea what to expect.

The place smelled of old pizza, stale popcorn, and sweaty hot dogs. Esther was already there, along with her sister, Suzanne. Maureen's sister Nadine stood at the counter, renting bowling shoes.

Esther had secured two lanes right next to each other. On one of the benches, Louise and her sister Gail sat, huddled and giggling. Maureen shook her head at the sight of them. That's how it was with those two: secrets and giggles.

Maureen caught up with Nadine as she turned away from the counter, a pair of red, white, and cream bowling shoes in hand. They looked well used. Nadine wore jeans and a blue cardigan over a white turtleneck.

"How do I allow myself to get roped into these things?" Nadine asked good-naturedly.

"Same way I do. Because Esther doesn't take no for an answer."

"Not much has changed since we were kids then."

"Nope."

Nadine waited while Maureen traded in her sneakers for a pair of bowling shoes, tucking the rental ticket into her back pocket. They sat at the nearest table, slipping on their bowling shoes and lacing them up.

Maureen looked around at the threadbare carpet, dark wood paneling, and the discolored drop ceiling. "Not much has changed since 1960."

Nadine followed her gaze. "I guess not. Look at all the black-and-white photos on the wall."

Esther caught their attention and waved them over.

"We better look sharp," Nadine said with a laugh.

They walked over, and the two of them hugged Esther and Suzanne and greeted their mother and aunt with a kiss.

Maureen said to Gail, "I thought you didn't like bowling."

Gail gave a dismissive wave. "I don't. I'm only here to provide the running commentary." Next to her, Louise laughed, which caused Gail to start laughing too.

"I hope we don't have to separate the two of you," Nadine warned, lifting an eyebrow.

Maureen and her sister went in search of a bowling ball to use.

"You didn't save your bowling ball from when you were a kid?" Nadine asked her.

"It's home in the attic. But I'd never get my fingers in those holes anymore. I was fourteen the last time I used it, and I'm too lazy to take it somewhere to get it drilled."

Nadine corrected her. "Not too lazy, too much on your plate."

Maureen agreed. "That too. Oh, I think I found one." She held up a ten-pound navy-blue ball whose shine appeared to have dulled over the years. But for tonight it would do. She supposed if she was going to be bowling regularly, she'd have to drag her old ball down from the attic and get it properly fitted to her fingers.

Within minutes, Nadine had also found a ball that would work, and the two of them made their way back to their assigned lanes.

"Can I keep score?" Aunt Gail asked.

Esther frowned. "No, Mother, you can't. We had a little problem the last time."

Louise elbowed her sister gently and chortled.

Gail protested, "It wasn't that bad."

"Mom, you didn't record the strikes and spares properly."

Louise put her hands on her hips and said in mock outrage, "Yeah, Gail."

"I hate it when people don't take bowling seriously," Esther muttered. Maureen grinned. She knew her cousin was only joking. Or she hoped so.

And then Esther announced, "I'll keep score." She slid into the seat where the paper scorecards and pencils were kept.

"Gee, you'd think in this day and age, there'd be electronic scorecards," Nadine mused.

"There are, but I prefer this way," Esther explained.

Maureen was first. She got up, picked up her ball from the rack, stepped forward with her arm swinging back, then launched the ball down the lane, where it rolled directly for the gutter.

"Oh boy," Esther said behind her.

On her second attempt, Maureen knocked down three pins on the end.

Relieved, she sat down next to her mother. Nadine was up next and fared much better.

After the first game, Maureen offered to get snacks, and Suzanne accompanied her to the snack bar to help. Once everything was organized and paid for, they carried the trays back to the lane. At the end of her next turn, where her score was dismal, she made a quick run to the restroom. On the way out, she was approached by a woman she knew.

Sylvia Pankowski's kids were of a similar age to Maureen's but her youngest had only started high school, and she was heavily involved with the parents' association at the high school. Maureen had gone to every parents' association meeting she could, but always remained in the back. Although she supported the organization and usually volunteered for fundraising drives, especially the bake sales, she never wanted the responsibility of being the one in charge.

"Hi, Sylvia." Maureen said.

"Maureen, it's funny I should run into you, because you've been on my mind." Sylvia was a few years older than Maureen. She was the same height but wore her hair short and in a contrast of colors: black with pale blond highlights. She wore gray eyeshadow and big gold hoop earrings.

Maureen frowned slightly. "Really?"

"Yes. You know how we sometimes have workshops planned throughout the year?"

Maureen nodded but was too embarrassed to say that she'd usually skipped them, except for the ones about keeping your children safe on social media.

"Once a year, we have a workshop on addictions, whether it be drugs or alcohol or whatever," Sylvia said.

Maureen had never bothered with that yearly workshop. In hindsight, she should have made that one her priority. She felt her cheeks go hot. It seemed as if everyone in Lavender Bay knew about Everett. She shifted from one foot to the other, slightly uncomfortable about the mention of her son's problems.

Sylvia was quick to reassure her, even going so far as to reach out and pat her arm. "Hey, no shame. I went through the same thing as you with my second child. Not drugs but alcohol."

"I'm sorry. I didn't know that."

Sylvia sighed. "It was a number of years ago, but it took us a long time to get him sober." She brushed the top of her index finger beneath her nose. "Anyway, I was wondering if you'd like to give a talk to the parents about what it's like to be the mother of an addict. I did it a few years ago, but they're sick of hearing from me." She laughed.

Maureen took a step back, alarmed. "I couldn't. I hate public speaking."

Sylvia didn't protest. "Most people do. It was only an idea I had."

Maureen apologized and said goodbye to Sylvia and wished her luck. As she turned to go, she felt guilty. Did she have something to say? Would other parents want to hear her story? She drew in a deep breath. Quickly, she turned around and said, "Sylvia, wait."

The other woman stopped and turned.

Maureen closed the gap between them. "I'm sorry, I changed my mind. I will do that talk."

"That's great. I know it's difficult when it's about your own family, but it might help someone else."

Maureen never wanted another parent to go through the hell she and Allan had been through. She'd have to get over her fear of public speaking, but she would do what she had to. If it saved one kid or spared one parent what she'd experienced, she could get over herself and get up in front of a group of people and tell her story.

CHAPTER FORTY-EIGHT

Allan stood with Maureen behind the stage of the McKinley High School auditorium. They stood in the shadows, and she was glad she wasn't visible. Her heart raced, and there was a fine sheen of perspiration around her hairline. She'd dressed casually in tailored pants and a blouse and wore a small gold necklace with the St. Anthony medal hanging from it. Everett had loaned it to her when he heard she'd be giving a talk. Touched, she kept checking to make sure it was still there.

Allan placed a hand on the small of her back. "Nervous?"

She nodded. "Uh-huh."

He spoke softly to her. The sound of his voice, in this tone, always had a calming effect on her. Tonight was no different.

Gently, he took her hands in his. His were warm and dry. "There's nothing to be anxious about. What you have to impart to these people is important. And some may not even realize it until after you've spoken." He rolled his lips inward. "And some might not even need this information until down the road."

His words skated across the surface of her mind, refusing to sink in, but she continued to nod.

A veteran of many dental conferences, Allan was used to speaking in front of crowds. The past few evenings, he'd helped her and coached her. She was grateful. He'd reminded her to keep her focus on the back of the auditorium. During practice runs, he'd slowed her down, reminding her not to race through her talk. And he even taught her some deep breathing exercises to help her calm down. But front and center was the idea of helping another parent or child and possibly preventing them from going through what they'd all gone through. That thought alone strengthened her resolve.

From where she stood, she heard Sylvia approach the podium and welcome the crowd. She adjusted the microphone, and a slight screech filled the air. She made mention of the full auditorium, and Maureen closed her eyes and groaned.

Allan reached over and rubbed her shoulder. "You're going to be great."

When Sylvia introduced her, Maureen took a deep breath, gave her husband a smile that said she was okay, and walked out onto the stage, into the glare of the floodlights. In her hand, she carried small index cards with her speech written on them. She thanked Sylvia, took her position behind the podium, and raised the microphone slightly.

Unable to resist, she scanned the auditorium and did not see one empty seat. Her heart thumped wildly.

"Good evening. Most of you know me. I'm a lifelong resident of Lavender Bay." She paused and drew in a deep breath. "But for those of you who don't, my name is Maureen Peterson, and I'm the mother of a drug addict."

***

Thank you for reading this book! If you enjoyed it, would you mind leaving a rating or a review on Amazon? Many thanks.

Also to keep up to date on new releases and to receive bonus material, please sign up for my newsletter at www.michelebrouder.com

Acknowledgements

This particular book was amazing to research. I happily went down the rabbit hole of women's contribution to the war effort by working in defense plants. I watched a lot of interviews and read a lot of material to create life at the aviation plant for Laura.

I am indebted to Jimmy Schichtel of the Lackawanna Historical Society who sent me a few years' worth of newspaper clippings regarding local men and women during World War II. It took me weeks to read through all the material and it gave me a great sense of time and place.

A huge shout out to Ed Cichon from Cazenovia Recovery for his detailed, thoughtful answers to my queries about residential rehab. I'm also grateful to Jharmar

Jean Francois of St Peter's Health Partners for walking me through the different options for rehab for drug addiction. He answered my questions thoroughly and patiently.

Any mistakes are solely mine.

ALSO BY MICHELE BROUDER

The Lavender Bay Chronicles
The Inn at Lavender Bay
Lost and Found in Lavender Bay
Second Chances in Lavender Bay (Coming in September 2024)

Hideaway Bay
Coming Home to Hideaway Bay
Meet Me at Sunrise
Moonlight and Promises
When We Were Young
One Last Thing Before I Go
The Chocolatier of Hideaway Bay
Now and Forever

Escape to Ireland
A Match Made in Ireland

Her Fake Irish Husband
Her Irish Inheritance
A Match for the Matchmaker
Home, Sweet Irish Home
An Irish Christmas
Happy Holidays
A Whyte Christmas
This Christmas
A Wish for Christmas
One Kiss for Christmas
A Wedding for Christmas
Audiobooks
Coming Home to Hideaway Bay
All books available in ebook, paperback, and large print paperback. Audiobooks coming soon.

Printed in Great Britain
by Amazon